PRAISE 1

Felicity Niven's writing is sharp and exquisite.

— JULIA QUINN, AUTHOR OF THE
BRIDGERTON SERIES

With her complicated and lovable characters, achingly tender love stories, and scorching steam, Felicity Niven has quickly become one of my all-time favorite authors.

— ALEXANDRA VASTI, AUTHOR OF *NE'ER DUKE WELL* (2024) AND THE *HALIFAX HELLIONS* SERIES

Niven is a masterful storyteller, deftly weaving beautifully drawn characters with taut, witty prose. A sensational new voice in historical romance.

— ERIN LANGSTON, AUTHOR OF *FOREVER YOUR ROGUE, THE NEW YORK TIMES* EDITORS' CHOICE

BED ME, DUKE

BOOK ONE OF THE BED ME BOOKS

A desperate Scottish countess seeks lovemaking lessons from a gorgeous rogue.

He can't stand her fierce resistance to his charms. She can't stand his dazzling good looks. But why bother standing when they'd both prefer to lie down on a bed together? Especially since neither has any intention of falling in love.

Captain Jack Pike leads a blissfully carefree existence as London's richest and most notorious rake. Becoming the Duke of Dunmore would ruin his fun. He doesn't even know where Dunmore is—Scotland, maybe? To add insult to injury, the savage Countess of Kinmarloch refuses to swoon for him. But why should he care? Jack only beds women married to other men, after all, and there's not a man in the British Empire brave enough to wed the feral countess.

A countess in her own right, Helen Boyd must marry the new Duke of Dunmore to save the people of Kinmarloch from starvation. If only the troublesome Jack Pike would go away and stop torturing her with his handsome face, perfect male body, and shameless flirtation. On the other hand, Jack might be just the man to teach the woefully inexperienced Helen a thing or two about seducing the duke and luring him to the altar. And as part of her training, there would be the added advantage of bedding the most beautiful man she's ever seen.

Friction leads to fire leads to forever-after in **Bed Me, Duke**, the first book in the steamy Regency romance series **The Bed Me Books** from author Felicity Niven.

Complete content warnings available at author's website: www.felicityniven.com.

BED ME, DUKE

BED ME, DUKE

THE BED ME BOOKS

BOOK ONE

FELICITY NIVEN

BLETHERSKITE BOOKS

Publisher: Bletherskite Books, PO Box 450824, Atlanta, GA 31145

ISBN: 978-1-958917-07-7

Cover Design by James, GoOnWrite.com

To all the Jacks I've ever known:
may you need less and deserve more.

And to all the Helens:
you are more than the sunrise and the stars.

CONTENTS

Chapter 1   1
March, 1819. Scotland.

Chapter 2   10

Chapter 3   23
Three weeks earlier. London.

Chapter 4   35

Chapter 5   41

Chapter 6   47

Chapter 7   58

Chapter 8   70

Chapter 9   81

Chapter 10   91

Chapter 11   96

Chapter 12   105

Chapter 13   115

Chapter 14   120

Chapter 15   130

Chapter 16   136

Chapter 17   144

Chapter 18   153

Chapter 19   161

Chapter 20   170

Chapter 21   176

Chapter 22   190

Chapter 23   195

Chapter 24   208

Chapter 25   216

Chapter 26   222

Chapter 27   227

Chapter 28   232

Chapter 29   242

Chapter 30   250
Chapter 31   259
Chapter 32   266
First Epilogue   277

More   285
Author's Notes   287
BED ME, BARON: PREVIEW   289
Acknowledgments   303
About the Author   305

ONE

MARCH, 1819. SCOTLAND.

"Jack."

He held still, sure it was a dream.

"Jack Pike."

He sat bolt upright in the bed, heart pounding, a young lieutenant again, startled out of sleep by his commanding officer.

The Countess of Kinmarloch stood across the room, holding a candlestick.

"What's wrong, my lady?"

"Naething. Nae a thing. I dinnae mean to frighten ye."

She hovered like a wraith in her nightdress. Jack himself was unclothed, not ready for battle stations. He clutched the blanket around his waist with one hand and reached out with other.

"Throw me my shirt, my lady. Behind you. On the chair."

Her burst of laughter fluttered the flame of the candle.

"Ye dinnae need to dress yerself for me, Jack Pike. I've seen yer chest. Ye were anxious enough to show it off to me a few days ago. I cannae believe in yer shyness now."

Oh. Yes. Wake up, fool.

Helen Boyd wasn't his superior officer. This wasn't a drill or an imminent threat to the ship. He wasn't a youth, still in the navy.

He was a man in his prime, naked in a bed. She was a woman who had confessed a degree of admiration for him and had come to his bedchamber in the middle of the night. A woman in his bedchamber was a common enough occurrence in the life of Captain Jack Pike. He should be in complete command of the situation, himself, and the woman in question.

But it was *her*.

She took a step toward him. He noted there was no movement of her breasts under her nightdress. Too small.

"And ye are clearly aware 'tis a handsome chest, ye vain man."

He made himself grin and lean back on the pillows, putting his arms behind his head, displaying himself and his handsome chest to her.

"I'm aware other females think highly of my chest, Helen, but I thought it might have escaped your notice."

She took two more steps, sat down on the edge of his bed, and her gaze dropped from his face to his torso.

She was looking at his muscles there, he thought. Or she was looking at the sprinkling of blond-brown hair that narrowed to a trail down to his navel and, lower still, to his cock, beginning to stir under the blanket.

Or perhaps she was looking at the scar just under his left nipple, the one he had sustained that time when he had been a little too intent on the chest of the lady on top of him and not on her foil-wielding husband who had come home far earlier than promised.

Now Helen would ask him about the scar and he would tell the lie he told all women, the one which featured pirates on the high seas, the lie which made most women stroke the scar before moving on to stroking something else on his body. Preferably something lower down.

But she didn't ask about the scar. And there was something in her expression he couldn't identify. It might be appreciation. It might be desire. Those sentiments were expected and welcome. But maybe…it might be…resentment?

No.

It was a trick of the candlelight.

Under the blanket, he began to respond more strongly to her presence, and he had to remind himself to keep his hands where they were, fingers laced together on the back of his head.

Easy, Jack. Don't spook her.

Because…Lady Kinmarloch in a nightdress, her brown hair in a plait. Lady Kinmarloch, smelling of grass and cider and soap. Lady Kinmarloch, the one woman he might bed in the duchy of Dunmore without worry he was taking advantage, since, after all, as she had reminded him many times, she was a countess. In her own right.

He had not had a woman in over a week, and a week was a very long time for Jack Pike. He had thought he was going to have to wait until he got home to London. But with each passing second, it seemed more and more likely he would bed a woman much sooner than that.

Tonight, in fact. Here, in Dunmore Castle.

At the very least, her scent would feed his thoughts when he took himself in hand after she left his bedchamber. Even if she had come to castigate him about something like the sins of his predecessor. Even if he were mistaken about the reason she was sitting on his bed.

But he didn't think he was mistaken. She wanted something from him, and usually, there was only one thing women wanted from him, only one thing they knew they could get.

However, she was not a usual woman. Not by a long chalk.

She looked away. "Jack, I must speak to ye."

With her gaze averted, he felt free to skim his eyes over her barely protruding breasts. He might, he just might, be able to convince himself he saw erect nipples under the well-worn and much-laundered muslin of her nightdress. The same small nipples he had forced himself not to look at when her shirt had been wet from the stream, days ago.

What would those nipples taste like? Which of her scents? Grass? Or cider? Or soap? Cider, he decided.

"First, I must ask that naething which passes between us tonight be spoken about, ever, to anyone," she said, still looking away. "Including yer master."

She meant the Duke of Dunmore. Well, there was no difficulty there. No one would ever know what happened in this bedchamber tonight between the two of them. He could assure her of that.

"My lady." His voice was a purr. "As I said this evening, I have no deep loyalty to the duke. He's not my master, really. We just know each other. As long as you don't want to lay a plot to assassinate the scoundrel, I promise you my complete discretion."

"I mean it, Jack Pike." She whipped her head around and glared at him.

He assumed his most serious countenance. "I won't tell anyone. You have my word, Helen."

He took an arm from behind his head and reached out and touched her lower back. She was all bone and muscle here, but there was warmth under the nightdress, and just a little lower down, her back began to curve out toward her bottom.

Her spine straightened under his hand, but she did not pull away. And was that a quiver? Promising.

She bit her lip before she spoke. "I have been thinking

about what ye told me. About how there are many beautiful young ladies at these balls during the London Season. And how the Duke of Dunmore could be easily persuaded to marry one of them." She swallowed. "I must marry well. Wealth or power. One or the other. Or both. I know I dinnae have much to offer, but my land splits the duchy. If the duke and I were to wed, our son would eventually be both duke and earl and the divided lands would be one again."

Damn. He was wrong about why she was in his bedchamber.

But still. He did not remove his hand from her back. It felt so good right where it was. And Captain Jack Pike could easily steer the course of this encounter in an entirely different direction. He could, and he would.

"Jack, do ye think that is enough?'

He blinked. "Enough for what?"

"For the duke to marry me."

"The duchy is not a rich one."

"Aye. But my grandfather would have wanted the lands united. And as the duchess, I might stop the clearances. Permanently."

He let his hand stroke downwards and now he was cupping the top of the near cheek of her small bottom.

"So you'll settle for power," he said absently. "But you have to realize the duke might need money from a marriage. The last duke did not marry wisely in terms of a dowry."

"Aye."

"It's nothing against you, Helen."

But I'd like to be against you. Very much.

She ducked her head. "Perhaps…I might have something else to offer the duke?"

Oh, yes. This was even more promising.

He moved his hand along the top of her buttock, finding

the divot that marked the beginning of her crease, placing his fingertips there lightly. "What would that be?"

She met his eyes and took in a stuttering breath. "I know what I am. What I look like. But if ye would be willing to train me, I might be able to enrapture the duke. Get him to compromise me. Then he'd have to marry me."

Jack wouldn't have to steer anything at all. She was bearing right at him, under full sail. He bit back his gleeful grin.

"Train you?"

"Aye. Train me in the carnal arts."

"The what?"

She shook her head. "Ye know."

"No, I don't." This might be the most fun he had had in months. No, years. He moved his hand around the side of her hip and stroked the top of her thigh with his thumb. As her leg tightened under this small caress, he asked, "What do the carnal arts consist of?"

Her voice had an edge to it. "What ye do with yer women, Jack Pike."

He sat up and leaned forward, his chest against her upper arm, and spoke in her ear. "Surely it's the same thing you do with your men."

"My men!" She stood suddenly, almost clipping his chin with her shoulder. He caught her hand, the one which was not holding the candle.

"Shhh, my lady. Sit back down. Give me that candle."

He took the candlestick and put it on the small shelf next to the bed. He looked up at her face, her brows drawn together, her eyes squinting.

"My men," she muttered.

"Sit, Helen." He yanked her down so she was sitting on the edge of the bed again. She tried to pull her hand out of his grip, but he held her fast.

"I've changed my mind," she snapped. "Forget I said

anything. Forget I was ever here. In fact, forget my name. I intend to forget yers as soon as I leave this room."

"Am I to understand you don't need my help, my lady?"

She stopped tugging.

"I wonder how far you'd get without me. You'll need some money to get to London. To buy some fine dresses. To get rooms. You'll need an introduction." He released her hand.

"Give me the money. I'll pay ye back," she hissed.

"How? How will you pay me back? You don't have a sixpence to rub together."

"I told ye my plan. I'm going to get the Duke of Dunmore to marry me."

"Oh, so now you think you can do that?" Jack laughed. "Without my help? Just a few minutes ago, it seemed to me, you were in a bit of despair that you wouldn't be able to— what was the word?—*enrapture* the duke?"

She trembled. Then she put her shoulders back, tossed her plait, and turned to confront him. This was the brave Helen he admired so much.

"Ye will train me, I will succeed, and I will be able to pay ye back."

"I am mystified as to why you think you need me." He shrugged. "I'm sure English love-making is not much different from Scottish love-making."

She scowled. Her large jaw jutted even more than it usually did and he knew she was gritting her teeth.

"I. Have. Never. Been. Touched. By. A. Man."

The statement hung in the air.

"Except by ye. When we—when ye kept me from falling into the stream. And ye petted me." She looked away. "And when I was drunk at yer table. And then when ye carried me into my keep. But I dinnae remember that."

He was rattled. "Er, that is to say, never? How old are you?"

"I am six and twenty."

Twenty-six and never touched by a man. By the time Jack was twenty-six, the perversions he had enjoyed, the countless women he had enjoyed them with…his mind was swimming.

She tipped up her chin and looked at the ceiling. "I am the Countess of Kinmarloch. And before I was countess, I was in the direct line. Even if I were pretty, a lad widnae have dared touch me."

He shook his head. "Even if you were…Helen, look at me."

She turned her head and stared at him sullenly, her heavy brow suddenly heavier than ever.

"I know what I am. Dinnae pay me any of your compliments, Jack Pike. I dinnae need to hear them. And ye dinnae need to say them."

"Am I allowed to speak the truth, my lady?"

She snorted. "Ye widnae recognize the truth even if it had its fangs sunk into yer bollocks."

He winced. "Ouch. You have just conjured an extremely unpleasant image in my mind. Not at all conducive to putting me in the mood."

"In the mood?"

"First, to say something nice to you. Second, to train you."

Her eyes brightened. "Ye will agree then to train me?"

She was not at all interested in his flattery, his opinion of her looks, how he thought he could harvest her spare body for his own pleasure, and that her face…that her face had grown on him and in a certain light and at a certain angle, she looked almost attractive. No, she was only interested in what he could do for her. How he could further her ends.

"I was considering it seriously until you began to discuss fangs and bollocks."

The light in her eyes went out. "Ye feel I am too rough and coarse for a gentleman like the duke."

"Well, you could stand to have a little polish put on you, but I think a little roughness and coarseness is good." He slid down on the bed, a little closer to her.

She looked at him with suspicion. "I dinnae care what *ye* think, Jack Pike. I care what the duke thinks."

"The duke? Well…" He considered. "The duke likes a little coarseness and roughness. Just not mention of sharp things and genitals. Together, in the same sentence. Very off-putting."

"His Grace might nae mind me?"

"Mmmm." He licked his lips. "Not at all."

It was the truth. Because he, Jack Pike, didn't mind her. Not one bit. And the Duke of Dunmore's taste was the same as his.

Exactly the same.

Because he *was* the Duke of Dunmore.

Two

Jack was surely going to go to hell for deceit, if not lechery. But he was going to enjoy himself on the way there.

"And His Grace has a particular fondness for nut-brown hair. Just like yours." He reached and found the end of Helen's plait and worried at the little piece of string tied there. Then it was undone and he was loosening the braid, brushing his fingers through her hair.

"Get away with ye," she said. But her voice was less belligerent than before. And she did not bat at his arm or drag his hand away. "Naebody likes brown hair. 'Tis ordinary."

"The duke does. And your hair is not ordinary, my lady. It's so soft." Jack lifted a hank and brushed it under his nose and against his lips. He wasn't lying. Her hair was like silk and it smelled of her.

He looked at her. She was watching him play with her hair.

"And he likes blue eyes. And fair skin. Like yours, Helen."

Her voice was low and breathy. "So will ye school me, Jack?"

"What do you want to know?"

"Everything."

"Everything?" He arranged her wavy hair around her shoulders. One finger stroked her earlobe. "What is everything?"

She shuddered. "Ye are going to make me say it? Kissing… touching…and *dàireadh*."

"And that last one is?"

"Rutting."

Rutting. His cock throbbed.

He should have taken Helen when he first met her, outside, with the sheep. Down in the mud, her lean hips in his hands, rain streaming off her rump as she pushed back into him and he thrust into her. Like a ram tupping a ewe.

The tenting of the blanket over his lap became more pronounced.

He ran the tips of his fingers along her hairline, to the back of her neck. "My lady, you would not need to know rutting. A simple kiss can be enough reason to force a marriage."

I would love to rut with you. Ask me again to rut with you.

She jerked under his touch of her nape. "If the duke dinnae marry me, I will have to wed Lord Reeves or some other man like him. I cannae think his kind cares much about pleasing a woman. And I think I should have one experience of pleasure in bed before a lifetime of duty."

"You think I would please you?"

She shook her head. "Ye are more in need of compliments than any woman I know, Jack Pike. Ye peacock. Aye, I know ye will please me." Her voice became raspy. "Looking on ye pleases me. And when ye touch me…"

He rested his hand on her collarbone. "And when I touch you?"

She looked straight at him, her eyes boring into him. "Ye drive me mad with desire."

"I do?" He had never had a woman confess her lust to him

like this. With no coyness, no blushing, no downward-cast gaze.

"I cannae think." Her black pupils were enormous, overtaking her blue irises. "My heart goes so fast, like now."

He lowered his hand to her upper chest. He felt her ribs moving with the thump of her racing heart.

"I feel piercing pains in my…"

"In your what, Helen?"

"In…in my breasts and…"

He slid his hand down to her small breast, almost lost under his palm. His fingers scrabbled over her nightdress and found a nipple and pinched it lightly. "And where else, Helen?"

She moaned and her whole body undulated as the nipple became stiff under his fingers and her head went back. "And… pains down below."

He moved his hand farther down her body and pressed against her mound with the back of his hand, feeling her maidenhair under the nightdress, pushing her thighs apart a little with his thumb and his pinky.

"Pains? Does it hurt?"

Her eyes were closed. "N-nae. But it drives me mad, the ache. I…I cannae think…"

He laughed. "Yes, you said that before."

"Jack." She jerked her head up and opened her eyes wide. She spoke in a voice filled with anguish. "Ye must show me how I can make the duke feel as I feel now. Shattered. Then he would do what I want him to."

"Does that mean, right now, you would do what I asked you to do?"

"A-aye."

"You would be wanton with me?" He grazed the top of her cleft through her nightdress with the knuckle of his middle finger. Her eyes closed again.

"Ungh." It was a grunt.

"You would marry me?"

Her eyes popped open, wide with alarm. He spoke quickly. "I'm just asking since that's what you want from the duke. A marriage proposal."

"If…if ye said ye would only continue doing what yer doing now if I accepted ye, I might be very tempted, *mo luran*. But nae."

He felt something. A strange little pain of his own. A twinge in his gut. But he winked and adopted a light, teasing tone. "Well, then it's good I'm not proposing to you."

"Aye." She took a deep breath. "'Tis good. I must do what…is best, after all…for Kinmarloch, for my people. I must marry for duty."

"I don't think," he said softly, flipping his hand and putting a bit of pressure on the top of her mound with the heel of his palm, his fingers continuing to trace her seam through her nightdress, her thighs falling away from each other. He could feel some wetness already seeping through the cloth.

"Ye dinnae…think what, Jack?" She was gasping, her eyes hazed.

"Right now, I don't think you are in a fit state to be trained for anything, Helen."

"N-nae?"

"No."

She shook her head. "Ye…must…"

"I think I must give you some relief. So you can concentrate your mind on giving rather than receiving pleasure."

Her voice was a harsh whisper. "Some relief, Jack."

He took his hand off her mound and shifted over and patted the blanket next to him.

"Get in the bed with me here."

She turned and slid up toward the head of the bed, lifting

her legs up off the floor and bringing them onto the mattress. The countess had done what he had told her to do. And oh, how he liked it.

"A trifle eager, aren't we, my lady?" He chuckled as he drew the blanket over her and put a hand on her waist to pull her even closer.

The chuckle broke the spell she was under. She stiffened and jerked away.

"If our situations were reversed, Jack, I widnae be making sport at yer expense."

"Really? You would be kind and ease my need?" Sweeping the blanket off his lap, he grabbed her hand and wrapped it around his half-hard cock and moved her palm and fingers up and down. Ungh. Her calluses gave his shaft a rough friction which was almost unbearably arousing.

Her eyes were wide. "I—ye know I know naething of this—"

He leered. "Are you frightened of my cock, Helen?"

Again, her jaw jutted. She curled her fingers around his hardening member, independent of his guiding hand.

"Ye know I am frightened of naething. Except empty bellies for my people." She gave him a fierce stroke. Too fierce. Far too fierce. She might tear his cock off if she became any fiercer. She was dangerous, this savage countess of the Highlands.

"I know, Helen," he said soothingly as he pried her fingers off his shaft. Carefully, carefully. "Now let me give you some relief. Then we'll settle into your training with clearer heads. And gentler hands. Much gentler."

She was still staring at his member. He pulled the blanket up over both of them. "Look at me, Helen."

Her small shoulders turned toward him and her half-moon blue eyes moved to his face. She squinted.

"I suddenly dinnae trust ye."

"You're a wise woman."

"Tell me what ye plan to do."

He put his knuckle to the soft skin under her chin and his thumb on the chin itself, gripping her firmly. "I plan to take off your nightdress so you're as naked as I am."

"A-aye."

"Normally, I would next kiss you for a good long while, but you're already quite excited, aren't you?"

Her face turned red. "I dinnae know."

"Do you like kissing, Helen?"

"I. Dinnae. Know."

"You've never been kissed?"

The thrust of her jaw. "I told ye already. Ye are the only man who has ever touched me."

"And I haven't kissed you yet, have I?"

She shook her head, breaking his grasp on her chin. "Yer a cruel man, Jack Pike." She turned and fumbled to get out of the bed.

"Wait." He grabbed her. "Why are you leaving?"

"'Tis naething to ye," she spat. "'Tis flirting to ye to say 'Oh, I havenae kissed ye yet, have I?' as if ye cannae remember. When ye know! Ye know of my lack of experience. So ye should know it would be an event of great significance to me. My first kiss. Well, yer cruel and don't deserve my first kiss. Ye haven't earned it. I will go back to my own bedchamber and tomorrow, I will kiss the first man I see and that will be that. Then ye can give me my training tomorrow night."

"Please, Helen. Don't leave."

She sniffed. He sensed a chink in her armor. He could be penitent and begging if that's what it took. Just another one of the many weapons in his vast arsenal.

"You're right. I *am* thoughtless and cruel. Don't go back to your bedchamber now and kiss the first man you see tomorrow. Because I would have to set up camp in the hall outside your room to make sure I was the first man you saw tomorrow."

"Ye widnae."

"I would."

"Ye have a lot of fine words, Jack Pike. Do ye ever do any of these grand gestures ye talk about?"

"I usually don't have to. As you already know, I'm a scoundrel. But I would make the grand gesture for you, Lady Kinmarloch. Your first kiss deserves it. But please don't make me sleep in the cold hallway. Stay here with me in this warm bed. I won't be cruel again, I promise."

She sniffed once more, but she lay back down. Thank God he hadn't lost his touch up here in the wilds of Caledonia.

He moved a piece of hair off her face. "I am at your disposal, my lady. May I kiss you?"

She put her fingers up to his mouth. She traced his lips. Her voice was soft. "The first time I ever saw ye…"

"Yes?"

"I wanted to lick the rain off yer lips."

"Yes." He stroked her hip through her nightdress.

"Then I wanted to kick yer teeth in."

He cast his mind backward a week, to their first meeting. He did not remember being overtly offensive.

"Why was that?"

"Because ye were so good-looking, ye made me hurt, here." She clutched between her breasts. "Like a perfect sunrise. Like stars on a warm summer night."

He blinked several times. This. From her. It was unexpected. As unexpected as hearing a tavern wench sing the Queen of the Night aria in a flawless soprano. Or a drunk sailor reciting word-perfect *Hamlet*.

He made his voice gruff and adjusted the top of the blanket over both of them. "That's foolishness."

"I'm sure ye have heard it all before, Jack Pike."

He shrugged. "Not really, no."

She squinted at him. "Those ladies ye dally with are fools then. First, 'tis true. There cannae be a man more handsome than ye. I cannae and willnae believe it. Second, ye love the compliments. Ye blush like a girl. And I think yer cock gets harder. 'Tis poking at me more now."

"Shut up, Helen."

"Aye, Jack Pike, ye may kiss me now."

She kept her eyes open as he leaned down. He stopped, his mouth inches above hers. "Most women close their eyes when they're being kissed."

"Most women are nae being kissed by someone as beautiful as ye."

She was the strangest woman he had ever met. She changed as quickly as the weather did up here. Loathing him one moment, worshiping him the next. By turns truculent, docile, knowing, innocent.

She held still, waiting, looking at him expectantly. He had better kiss her now while she was still adoring him.

He kissed her and tasted cider.

"Kiss me back, Helen," he murmured and when he brought his lips down against her mouth for a second time, her own lips were pursed and hungry, devouring.

It was quite a long kiss, he thought, but when he lifted his head, her mouth chased his, her neck straining, her shoulders and head coming off the pillow.

He pushed her down. "That's enough kissing."

Her body went rigid. "I hate ye, Jack Pike."

He sighed. "Why do you hate me now?"

She shook her head. "If ye dinnae know, I widnae tell ye. What's next? Oh, aye, we skipped over the nightdress." Before he could stop her, her hands were at her hips and she sat up and whipped the nightdress up over her head. She threw it on the floor as she lay back down.

"There, I am as naked as ye now."

"Why are you angry, fair Helen?" He stroked her arm. She was almost hot to the touch. The grass smell was stronger now. Her skin was very pale, almost translucent, with tracings of blue veins here and there. Her breasts were…well, there was no way around it. They were small. Achingly small, but tipped with beautiful, dark-pink peaks. He ran his hand down her flank, feeling each rib with his fingers, and finally found a buttock and squeezed.

Her voice was strained. "I. Dinnae. Want. To. Talk. About. It."

"Shall I give you some relief now?"

"Aye."

He moved his hand to her mound, felt the tickle of her maidenhair, and discovered her legs already spread apart.

He leaned down to kiss her but she turned her head away.

"Kiss me, Helen."

She shook her head. He took his hand off her mound.

"Kiss me," he commanded.

She turned her face back to him and he was shocked to see tears in her eyes.

"Ye. Said. That's. Enough. Kissing."

He suddenly realized every time she spoke in this staccato cadence, these choked words, she was keeping herself from crying. But she hadn't been able to keep herself from crying this time. For whatever reason, *that's enough kissing* had hurt her more than anything else he had ever said or done during their acquaintance.

"I meant at that particular moment."

"Do ye know what yer problem is?" She got up on an elbow. "Ye have nae imagination. Ye should be putting yerself in my mind. Thinking 'oh, if I were an untouched maiden, I would want such and such.' And in my case, that might be unlimited kissing. But nae, ye do what ye want. Ye treat me as if I were a trollop who had been pleasured by hundreds of men."

Jack's temper flared. "And you? Are you thinking of *me?* What I want?"

"Do ye think I have ever told any other man they are like a sunrise or the stars?"

"So you don't really think that? You said it just to please me?" he growled.

"Nae, 'tis true. 'Tis what I think about ye. But even if it were true about any other man, I widnae have told him. Only ye. Because I thought ye would like it and would want to hear it."

He had liked it. He had wanted to hear it. Her words had stroked and soothed a wounded part of him he kept stuffed away. But how had she known?

"Why did you think I would like that?"

"Because 'tis how ye yerself talk to women. Ye give yerself away."

He shook his head. "I'm a scoundrel."

"Be careful, Jack Pike. Ye keep saying that, someday ye will believe it." She sat up. "I'm going back to my own bed."

He grabbed her arm. "No. I'll give you unlimited kissing."

"'Tis late. I'll give myself my own relief, and ye can train me tomorrow." She wrenched herself away and leaned over, feeling on the floor for her nightdress.

"Who knows what will happen tomorrow, Helen?" He stroked her naked back, her delicate spine and ribs cushioned only by muscle and skin. "I could be set on by a wolf and killed. You would never get your training."

She sat back up and met his eyes. "Or I could meet a mercenary Highlander heading home from the wars. One with an enormous cock who thinks I'm the perfect sweetheart for him. And he could give me my training."

Even though he knew she was taunting him, he did not

like the sound of this mercenary Highlander and his enormous cock. Not at all.

"The wars are long over."

"There are nae more wolves in Scotland, Jack."

"I know what the duke wants, Helen. A mercenary wouldn't." He willed himself not to let his gaze slip to her breasts but to keep his eyes on hers.

She shook her head. "Och. Ye look at me with those earnest puppy eyes, *mo luran*, and what am I to do? How can I leave yer bed?"

"You can't."

"Well, hurry up. 'Tis late. The dawn will be here before ye know it."

"You can't hurry a painter, Helen." He stroked her cheek with one finger. "Or a poet. Or a lover." She snorted. He leaned forward. "May I kiss you?"

"Aye," she whispered, suddenly all softness.

Still sitting up together, he kissed her. And on this kiss, he parted her lips with his tongue and delved into her sweet mouth which tasted even more of cider than her lips. And as he explored her mouth and brushed one of her nipples with his thumb, her hands came up to his face and she began to kiss him back, whimpering into his mouth. He pressed his body against hers, wrapped his arms around her, and lowered her back down to the mattress.

He got on top of her, his knees between her legs, his cock nestled in her cleft. He tried to keep her clearly in his mind and to ask himself, *What does Helen want?*

He kissed along her jawline to her ear and whispered, "I love kissing you, Helen."

That had been the right thing to say. Her breathing got heavier. He felt her hips pushing up against him.

And he was surprised to find it was true. He did love kissing her. He captured her mouth with his again and delighted at the voraciousness of her probing tongue, the growls in the back of her throat, her rough fingers raking his back as her body strained under his. God love the woman. She was the lustiest virgin in the empire.

He kissed his way down the surprisingly soft skin of her throat, stopping to lavish attention on the point where her pulse beat rapidly in her neck while she moaned. And lower down, he found himself charmed by her breasts. Such perfect, firm bits of flesh. And her pert, dark-pink nipples became even more pert under the ministrations of his tongue and his lips and his teeth.

But he had been wrong with his guess about the taste of her nipples. They did not taste of cider. Close, but not quite. They tasted of applesauce, warmed by the fire.

Her moans were so loud and heated that he wondered if he should just stay here and continue to feast on her breasts. But, no. Her hands were in his hair, and could it be? The countess was pushing him down and away from her chest?

"Oh, Jack. Do that, but lower down," she groaned.

He lifted his head. She lifted hers as well. "Why did ye stop? What's wrong?"

"You told me you were untouched." He heard the snarl in his own voice. She was a liar, after all. He didn't expect or want a woman to be a virgin for him, but he had never thought Helen would lie about it.

"Aye?"

"How do you know what men do with their mouths *lower down*? You didn't learn that from watching sheep."

"The blacksmith…" She bit her lip. He thought she was blushing but the candle was flickering and he wasn't sure.

"The blacksmith licked you between your legs?" He was pushing himself off her, away, but her hands clamped his shoulders and held him. For being so slight, she was very strong. From grabbing and heaving sheep around, no doubt.

"Ye know that's nae true, Jack. Ye are being silly. Years ago, I saw the blacksmith up the side of the mountain with his head in his wife's lap, under her skirts. She was making little noises. I guessed what he was doing."

He relaxed back onto her, his own body trembling with relief. He hadn't been wrong about his savage countess. She really was all brutal truth and innocent desire.

He raised his eyebrows. "You guessed?"

"Aye. D-did I guess right?"

"I don't know what the blacksmith was doing under his wife's skirts, but I will promise you one thing, Helen Boyd, Countess of Kinmarloch in her own right."

"What?

"The noises you'll make with my head in your lap? They will not be little ones."

He gave her his most wicked grin.

And was delighted to see her grin back at him.

"Aye, *mo luran*," she said and ruffled his hair.

He still didn't know what *mo luran* meant. And he didn't care. It was Helen Boyd's name for Captain Jack Pike, and it made his cock hard.

THREE

THREE WEEKS EARLIER. LONDON.

J ack lay on his back, watching Marina dress. She had opened the drapes of one window to let in the morning light and to show herself off to him, he was sure.

And by God, she was right to do so. The sun glinted on her thatch of red-gold maidenhair and bathed her lush, curving body with a glow. And it wasn't just Lady Garvey's flesh he enjoyed, the ripple of the cheeks of her bottom when she got up on all fours on the mattress, arching her back for him, as she had done last night in his bed. It was also those satisfied sighs she made when he took her. Those screams when he buried his face in her scented quim. Those groans when he clutched one of her abundant breasts—

"Jack." He looked up. She was fully dressed. "Stop stroking yourself under the covers."

"Why?" He threw the sheet to one side. "Do you want to do it, Marina?"

She eyed his cock. Unless he was very much mistaken, she licked her lips, just a little.

"Under other circumstances, I'd say yes. But I must get home. Lord Garvey is due back in London this evening."

"So, no more fun for Jack while your husband is in town?"

"Do you know what day it is?"

"No."

"It's been a month since you first took me to bed."

Had it been? Yes, it had. And it had been an extremely pleasurable month. But he knew what that meant.

He groaned, "Are you telling me I've had my goodbye fuck without even knowing that's what it was?"

"It's not my fault you don't know your own calendar. And it is *your* calendar. You made me well aware of it when you unlaced my stays for the first time."

Yes, his unwritten rules. His often unspoken rules. But he had known Lady Garvey's reputation for taking lovers and keeping them, and he had thought it wise to let her know from the start she wouldn't be sinking her claws into Jack Pike. One month and that was all.

How fortuitous that her month with him had coincided with her husband being out of town and he had had her so many times. Although risk could heighten his pleasure, he had been more than happy to trade that thrill for the delight of playing in bed with Marina for hours at a time.

"Unless." She leaned over and ran her soft, delicate fingers over his shaft. An involuntary grunt escaped his lips. "You want to make an exception. In my case."

"No." He moved, taking himself and his member off the bed and away from her. He started looking for his trousers in the tangle of bed coverings on the floor.

Yes, coitus with Marina was intoxicating. But the affair was over. The month had passed, and today he would start to work on finding another desirous lady of the *ton* who would welcome his transitory attentions. It shouldn't be difficult. It never was for him. Women were weak. Easily seduced by a few compliments. Naughty smiles. Fleeting, stolen touches at the waist, the neck. And he knew his looks didn't hurt.

"No, I didn't think you would." She came up behind him and squeezed a buttock as he leaned over. "But thank you for proffering such a lovely view to me on my way out the door."

He found his trousers and straightened up with them in his hand, giving her his standard devilish grin as he looked over his shoulder at her breasts on display in her low-cut bodice. "My pleasure."

She simpered. "No, Jack. Mine."

"Give my regards to the viscount, Marina."

"I'm Lady Garvey from now on. Don't forget it, Captain Pike."

Then she was gone, the cuckolding harlot. And he was still hard. Damn it.

"You know—" Phineas Edge, the Earl of Burchester, stopped himself midsentence. Uncharacteristically.

"What, Phin?" An irritated Jack rustled the newspaper. They were in the reading room of their club and Jack had been perusing the pages which dealt with gossip and society gatherings, looking for names of attractive women who might be ripe for a dalliance.

"You might be less convinced that all women are deceivers ever, if, just once, you bedded a woman who wasn't already married."

Jack snorted. Phineas had said this to him before.

"Not that I'm suggesting a debutante to you, Jack. I wouldn't wish you on one of those innocents." Phineas chuckled.

Jack crumpled the newspaper. "The debutantes are safe from me. And on first glance, the matrons who are in town also have nothing to worry about. A very unpromising bunch. It looks like I'll be making do with the damned brothel until the Season is in full swing. What say you to Madame Flora's tonight?"

Phineas sat back in what he called *the chair*. Phineas and one of their mutual friends, George Danforth, often clashed over *the chair* since George also thought it was a superior seat. The serious young Baron Danforth had resigned himself to a different wing chair today and was in a corner, reading a thick book.

Phineas ran his fingers through his mane of prematurely silver hair. "Someone else might have wanted to read that paper, Jack."

Jack growled but he attempted to flatten the newspaper with the side of his hand.

"In truth, I'm not fond of your company when you're so cross." Phineas sighed. "You are, without fail, once a month, the worst kind of malcontent. Quite like a woman yourself with your lunar moods. But for you, it's always because it's that delicate time when you are *between*, isn't it? Between mistresses." He cocked his head. "Because why fuss about going to the brothel? You can afford it, Jack. You can afford it three times a day, every day of the year, for years on end, you rich wretch."

"Yes. Although you know I like to watch my pennies."

"It's the very little bit of the Scot in you, I dare say. And it's part of why you're so rich. But going to a whore—it doesn't satisfy you, does it?"

"If you're implying I can't get it up—"

"Of course not." Phineas rolled his eyes. "I've come behind you a few times, wiping away the tears of your discarded wives of other men." He grinned. "They tell me all about you and your cock before I soothe them with my own special prong. I know getting satisfaction is not a problem for you."

"Then what the devil do you mean?"

"You tell me, Jack. Why don't you like going to the brothel?"

"Because—"

"Because you want a woman to want you, more than you want her."

"No." Jack leaned forward, ready to refute Phineas. Because that wasn't it, was it? Yes, he liked attention. But the whores paid him attention. For an hour or two. Maybe it was that he liked *genuine* attention.

"I think," Phineas said. Again, an uncharacteristic pause. He must be weighing his next words carefully.

Blast Phineas. It was none of his business why Jack did what he did.

But they had known each other a long time. Been lieutenants together years ago on the *HMS Endeavor*. Seen action and faced death together. Phineas had been decommissioned when he was suddenly made the Earl of Burchester. Jack eventually rose in the ranks to become captain of his own ship. It was how he had made the beginning of his fortune which had grown exponentially with some clever and risky investments. And after the wars, when Jack had resigned his commission and settled in London, he had found the Earl of Burchester the same stalwart and jovial companion he had been when they had roamed the Atlantic together as young men in the Royal Navy.

Phineas finally spoke. "I think you want women to fall in love with you. That's what I think."

Jack shook his head.

Phineas persisted. "You want them to fall in love with you and just as they do, you want to break it off. You want to be the heartbreaker, not the heartbroken."

Jack scoffed. "Who doesn't?"

"You might be surprised."

"Not you, Phin!"

"Oh, hearts are not involved with me." Phineas thumped his chest. "They all know what they're getting with me. A bit of fun. A romp. A good giggle."

"That's what they get with me, too."

"No, Jack. That's not true. They think they're getting unplumbed depths with you. You're a dashing hero, after all. That's why they're so angry when you turn out to be just as shallow as the next fellow." Phineas smirked. "Besides, most of my women are widows, not matrons. I am the relief between husbands. You are the relief *for* the husbands. Is it any wonder your women expect a grand romance since they are risking so much to bed you?"

It was long past time for Jack to change the subject.

"The question still stands, Phin."

"What's that?"

"Madame Flora's. Tonight. Yea or nay?"

"Are you paying?"

"For you? Never. You rack up all kinds of extras."

"That was only the one time, Jack. And believe me, it was worth everything you paid for it."

Jack crumpled the newspaper again and threw it at Phineas.

Suddenly, a shadow fell over both of them.

Jack and Phineas looked up.

"Edmund," Phineas said, grinning. "Save me from this starboard bow assault by newsprint."

Edmund Haskett, Earl of Longridge and heir apparent to the Marquess of Sudbury, loomed. Edmund was tall and large. Outlandishly so. Very intimidating. Reliably foul-tempered. Always destined since birth for the peerage so he had never served in either the army or the navy. But Jack had often thought what a phenomenal soldier Edmund would have made. He would have scared the French into surrendering with his hulking size alone.

Jack saw Phineas straighten up, push his shoulders back. He always did when Edmund was around. Didn't like his relative stature. Never had. Although Phineas would be the first to say his height was average for an Englishman and he was just cursed with unusually tall friends.

Edmund bowed. "Your Grace." His deep voice filled the reading room of the club. The chatter among the other gentlemen in surrounding chairs suddenly hushed.

Edmund sat. As always, he made ordinary furniture look doll-sized.

Jack glanced around the room to see if either the Duke of Thornwick or the Duke of Abingdon, both members of the club, were standing nearby. No, they weren't in the reading room.

The silence stretched.

Jack looked at Phineas. Phineas was looking at Edmund.

"Did Norman MacNaughton die?" Phineas asked in a low voice.

"Yes. This morning."

No. No. Jack's bones dissolved and he slumped back into his chair.

Norman was dead. His cousin. His vile, contemptible, piece-of-shit cousin was dead. But Norman was young, three or four years younger than Jack. And the last Jack had heard, he was in good health.

"It's a mistake," Jack got out.

"No," Edmund grunted. Definitively. "Choked to death on his breakfast."

Phineas stood and turned to Jack and bowed. "Your Grace."

"Sit down, Phin," Jack hissed. "Edmund's having a joke."

Phineas looked down at Jack. "Have you ever known Edmund to have a joke? If it were me coming to you with the news, I could see it. But Edmund?" He gestured at the dark-haired man who was hunched over, his elbows resting on his thighs. "It must be true, Jack. You are the new Duke of Dunmore."

"I…" Jack searched Phineas' serious face and Edmund's scowl. He got no reassurance from either of their expressions.

No, no, no. He couldn't be the Duke of Dunmore. He was never going to be the duke. Norman was supposed to have a dozen sons with his deceitful, beautiful whore of a wife and put Jack well out of the running. It was just like Norman to have failed at even that. The arsehole.

"I need a drink," Jack finally gasped out.

Phineas disappeared and seconds later was back with glasses and a bottle of amber liquid.

"It's appropriate, I think, to toast the new Duke of Dunmore with some whisky."

Jack grabbed a glass as soon as the whisky was poured and gulped it down. He held the glass out, his hand shaking. "Another." The glass was refilled. He was drinking the second finger as Phineas and Edmund both held out their glasses and intoned, "To the Duke of Dunmore."

Jack was aware other men were saying "hear, hear" and several were leaving the reading room, ready to spread the news to men in other parts of the club and also among the *ton* in general. By afternoon, it would be everywhere. Because it was juicy news, indeed. Captain Jack Pike, the ruthless navy captain who had untold riches after the wars, was now the Duke of Dunmore.

"Where's everyone off to?" George Danforth joined the three men, his book in his hand. The grave baron with his regimented mind, his outmoded wig, his dark eyes that missed very little. "Did something important happen?"

"Jack's the new Duke of Dunmore," Phineas said and sat quickly, likely to remind George of his prior claim on *the chair* today.

"Your Grace." George bowed and pulled up another chair, glaring at Phineas and shaking his head when Edmund lifted the whisky bottle. "Norman MacNaughton is dead, I take it. He would have to be, wouldn't he?"

"Yes," Edmund said.

"Well." Jack wiped his mouth. "I hated Norman, but I never wished him dead."

Phineas studied Jack over the top of his whisky glass. "Even though you would have been well within your rights to."

"Well, yes. But wishing him dead would mean I had to become the duke and I was rather hoping to avoid that." Jack laughed and he knew the laugh was a bitter one.

"Yes." Phineas was about to say something else, but he clamped his mouth closed.

Edmund raised his glass. "Welcome to the peerage, Jack Pike."

George raised his forefinger, as if to lodge an objection. "MacNaughton."

"Indeed," said Phineas. "You won't be Jack Pike anymore, will you? You'll be Jack MacNaughton. Or John MacNaughton. You'll have to revert to your father's name."

Jack's own father, a worthless drunk, had died when he was five, and his mother had quickly married Sir Oswald Pike. Jack had chosen to take his stepfather's name years ago. His commission had been paid for by his stepfather under that same name. But as the ninth Duke of Dunmore, he'd have to go back to being a MacNaughton. The Duke of Dunmore had been a MacNaughton for as long as the title had been in existence.

"But I suppose most of us will just call you Dunmore." Phineas poured more whisky into Jack's glass.

Jack attempted a smile. "Well, call me Your Grace, and it won't be that much of a hardship for you to remember."

Suddenly, he was struck by a possible way of escaping his fate. "Wait, we're forgetting. I am not necessarily the duke."

"Why do you say that?"

George answered for Jack. "The Duchess of Dunmore could still bear a son."

Phineas frowned and looked at Jack. "Have you heard rumors Elizabeth is with child?"

Jack turned away, grinding his teeth. "I think I would be the last man in the world to hear any rumors about that woman."

"Yes, everyone keeps their mouths shut about Her Grace around you, don't they? But people have no reason not to talk in front of Phineas Edge. And I can tell you I have heard no gossip in that direction. Although I have heard she has a new lover—"

"I would remind you that my friends keep their mouths shut about the Duchess of Dunmore around me because I promised that anyone who mentioned her would get a blade in his neck."

"Calm down, Jack. I won't say anything else about Elizabeth, all right?"

Jack put his third whisky to his lips and felt the glass knock against his teeth. He was trembling.

Elizabeth. He didn't like to think of his cousin's wife—now his widow—as Elizabeth. If Jack had to think of her, much better to think of her as a heartless, betraying trull. Because she was one.

He tossed the whisky back. The burn in the back of his throat did nothing to ease the peculiar ache in his chest.

"Dunmore," he mumbled. "Where is it, do you know?"

"Scotland." Phineas raised his eyebrows. "Hence, I thought the whisky was fitting, Jack."

"Blast. I know it's in Scotland. But where?"

"It's your duchy, Jack. Not mine."

"The Highlands." George was thoughtful, lying back in his chair, his forgotten book hugged to his chest, one finger still holding his place. "Beautiful scenery, I hear. Brutish people."

"I suppose I'll have to go up and have a look at it."

Edmund grunted. "You should go as Jack Pike, not John MacNaughton. Get the lie of the land. Find out all the secrets. I wish I could do that with Sudbury."

Jack shivered. "Scotland. In March. I would be a glutton for punishment."

"Gluttony is not the sin I would ascribe to you, Jack," Phineas teased.

Jack forced a grin back on his face. Maybe the whisky was doing something to improve his mood. "You know, before my uncle died, he told me there would be a neighboring young countess. Some barbaric and ancient Scottish splitting of the titles and the land when the duke before him died. My grand-father was her grandfather's cousin. Perhaps I might use my scouting trip as a chance to get to know her."

"A countess and a third cousin, eh? That's the Jack I know and love." Phineas clapped Jack on the shoulder. "Go to your new pastures and satisfy your itch for the fair sex. A coupling or two with a pretty Scottish lass will get your blood coursing. Just be sure you're back to London in time for the last few months of the Season."

"Why's that?"

"The marriage mart, Jack. Barring the duchess being *enceinte*, you'll be a new duke by then. The debutantes will be running riot if you don't show up."

"I'm never getting married. You know that. I've told you a million times."

Phineas leered. "You need to make an heir, Jack."

"How about you? You need to make one, too, Phin. And you, Edmund. And you, George."

Edmund shook his head, slowly. "No."

George frowned. "I have to get my sister married first. And you forget I'm several years younger than the rest of you." Yes, it was easy to forget how young George was since he was far more serious and responsible than the rest of them. Wearing his wig, following his rigid routines, always preparing his ponderous speeches for the House of Lords.

Phineas scoffed. "I was twelfth in line when I was born. The title is lucky to have me rather than the other way around. I'm not rushing. I feel no obligation to anyone."

Edmund growled. "Like you, Jack, I will never marry. My cousin will be the marquess after me. Or his sons."

Phineas sat back with a smug grin. "Just wait. You'll all find some soft little thing who makes you dizzy with a bat of her eyelashes and you'll be married before you know it. Come now, Jack. You must be back in town for the important balls of the Season. What fun it'll be. You all done up as a duke. The young ladies salivating over your good looks. The mothers salivating over your title. The fathers salivating over your fortune."

"I have no interest in making the fathers salivate, Phin."

"Well, if you don't want to get coated in drool, you had better give all your money to me, Jack."

Four

"Lord Reeves."

"Lady Kinmarloch."

Even though the room was warm, much warmer than her own keep, Helen Boyd shivered.

She had known the man in front of her all her life, and she had never liked or trusted him. He had a cruel set to his mouth, the lips thin and always wet. The rest of his face was soft, pale, and relatively unwrinkled, despite the fact he must be forty years of age. This was not a man who went out in the weather. This was a man who sat in a warm room like this one and made other men go out.

He did not offer her a chair or refreshment of any kind but took his own seat and raised a goblet to his lips, appraising her.

Her nose twitched. Mulled wine. Helen could smell the spices, those damned exotic spices she would never be able to afford again. She had drunk mulled wine once-upon-a-time, though, when her grandfather was still alive. She had the memory of the taste of it in her mouth. She felt the back of her throat tighten, and her mouth was flooded with spittle.

That must be why Reeves' lips were always moist. He had

mulled wine, beef, all the bread he wanted, things to make your mouth water. It was a wonder Reeves wasn't fat. But he wasn't. He was lean, like she was, despite his good food, his money.

"My lady." At least he addressed her correctly even though the rest of his behavior was that of a boor. "What brings you to my barony?"

She smoothed the front of her bodice. She wore her best dress, although it hung loosely on her now. The wool was brown, her least favorite color. But that was why the dress had lasted this long and was the least patched, the least stained. She hated wearing it.

The roughness of her palms snagged against the cloth. She looked down at her red, much-worked hands. Then she raised her head and squared her shoulders. Yes, don't let her appear as some favor-seeker, some beggar. Even though that was what she was.

"Lord Reeves, I would like to borrow some money."

He stilled in the midst of raising the cup to his lips again. "And I would like to be king of England."

If he had smiled, she would have known what to do. She was prepared for a gibe. She would have forced herself to laugh at what he thought was wit and approached the request a different way.

But Lord Reeves did not smile.

Damn these English. Because that was what he was, of course. He may have grown up in Scotland, but his parents were English, his father having been made a greater baron of the lands south of Kinmarloch some thirty years ago. And he spoke with the flat and humorless accent of his southern heritage. No burr for Lord Reeves.

"Once I sell my spring wool, I will pay ye back."

"The spring wool from your forty sheep? Surely, you need that money to make it through next winter."

Yes, damn him, she did. And how did he know she had only forty sheep? Thirty-nine to be precise, since a ewe had disappeared last week despite her and Luran's careful watch.

"My people need food, Lord Reeves."

"The current Duke of Dunmore has made clearances. My father made them years ago. If you or your grandfather had, you would not have people you needed to feed."

He stood and walked to her, his eyes on her chest. She willed herself not to recoil, not to back away. Not to squeak. She was a countess. In her own right.

"I would say you were in need of food, too, my lady. Your bosom is so shrunken. Is there famine in Kinmarloch?"

She leveled her gaze at him, waiting for his eyes to move up to her face. Finally, they did.

"Nae," she said. And it was true. There was not famine. Not yet.

He sighed and walked away from her and refilled his cup from the ewer next to his chair. "This is why these old Scottish peerages are so foolish. A soft-hearted, brainless woman can inherit a title and have the responsibility of making prudent decisions when so many men might die."

She let his insults slide off her. She did not care about his good opinion, only his money.

"I have made prudent decisions, Lord Reeves, the same as my grandfather who was both the Duke of Dunmore and the Earl of Kinmarloch when he was alive. I have just nae made the same decisions ye have."

"You think keeping your farmers as farmers when you so desperately need grazing land is prudent? All your people should have been moved years ago to the coast where they could fish or harvest kelp or croft in some other way."

"Ye know my land dinnae touch the sea."

"No, it doesn't, does it? You lost that bit when your grand-father died five years ago, didn't you? Then you should have

moved your farmers someplace else where they might scratch
out a living. Glasgow. The New World."

"I dinnae have the money for that, my lord." And it was
cruel to tear people away from the land they had lived on for
centuries.

"Yes, I see your difficulty. But it's your difficulty, isn't it?
Not mine." He turned his back to her and faced the fire.

She almost turned then herself. Almost turned and walked
away, leaving the warm room and the warm house of this
unspeakable worm. She would resaddle her horse herself, not
wanting any favors from Reeves' grooms, and ride the many
miles back to her keep.

And once in her keep, she would do what? Have Mags
make up the pallet in front of the fire while she herself heated
the groats. And after a few shared spoonfuls, she and Mags
would lay down on that pallet, her keeping the girl in front of
her to get most of the heat, she with her back to the cold of the
keep. Please let it not rain tonight.

"But."

The word arrested her.

"But?" She could not keep the hope and the plea out of
her voice and she hated herself for it.

"I might be willing to make your difficulty mine. I am long
past due to take a wife."

He spoke slowly, almost in a lazy manner, as if the idea had
just occurred to him. But for Helen, the words dangled, sharp
and pointed, full of menace, like a suspended sword. No, no,
no. Not this.

"I had thought to go to London," Reeves went on. "To
rent a house. To make the acquaintance of some young ladies
there. Perhaps make an offer of marriage to the daughter of a
merchant. Or to the daughter of an impoverished earl,
desperate to dispose of one of his female offspring. I do not
need a large dowry. I just need an obedient wife who is willing

to come live in this godforsaken place. A fertile wife. But perhaps I need not travel so far afield."

He turned to face her. "Because, after all, there is a woman here, in front of me. An ugly woman, but one with land. Barren, rocky land I know can turn a profit as grazing land. And she has a title which would one day go to my son. He would be an earl, himself." His eyes ran over her body. "But is the woman as barren as the land? I think I would have to plant some seed and make sure it took root before committing myself."

He had made it easy for her, thank God. He had not wooed her with pleasantries or undertook any effort to make himself appealing. He had made the crudest offer possible—that he would take her, likely in this room, right now, and if she met with his approval and if she became heavy with child, he would marry her.

She had her dirk strapped to her leg. She allowed herself to imagine a future in which she pulled that dirk from its sheath and charged Lord Reeves with a battle cry, sinking the dirk into his belly and twisting it so his intestines spilled out onto the floor of this warm room.

But…Mags and everyone else who depended on her. And her title would become extinct when she was executed by the crown for murder. And the people of Kinmarloch would be at the mercy of some other man she did not know.

She took a breath and summoned the strength of the Mac-Naughtons so she could manage to bite her tongue, to say what was needed to get her money. She had not known how much strength it took to submit.

"I think ye should go to London, my lord. Since I am so ugly, ye widnae have difficulty finding a prettier woman, one ye deserve. Ye might even find a widow, one who has already borne a child, and ye would then have yer surety she could do the same for ye."

He said nothing. She took another deep breath.

"But in case ye dinnae find a woman to yer taste in London and ye returned here unwed, might I borrow some money so ye dinnae come back to find me famished and wasted and unable to fulfill my potential future duties as yer wife?"

She had not told an untruth and said she would marry him. Or couple with him. Although it might come to that. But she would not think on that possibility now. She would only think on the money and the food the money would buy.

The seconds stretched out as Reeves considered her and her proposal. Finally, he drained his goblet and set it down with a loud clank.

"I'll have my steward give you some money and write out a note for you to sign. You do know how to write your own name, don't you?"

She gritted her teeth.

"Aye, my lord. I do."

FIVE

Jack ate his first dinner as the possible future Duke of Dunmore alone. Afterwards, he went and lay on the sofa in his drawing room and considered going out and paying to have something really filthy done to him at Madame Flora's. It would fill an hour or two and sate him temporarily.

Phineas had turned down going to the brothel since he currently had a randy widow keeping his bed warm for him. George had never liked using whores and had been entertaining the same mistress for the last three months or so, also a widow. And Edmund had also refused to come along. He had not said why, but Jack knew Edmund had a difficult time convincing Cyprians to accommodate his phallus, an organ as outsized as the rest of him. Madame Flora must not have any in her employ currently who were willing.

But Jack might visit the brothel alone. Most men did, after all.

He thought idly about maybe going to Scotland. What he might pack. How much whisky he would drink once there. And would he find a lusty Scottish lass to frolic with him? Of course, he would. Dozens of them. Women loved him. His charm and his looks would not be any less in the far reaches of Scotland.

And there was that countess up there. If she were not too unattractive, he would sneak her away from her earl for a little fun. Why shouldn't he give some pleasure to a countess in the middle of nowhere? There could be nothing to stop her from dallying with him, apart from her duty to her husband. But Jack knew ways of making that duty seem very small in comparison to his cock. After all, women had no sense of loyalty. They were all faithless. Just like his mother had been. Just like—

No. Think of something else.

Scotland. Scotland might be a bit of an adventure for him. And he would *not* go as the possible future duke. Edmund's idea of going as Jack Pike was damn near verging on brilliant. Yes. He would go as Captain Pike. Let him stretch out his time as a carefree and notorious rake as long as possible.

He turned on his side.

Because damn being duke. Damn the duchy of Dunmore. If only he could go back in time to this morning when his sole problem had been finding his next mistress.

He heard a knock, his butler's voice, some rustling in the front hall. Jack had an unexpected caller. He got to his feet, combed a hand through his hair, felt his cravat to make sure it was straight.

"Her Grace, the Duchess of Dunmore," his butler intoned at the drawing room door and withdrew.

The woman he had just banished from his thoughts. Here, in his house.

Elizabeth was as lovely as ever. Her raven-black hair. Her large violet eyes. That beauty mark next to her full lips. Her short stature which still offered a gorgeous, perfect bosom.

One breast of which, he knew, had a beauty mark next to the areola to match the one by her mouth.

He cursed himself. Why had he just pictured the naked breast of the woman he hated?

"Your Grace." He bowed. "I offer my condolences."

"*Your* Grace." She curtsied. "I offer mine."

"I do not need condolences. And I am not Your Grace yet."

"No. That's true." She smiled sadly. "I suppose everything hinges on whether or not I have my courses in the next few weeks. And if I am with child, whether or not I then give birth to a son."

"Yes."

She nodded and for just a moment a crease appeared in her forehead. "I can't decide if you would like that, Jack."

He couldn't decide, either. He did not want to be duke. He liked his easy life, his wealth, his mistresses. But right now, some childish part of him was liking the fact that if he were made duke, the woman in front of him would be shut out of most of the privileges she had enjoyed for the last five years. She would be relatively poor, and he would still be rich. And a duke.

He studied her more carefully. He had not seen her in nearly a year. His initial impression of her as being as lovely as ever held up under closer scrutiny. She was ruinously beautiful. And as always, he felt his knees go weak. His chest ached. His mouth went to dust. And yes, shamefully, his cock got hard.

She was in a dress of dark-purple silk which made her eyes appear even more violet. But he was surprised she was not in mourning.

She saw him looking at her dress. "I was not prepared. My modiste will have a bombazine ready for me by tomorrow. But it is unseemly for me to be here in the first place. I didn't think not wearing black would compound the impropriety."

"I suppose you're right."

"But I knew you would not come to me, Jack, so I must come to you, whether or not it is seemly."

He took a deep breath. "Did Norman really choke on his breakfast?"

"That's what I was told. I wasn't present." She trilled a caressing, lyrical laugh. "And I will tell you, in confidence, there is no chance I am with child. At least, not with Norman's child."

His pleasure that at least his cousin had not enjoyed Elizabeth's body in the weeks before his death was destroyed by the reminder that she was an adulterer. Inconstant, like every other woman. Always ready to lie with whom she liked, whenever it took her fancy.

Indiscriminate and lustful. Just like me. But I am not married. I am not a duchess. I am not tasked with bringing a legitimate heir into the world. It would be just like her to have a son by someone else and have him become duke.

The small part of Jack that wanted to be duke became a little larger.

Because the title belongs to my *family, doesn't it? Not some bastard she's going to palm off on the duchy.*

She smiled, a small smile. "But one cannot say that openly, of course. So we will wait, won't we?"

"Yes."

"I would much rather be married to a duke than be mother to a duke."

She said it so simply. Guilelessly. It was what had charmed him about her initially, that she had seemed so direct. He had thought it meant she was truthful.

"Is this a marriage proposal?" *You conniving strumpet.*

"It might be. Would you be agreeable, Jack?"

He made a lazy smile come to his lips. "I am always agreeable."

"You know what I mean."

"If you think you can feel me out on the matter, see if I will say yes before you make your proposal, you are mistaken."

She stared at him through her long dark lashes. "I am trying to decide how long you want to make me pay. If it's a short time or a long time."

"I'm not interested in making you pay. But I am very interested in my own happiness. And I have to ask myself, would I be happy with a woman who left me for my cousin? If that woman came back to me once I had her husband's title? Well, the question really comes down to the woman. She's as beautiful as ever. She's as beguiling as ever. I want to bed her as much as ever. But she's a liar. A cheat. A thief of my heart. So…" He shrugged.

"Do you really want to bed me as much as ever, Jack?" She stepped closer to him. "Did I really steal your heart?"

"You should go, Your Grace."

"Once upon a time, you called me Elizabeth."

"Once upon a time, I thought I was in love with you."

"Can you honestly say you're not in love with me now?"

"What do you know of honesty?"

She smiled. "I'll leave, Jack. I can see you're in one of your stubborn, querulous moods. And I remember the best way to handle one of those. I'll let you sulk and stew, but I'll promise a reward if you come to your senses. Tonight, think on me. Think on what we shared together. And I'll see you tomorrow. You will come to me, won't you? In the afternoon?"

Her hand was on his chest, touching his shirt just under his cravat, toying with a button.

"Yes," he answered in a hoarse whisper, knowing, with a despairing certainty, that tomorrow he would go to her as she asked. And he would bed her. And he would rise from that bed a baser man, hating himself and his weakness.

She smiled and curtsied and left the drawing room and his house, but it felt like her hand was still on his chest, over his heart.

He did not go to Madame Flora's that night.

He also did not sleep that night. When the sun rose, he ordered his valet to pack his warmest clothes. He was headed north to Scotland. He would wait out the weeks up there until his fate was set. He would go wherever far-flung Dunmore was. Away from Elizabeth. Away from her face and her breasts and her quim.

And he would go as Jack Pike, just as Edmund had suggested. He wasn't the duke yet, after all. One of his coachmen had served under Jack's command in the navy and would not blink at Jack's subterfuge. The former sailor would follow orders, keep his mouth shut, and remember not to call Jack by a title or refer to him as the possible future duke.

Yes, let him travel to Dunmore as Captain Jack Pike. Elizabeth could be pregnant or not. She could have a son or not. He could be duke or not. He had no control over any of that.

But, by God and by England, he still had control over his own cock.

Six

"The duke has died?"

Helen took a step back from the man who had just given her the news. She had gone to buy food from one of the few farmers left in Dunmore. She knew a Kinmarloch man would pity her and sell her what little he had at an unfairly low price, and she could not do that to one of her own people.

"Aye, my lady."

"Who is the new duke?"

"Well, there is thought to be some question about whether the widowed duchess has a child in her belly, but the word is that the duke will be John MacNaughton, the last duke's cousin."

"And is this John MacNaughton married? Will there be a new duchess?"

Please let there be a new duchess. A woman who might come to Scotland. A woman she could meet. Not like the last duchess who, just like her late husband, never came to Dunmore, never answered Helen's letters.

Yes, let there be a new duchess, a sympathetic woman who

felt as Helen did and whom she could talk round, explain the desperate need and the injustice of separating the people from the land their families had known as their own for almost a millennium. And then the wife could convince the new duke to stop the clearances, to cease using Kinmarloch as a throughway for Dunmore sheep, and maybe even to loan Helen a small sum. To relieve her, a little, of some of her burden.

The farmer shrugged. "I dinnae know about a duchess. MacNaughton's London man should be here tomorrow and ye can ask him yerself whether the duke is married. Word was sent from Cumdairessie that the London man is staying at the public house there. As ye can imagine, the castle is in an uproar, food being sent for, a call out for extra servants. There is thought that this Englishman may be clearing the way for the duke's arrival and, as ye know, there has been nae duke here in residence since yer grandfather died."

Helen looked at the single coin in her hand and gave it to the farmer and hefted the bag of potatoes onto her back.

It had been the last of the money from Reeves' steward.

But a new duke. This might change everything. She had to force herself not to break into a run on the way back home.

"Mags!" she called when she was still ten yards away from the keep.

Mags met her at the door. Despite her limp, the girl did her best for Helen and made sure the keep was tidy, the fire was lit, the tea was made. She was seventeen and growing into her womanhood even though Helen could feed neither Mags nor herself well. Mags was a beauty with her red hair and green eyes, her graceful figure.

For the thousandth time, Helen had the thought that Mags should have been born a countess, not Helen.

"Potatoes, Mags."

Mags smiled radiantly. "Aye, my lady. Good."

"And there is to be a new Duke of Dunmore."

"Is there? Let me get started on the potatoes now."

"Ye seem happier about the potatoes than ye are about the duke."

"Should I be happy about a new duke?"

Helen followed Mags into the keep, noticing Mags' limp was more pronounced than usual.

"Does yer leg hurt worse today?"

Mags shrugged and went to get her knife to peel the potatoes.

"Will ye let me look at it later, Mags?"

"Aye."

Helen took out the potatoes they would eat for dinner tonight.

"I am hoping it will be a good thing. Maybe the duke will have a duchess and he'll bring her here. And I would be able to talk to her. Get her to help us. The new duke might do some good."

"Maybe, my lady."

"But he might nae be married. The man who told me dinnae know."

"If the new duke is nae married, ye could marry him yerself, my lady. Then ye widnae need to convince the new duchess of anything. Ye would *be* the new duchess. And ye widnae need to go to Lord Reeves for money again."

The neatness, the rightness of it made Helen almost drop the potatoes she held in each hand.

To be Duchess of Dunmore *and* Countess of Kinmarloch. Then things would be as they had been before, as they had been for centuries.

She looked at the girl who was intent on sharpening her little stub of a knife so the peels would come from the potatoes with the least amount of flesh wasted.

Why had Mags seen this as an answer and Helen hadn't?

Helen was the one tasked with coming up with the plans and the schemes to allow them to survive one more month, one more season, one more year.

Because Mags was blind where Helen was concerned. Mags didn't really see Helen. Not how a man would see her. Not how men *did* see her.

Helen knew, deep in her heart, no duke would ever want her. Couldn't want her.

But, still, she could pretend to have hope. And for her own sake and for Mags' sake and for all of Kinmarloch's sake, Helen must at least try to become a duchess.

WET, cold. Hoarse from yelling at the sheep. Lungs burning, muscles aching. After six hours out in the weather, she and Luran had finally chased her own sheep east, off the lands of the duchy of Dunmore, back onto the safe grasses of Kinmarloch.

Several times today, Helen had wanted to throw herself down in the mud and scream in frustration. She wanted to do that now. To lie down. To rest. She was so tired. And after all, she could not be any wetter than she already was. But the thing that stopped her, besides the coldness of the ground, was the knowledge that she *could* be muddier. And she would be the one washing the mud out of her clothes tonight.

Yes, best not to lie down and wallow. There would be, as always, a price to pay for that.

She began the long, slow trudge home to the keep, behind her own small flock, Luran racing back and forth to make sure none strayed. She might be lucky and some tea would be waiting for her, fixed by Mags. There would be no hot bath but there might be a clean bit of cloth she could use to wipe off the mud. A peat fire. Potatoes. More than many others had.

And after that, if the rain stopped, she would gird her loins, put on her brown dress, and go see the duke's man at the castle of the duchy of Dunmore. He should have arrived by now.

She heard something. She looked around. Behind her, several hundred yards away, a rider on horseback came through the duchy's lands toward her. Probably from the castle.

He was here. The duke's man was here, and he was going to meet her when she was exhausted, cold, wet, and wearing muddy breeches. Damn it all to hell.

She stopped walking. At least, she could rest while she waited for him. Luran would continue, good boy that he was, chasing the sheep back to the paddock.

The man had a good seat, she noted as he slowed his horse. Still at least fifty feet away, he shouted at her.

"Ho, boy, whose sheep are these and where are you taking them?"

She waited until he came closer to answer. After all, her voice was already hoarse.

'They are the Countess of Kinmarloch's sheep."

As he pulled his horse to a stop, she heard the most glorious sound she had ever heard. A full-throated laugh. It rippled over her like sunshine rippled on her own loch in the summertime.

She hadn't ever laughed like that. She hadn't ever met anyone who laughed like that. She wanted to be drenched in that laugh, feel it against her skin.

The man dismounted in a smooth, even move. He swept off his rain-soaked hat and bowed.

"My apologies. I saw the breeches and assumed. I must have been blind. Of course, you're no boy, but yet another female jewel in this crown of Scotland."

"Are ye the man sent by the new Duke of Dunmore?"

He was only a few yards away. He straightened from his bow.

Her chest began to hurt.

Tall with broad shoulders. Dark blond hair. Light brown eyes flashing above perfect cheekbones. White teeth gleaming in his grin. A square jaw covered in barely visible stubble.

Handsome. Devastatingly, crushingly handsome. And very, very secure in his knowledge of his own beauty. How could he not be?

There was rain dripping from sculpted lips now that his hat was in his hand. She'd like to lick the rain off those lips.

The lips moved. "In a manner of speaking. My name is Jack Pike. Who are you?"

She was embarrassed to find her own tongue just slightly protruding from her lips. She hastily tucked it away and used it to answer him. "My name is Helen Boyd."

He put his hat back on. "Helen, the lovely shepherdess of Kinmarloch. Fair Helen."

His eyes roved over her body. For the first time ever, she regretted wearing breeches while out with the sheep. Oh, to be in a dress and not to have the shape of her legs and her bottom exposed to this man. Because she knew whatever this beautiful man wanted, it would not be her and her meager hips.

And in addition to her chest ache, his eyes were making her feel warm in quite an unaccustomed way. In a way she didn't like. It made her want to kick him in the face and dislodge one of those white teeth. But sadly, a hole in his smile would not make him any less handsome.

He grinned even more broadly. His voice was silky, warm. "Scotland isn't quite what I expected. I came up here thinking to find big men in skirts and instead I find a beautiful woman in breeches. I'm not complaining, mind you, I'm just surprised."

She snorted. Beautiful woman, indeed. He had the lying,

smooth tongue of an Englishman. No one had called her beautiful since her grandfather had died five years ago. She knew what she looked like.

"They are kilts, nae skirts."

"Fascinating," he said and walked closer and leaned down. His body was so near hers. A thrill coursed from her head to her toes as her breath hitched in her throat.

The man purred, "I would love to take you somewhere dry and warm where we might speak more on this subject."

"And I would love to—" *believe ye, ye tempting piece of masculine perfection* "—nae starve next winter. My sheep still need me. So, I will bid ye farewell."

She turned. She would wait until she was clean and rested to speak to him again. When she might be better prepared to deflect his lying, sweet words. And better prepared to look at his face. *A face that launched a thousand ships.*

She heard him sigh.

"Fair Helen, Miss Helen Boyd, will you tell me where I can find the countess, Lady Kinmarloch? Perhaps, if you are headed back with her sheep toward her lands, I could walk with you and you could point out the way to her castle?"

She turned around. "Ye are on her lands right now."

The man scrutinized the landscape, looked at the mountains. "Surely not."

"Aye. The duchy ends a furlong back the way ye came." She pointed.

He looked behind him. "Mmm. I'll have to look at the maps more closely."

"And ye have found the countess," she said heavily.

His head whipped around. "The countess?"

She drew herself up. "I am the Countess of Kinmarloch."

"You? But you're herding sheep—"

"—while wearing breeches. Aye."

"Er, I hadn't realized, I wasn't made aware—"

"Kinmarloch is a poor place, Mr. Pike. But ye can assure His Grace that the duchy of Dunmore, which his predecessor has undertaken to clear of farms, is slightly less poor. Ye can tell him the duchy has plentiful pasturage, and the Countess of Kinmarloch is doing her best to keep her sheep off his land." She gestured at her mud-stained breeches. "Personally."

"My lady." His bow was deep, much deeper than his first one. At least this scoundrel knew what was owing to her.

"And ye can tell him he should come up here himself and see how his cousin has destroyed this place by proxy. See what has been done in the name of the Duke of Dunmore."

She turned and walked in the direction of her small flock. Luran looked back at her and barked once. She made a movement with her hand and whistled, and he resumed his long, loping circles around the sheep, keeping them together.

The man followed her, leading his horse.

"Did the previous duke never visit from England?"

"Nae, he dinnae. We thought he might, we hoped he would. Instead, he just had his men—men like yerself—clear the farms and burn the villages."

"Burn villages?"

"Aye."

"My lady, please explain to me how you came to be the Countess of Kinmarloch and a MacNaughton will be the Duke of Dunmore when I believe your grandfather held the titles of both duke and earl together."

"The earldom of Kinmarloch is an ancient one, Mr. Pike, and so the title—"

"Please call me Jack, my lady."

The rain was a little heavier now. "Many ancient titles in Scotland can pass down the female line. My mother was my grandfather's only child—"

"Then your father was earl?"

"Nae." Was the man not listening? She turned to look at

him and saw he had dropped behind her slightly and was looking at her bottom.

"Mr. Pike," she said loudly. His eyes came up slowly. Then the grin. The man had no shame at being caught ogling her like she was a tavern wench. At least he wouldn't be able to see her blush in the rain.

"My mother, if she had outlived my grandfather, would have been countess in her own right. As I am. My father, William Boyd, would have been my mother's consort."

"So, your husband is your consort?"

"I have nae husband." She hated herself for her weakness, but she could not resist glancing at him as she said that. Suddenly, she wanted him to flirt with her again, as he had when he had offered to talk to her in a warm, dry place. Or to look at her bottom again. Maybe it was not as ill-formed as she thought. But he was looking down at the ground now, intent on keeping his very fine, well-polished boots out of as many puddles as possible.

"My father died a month before I was born and my mother died giving birth to me. I was her only child, just as she was my grandfather's. The title of Kinmarloch came to me after my grandfather's death five years ago. As I said, that ancient title can descend in the female line. But the title of the Duke of Dunmore is only two hundred years old and must pass to male heirs. My grandfather's first cousin's son was duke for a few months before he died. Then the title went to *his* son, my third cousin Norman MacNaughton who is also dead now. Yer master, yet another third cousin, will have the title soon. Another MacNaughton who has spent his whole life away from Scotland and knows naething of our life here."

"Perhaps that is why the purported duke sent me, my lady. To learn a little of the Highlands."

"What does that mean?" She paused her forward motion and frowned. "Purported?"

"It means he's thought to be the duke but he's not the duke. Yet."

Purported. She would remember that. She started walking again. "Aye. The widowed duchess. Do ye know if she is with child?"

"No. I don't." His answer was abrupt, angry.

"For the sake of the Highlands, I hope she is nae carrying an heir. We dinnae need a bairn made the Duke of Dunmore with corrupt men doing things in his name. But tell me, is yer master married? And if John MacNaughton is named duke, will he come here? We are eager to meet him."

"You're eager? Why is that?"

She bit her lip. She could not tell this Jack Pike what she had allowed herself to hope since talking to Mags yesterday— that the duke was unmarried and she might convince him, for the good of both their peoples, to marry her. So she could sway him to stop the clearances. And so their son would someday reunite the earldom and the duchy under one title-holder and the somewhat greater riches of the duchy could be used to support the impoverished earldom.

She could not tell Mr. Pike any of this. First, because he might take word of her back to the duke. She may not know much about men, but she knew they didn't like to be told to do things or made to feel they must. And there could be nothing flattering in what Jack Pike might say about her to the duke. Second, she could not tell him she hoped to marry his master because…because…because Jack Pike was arousing very strong feelings in her.

Oh, to be in a warm, dry place with this man.

Naked.

"Aren't you pleased I came in his place?" His eyebrows were raised in a leer, his lips curved in a sly smile. The damn man knew what she was thinking. Or feeling. About him. "I can be most amusing, Lady Kinmarloch."

How dare he? No man had ever had the gall to speak to her this way. Or look at her this way. The Countess of Kinmarloch in her own right. A proud title for a proud woman.

But she was still a woman. And this man made her wet with desire between her legs.

How she hated him for that.

But she needed Jack Pike, his information, and maybe his help. He might be her path to the chance, as slim as herself, that she could get the duke to marry her.

"Come have tea, *mo luran*," she said to the most beautiful man she had ever seen. "Come see the keep of the earldom of Kinmarloch."

SEVEN

Dinnae expect too much, she had said. And Jack hadn't. A countess in muddy breeches, looking half-starved, herding sheep? Most assuredly, he was not expecting much.

But he was not prepared for the wreck of the castle he encountered. Only the keep still stood intact, and it was cold, damp, and leaking rain. One small fire was lit, barely heating the cavernous space.

"Mr. Pike, this is Mags." Mags was a tall, slender girl with a limp, red hair like a sunset, and a face like an angel. "Mr. Pike is the new duke's man. The purported new duke's man."

The girl bobbed.

"I am enchanted to meet you, Miss Mags. I continue to be astounded by the beauty of Scotland's women. You put me in mind of Hestia, the Greek goddess of fire, seeing you stand by the hearth that way."

He was pleased the young woman's eyes met his and she smiled and blushed before she went back to making tea. Now, there was a proper response to Captain Jack Pike. He turned to Helen, as if to say, *See, that's what a normal female does when she receives a compliment from me, you cold-blooded, breeches-wearing harpy.*

But the countess was scowling. Her heavy brow was knitted. She took him by the elbow. "Come this way, Mr. Pike. Let me show ye the outer walls." She yanked him back outside.

In the rain, Helen pushed him against one of the outer walls she was meant to be showing him and leaned close. "Ye are to stay away from Mags. Do ye hear me, Mr. Pike? I want yer word on it. Nane of yer flirtation and fooling."

He peeled Helen's fingers of steel off his elbow. "I was not flirting. I was complimenting. A small tribute. She's just a girl. What do you take me for?"

She put her fists on her narrow hips. "I take ye for a man. A cocksure man with a smooth tongue and pleasing ways. A filthy animal of a man who is used to getting what he wants because he's pretty and his talk is pretty. But Mags is under my protection." She looked pointedly at his groin. "Take yer prick to the public house at Cumdairessie and get it wet there. But nae here. Nae in Kinmarloch."

"Now, my lady, are you saying I can't speak sweetly to any of the young women of Kinmarloch?"

"Aye."

He laughed. "What about Dunmore? Can I engage in flirtation and fooling there, as you put it?"

She squinted at him. "I cannae tell ye what to do in Dunmore. But I will remind ye that ye are the duke's man and ye represent him. The women and girls of Dunmore are under his protection, and therefore, yers. And if John MacNaughton is a good man and a good duke, he would hang ye up by yer thumbnails if ye were to take advantage."

Oh, damn.

Damn, damn, damn. Fuck.

It had not even crossed Jack's mind. Of course, if he became the duke, he would be a swine, an absolute villain, if he were to couple with a woman who lived in his duchy. Because the woman would feel obligation. She would come to his bed because he was the duke, her lord and master. Not because he was Jack Pike, master of the bedchamber.

And even if he were willing to be a villain, and he very well might be if he stayed chaste long enough up here in Scotland, there would be no pleasure in it for him. No pleasure besides the same fleeting pleasure his own hand gave him.

Because he would not know if the woman really wanted him.

Fuck.

The tiny part of Jack that wanted to be duke had doubled upon his arrival here today, despite the cold and the rain. There was beautiful scenery to be had in Dunmore and Kinmarloch, both mountainous and feminine. Barring the countess, of course, whom he had flattered and flirted with and gawked at merely as a matter of courtesy, but who was clearly a dirty, savage example of her species. And who vexed him with her resistance to his charms.

Yes, he *had* been thinking maybe it wouldn't be so bad to be duke of this brutal, wild place.

Now, after what this killjoy of a shrew had said? That part of him that had wanted to be duke? It shrank. Considerably. To nothing.

Yes, yes, there was the public house in Cumdairessie she had mentioned. The town was outside the duchy, and he had enjoyed himself there last night with a buxom Scottish doxy who had been willing to do far more for far less money than the whores at Madame Flora's. But the town was four hours away by horseback. Four hours. A daily fuck would be impossible.

He would live as a monk in Scotland.

He grimaced. If he became duke—oh, please, let Elizabeth

be pregnant—he would have to do as his cousin Norman did. Stay away from Scotland.

"Are ye listening to me, Jack Pike?"

"Yes. I'm listening. I will not besmirch any of the maidens —" Helen opened her mouth. "—or any of the other women of Kinmarloch."

She closed her mouth.

"Now, can we get out of the rain, my lady?"

Helen turned on her heel and stomped back into the keep, and he followed her. The dog ran up and herded him inside.

Not that it was much drier in the keep. He looked up. Surely something could be done about the leaks?

Helen sent the angel girl Mags away to some other part of the keep and invited him to sit in a chair which was settled in a dry patch. She directed the dog, who had been circling Jack, to lie by the fire. The dog got down on his belly but kept his head up, his tongue out, looking at Jack with suspicion.

Jack sipped his tea gingerly. It was weak. Very weak. It was hot water, basically, which had been briefly introduced to a few leaves of tea. Of course, tea was expensive and it was a miracle it had been offered to him at all, given the poverty he was surrounded by.

Helen made no apologies. She blew on her own tea and gulped it greedily. She must be used to the weak brew and didn't know what real tea should taste like.

"My lady, is this where you grew up? The keep?"

"Nae, I grew up in the castle of Dunmore. With my grandfather. But of course, once he died, I dinnae have the right to live there. I came here. And people hadnae lived here for two hundred years." She smiled. The first smile he had seen cross her face. A tired smile. "Ye should have seen it when I first came. I spent the first week just mucking out the sheep shit."

He couldn't help it. He smiled back. A countess who said *prick* and *shit*. Damn, this place suited him in so many ways.

"But why hasn't the roof been fixed? Why isn't there a man to help you with herding your sheep?"

"A good many men went off to fight Napoleon and America and dinnae come back. But even more left once the clearances started in Dunmore under the last duke. We are mainly women and children. But there are some men, mostly farmers who are busy on their farms. We have a good black-smith in Kinmarloch, and he and his son Duncan are a blessing."

'The clearances?"

"Aye."

"Explain the clearances to me."

Her eyes widened. "I thought ye were the new steward."

"Not exactly, no. I'm more of a personal representative for the duke-yet-to-be-named."

"Do ye have John MacNaughton's ear?"

"I can fairly say I have both of them."

"And ye really dinnae know what I'm talking about?" Her tone was incredulous.

"I know very little." He knew nothing. But this imperti-nent countess was not to know that.

She gestured with her cup. "This is poor land for farming. Yet, there are farmers here and they have been here for centuries. There is a great deal more money nowadays to be made in sheep since the price for wool is high. Many, many lords have had the farmers cleared off their lands to make way for more sheep."

"Like you have."

She stared at him. "I dinnae do that. That's why I'm so poor. There have been nae clearances in Kinmarloch. And the clearances in Dunmore started only after my grandfather died."

"But you have sheep."

"Forty sheep. Barely a flock. Just enough wool to keep groats on the table, peat on the hearth."

"Tell me about the burning of villages you mentioned."

Her jaw clenched. There was a glimmer of something in her eye and Jack felt the same cold fear he had felt at the Battle of Lissa.

"A village would be cleared. The people sent away. But then people would return and live in their old houses. Some thought it best to burn the villages so nae houses would stand."

"I see."

She took a deep breath. "There is—there was a village which was half in the duchy and half in Kinmarloch. The whole village was burned by the duke's men. My people hadnae left, hadnae been ordered to do so by me. They had a right to stay. And I dinnae know of the planned burning."

Jack could sense where this was going and his gut twisted.

"There was a sick girl in one of the cottages."

"Oh, my God." He didn't know if he meant the words as a prayer or a curse.

"She lived, but her leg was badly burned."

Jack bowed his head for a moment. "I'm glad she lived."

"Aye."

"Were—were you compensated for the loss of the village?"

"Compensated?"

"Given money?"

"There is nae enough money to compensate for that rape of my land."

"Were you offered any?"

She stood, her eyes burning into him. "Nae. And I widnae accept it. Because how can I let my people think there is a just price for their homes, their safety, their livelihoods? It widnae be right."

"You have a great deal of pride."

"Aye. It may be the only thing I have. But I would let it go if…"

"What?"

"Never ye mind. More tea, Jack Pike?"

He accepted more tea—more warm water—because it would not do, not at this moment, to make any move which reflected badly on this woman's hospitality.

"I must discuss something with ye."

"Yes?" He sipped his water.

"The duchy is divided by my land. The duke's sheep are often led through Kinmarloch to get to the pasturage which is owned by the duchy on the far side. There is a way to go, through the foothills of the Benrancree mountains, but the duke's shepherds dinnae direct the sheep that way because 'tis longer. And the passage they use through my farmers' lands ruins what little they can grow."

"That is a problem."

"Aye. I'm glad ye think so. It must stop."

"I will speak to the duke. Or to whomever will be acting as duke if there is…"

"A baby in the belly of the duchess."

"Yes. Why didn't you complain to Norman MacNaughton, the last duke?"

"As I told ye, he never came here. I complained to his steward, his other men, his shepherds. About the sheep, the clearances, the burnings, the injuries done to a young girl. I wrote many letters to London. I heard naething. And there is nae money for me to go to London myself and make my case."

Jack cleared his throat. "I will make your case."

And then something happened. She was still standing, her cup in both her hands, close to her chin. The firelight flickered across her features. And despite her gauntness, her too large jaw, her too large and bony nose, her too large forehead with its heavy brow, she was…what was she? The first word which came to Jack's mind was *beautiful*. But she wasn't. Not at all. Not like other women. She was something else entirely. Something noble and brutal and…

He didn't know what it was, but it took his breath.

She moved her cup down. "Thank ye."

"You're welcome," he murmured.

"I'm glad to find yer nae just a pretty face and pretty words, Jack Pike."

He choked out a laugh. "I haven't done anything yet."

"But ye listened to me. Which is more than anyone else from the duchy has ever done."

A moment of quiet. Something surged and pulsed in that moment. There was something unfamiliar here. Something uncomfortable. Something pure which hurt him deep inside.

There was only one thing for it. He would have to ruin it.

He stood. He put his cup down and leered. "Well, I am always willing to listen to a fair lady who plies me with tea in her keep. I will have to return your hospitality."

That had done the trick. She stiffened and was the ordinary woman in muddy breeches again. "I dinnae think that's necessary, Mr. Pike."

"Jack," he corrected her.

She said nothing, staring at him.

He went on, rubbing his hands together, grinning. "But I think it's necessary. You owe me that if I am to make your case to His Grace. You'll come to dinner at Dunmore Castle tomorrow night. You can show me around since you grew up there. The secret passages. The dungeons."

She nodded, but he could tell from the narrowing of her eyes and the set of her jaw, she would very much like to show him the dungeons. Personally. And then throw him into one, slam the door shut, and hurl the key into the deepest, coldest loch in Scotland.

The Countess of Kinmarloch hated Jack Pike, that much was clear.

The dog jumped up from the hearth and barked, Helen raised her hand to make him sit, and in the next ten seconds, it became clear she hated someone else much, much more than she hated Jack Pike.

A man entered the keep without knocking. Not asking permission, not taking his hat from his head.

"Lord Reeves." Helen made a very small curtsy. Her voice was as cold as the rain outside.

The man was thin and well-dressed in a heavy tweed great-coat. He glanced at Helen for only a moment and then his eyes went to Jack. "Are you the duke's man? Are you Jack Pike?" His accent matched Jack's.

"I am."

"Well, I am Lord Reeves, the greater baron of the land south of here. I was told at Dunmore Castle that you had come this way. I saw your horse outside. You should be careful. The peasants will steal your mount."

Jack could feel Helen bristle at his elbow. He moved half a foot closer to her, but he did not bow to Reeves. He would not. Reeves was in the keep of a countess, and a countess ranked above a greater baron. This man should bow to Helen. Then, and only then, Jack would bow to him.

He was glad to see Reeves did not know how to react to Jack's silence and his obvious refusal to perform an act of obeisance.

"I wanted to meet you," Reeves said after a long pause. "To learn more of the duke's plans."

"The duke has not been named, as of yet. There is an unsettled question of an unborn heir apparent."

The man licked his already wet lips. "Then why are you here?"

Why was Jack here? He had thought it was to escape Elizabeth and the siren song of her body and her face. Or to have an adventure as he had had when he was a young sailor. But now, a strange thought came into his mind.

I'm here to protect Helen.

Here to protect a woman he had just met. A woman who, until a few moments ago, he would have thought needed no protection. And would surely reject any offer he made in that direction.

He came up with another answer for Reeves. "It is thought very likely John MacNaughton will be the duke, and he was anxious to find out what his soon-to-be duchy and the surrounding Highlands were like."

"Ah. Well, as you can see," Reeves gestured vaguely, "it's a shithole."

No. No. The countess could say *shit* if she wanted to, in her own keep. This man could not say it in front of her, however.

"There is a lady present."

Reeves laughed. "You will soon find out there are no ladies in Kinmarloch. There are women though. Mostly ones that look like men. Except for that lovely little redhead." The man turned his head and scanned the keep. "Where is the shy vixen?"

Jack felt Helen next to him stand up straighter, take a deep breath.

Good woman. Castigate the arsehole.

"I have naething to offer ye, Lord Reeves, so I think ye should leave."

Why was she being so restrained with this scum? Why didn't she cut him to pieces with her tongue like she did to me?

"Not even the money you owe me, Helen?" Reeves had an unpleasant smile.

Jack took a step toward him. The dog came up out of his sit and joined Jack, his teeth bared at Reeves, his body tight against Jack's calf. Jack heard a growl but he wasn't sure if it came from him or the dog.

Reeves retreated toward the door. "Mr. Pike, I will be telling John MacNaughton of your insolence to me."

"Please do, Lord Reeves. MacNaughton and I have known each other a long time. Yes, please tell him. He'll be sure to listen to a man like you before he listens to me."

The man ducked out the doorway and was gone.

Jack turned to Helen.

"Thank you, *mo luran*," she murmured, but she was looking at the dog.

Jack boiled over with an inexplicable fury.

"You owe that man money? How could you think of going into debt to a bully like him? Don't you know he will take every opportunity to abuse you because of it? Hell, I can tell that, and I've only been in the man's presence for two minutes."

Helen raged back. "Ye think I wanted to borrow—I had nae choice—ye made him angry, Jack Pike. What do ye think that will cost me in the future? Ye will go back to London and I will stay on here, surrounded on all sides by men with the power and the money to destroy me and Kinmarloch. I must step carefully. Ye dinnae think I was nae dying inside, wanting to spit at him, curse at him, claw that warm coat from him for my Mags, lop off his head with a claymore?"

Jack chuckled. He would have liked to have seen that. Very much. Helen hefting a sword over her head with both hands and Reeves' blood spraying onto the walls of the keep.

"How much do you owe Reeves?"

"Why?"

He drew himself up to his full height and used his captain's voice. He hadn't used it in four years.

"Tell me, Helen," he boomed.

She was not fearful, she did not cringe or step away. She

snapped out an answer, just as he would have expected his first lieutenant to answer him. "Sixteen shillings."

Jack dug in his pocket for his purse. He took out a pound coin and shoved it at her. "Here."

She didn't reach for it.

"Take it. Take it. Don't be a fool. It's not a gift. You'll owe it to me. Be honest, wouldn't you rather be in debt to me than that vile shit?"

"There's a lady present."

He did not understand at first, but then he saw an almost-smile twitch her lips.

"Yes. There is. Forgive me. Lord Reeves is vile…feces. My lady, take the pound."

She did not. The almost-smile was gone.

"We have had a short acquaintance, Lady Kinmarloch. You don't know me. But I know you already know I'm a better man than Lord Reeves." He thrust the money at her again even more vehemently.

She put out her hand and took the coin from him. Begrudgingly. Then she fixed her fierce half-moon blue eyes on him and grinned.

"Well, yer one that is certainly easier to look at, *mo luran*."

EIGHT

The next day, Jack was very busy. The busiest he had been since he had resigned his commission.

A meeting with the steward, a sour man named Macsomething. All clearances were to be halted. Yes, Jack knew the duke had not been named yet. But—he flourished a letter signed by John MacNaughton saying Jack Pike was to act for him in his name—nothing new should be done until the duke *was* named. And if that duke turned out to be John MacNaughton, as it most likely would be, and he found out his wishes had been ignored, the steward would almost certainly lose his position. The steward grimaced and whined his agreement. No new clearances. Although there were still too many farms in the duchy and pasturage was—

Jack cut him off. He did not like the man's tone, his protestations. If he became duke, he would look for a new steward.

Next, a ride out to the pastures of Dunmore to speak with the shepherds and make it clear they were to use the hill passes to go to the other grazing sites in Dunmore. No more cutting through the farmlands of Kinmarloch. Jack didn't care that it added two hours to the traverse.

One man stepped forward. "If a hut and a paddock could be built on the far piece of the duchy, some shepherds could stay the night with the sheep. Less travel for them back and forth. Less wasted time. Fatter sheep."

Jack grunted. "What's your name?"

"MacLeod."

Damn. Was everyone in this rain-soaked part of the country a Mac this or Mc that? He would never be able to keep the names straight.

"I'll see it's done," Jack said.

Back to the castle to see the steward again and to arrange for the building of the hut and the paddock as suggested by the shepherd Mcwhozit.

"But ye said naething new should be undertaken, Mr. Pike."

Jack growled. "I am paying for it. If the duke doesn't like it when he becomes duke, I'll tear it down myself."

A discussion of masons and materials and roofs followed.

By dinnertime, he had almost forgotten he had insisted Helen come for the meal. He bathed quickly and then realized he was long overdue for a shave.

He had a moment when he held the razor to his own jaw and regretted he had not brought his valet with him. But he had not trusted his valet enough to keep the secret that Jack Pike was really John MacNaughton, purported future Duke of Dunmore.

He could shave himself. Of course, he could. Hadn't he done it for years on board a rolling ship? But he was out of practice and nicked himself twice.

He put on clothes he had not worn since leaving London, clothes he had thought he would have no occasion to wear in Scotland but his valet had packed anyway. A dark tailcoat, a fine linen shirt, crisp cravat, embroidered waistcoat, closely-fitted trousers.

I deserve a good dinner after today. Clean clothes, a bath, a shave. It has nothing to do with the fact that my dinner guest is Helen Boyd, the Countess of Kinmarloch.

He paced the carpet of one of the castle's drawing rooms, waiting for her to come, ready to pour her a glass of sherry or whisky or whatever she wanted. He waited. He waited.

He went out into the Great Hall and accosted the manservant there. "The countess. Should I have sent the carriage for her?"

The man blinked. "The countess is here, Mr. Pike. In the kitchens."

"What's your name?"

"MacDougal."

Of course. "Where are the kitchens, man?"

In the warren of rooms under the castle, Jack followed his nose to the kitchens. And there was Helen Boyd, Countess of Kinmarloch, in a loose brown dress, sitting on a stool, laughing with a large woman in an apron splashed with some sort of gravy. The cook, presumably.

"Good evening, my lady," Jack said and bowed.

Helen turned to him. Her eyes were shining. "Mr. Pike, Mrs. Mac says we are to have goose tonight. Ye havenae eaten goose until ye have eaten Mrs. Mac's goose. 'Tis wonderful."

Mrs. Mac, the large woman, shook a spoon. "I remembered ye liked my goose from yer grandfather's days, my lady."

"I look forward to it," Jack said smoothly, smiling. "So far everything I have eaten in the castle has been delicious. Now I find out why. Because the cook herself is a delicacy."

Helen rolled her eyes as the other woman tittered and blushed.

"I didn't know you were here, my lady," Jack said.

Helen smirked. "Aye. I snuck in the postern and came through the dungeons."

"Let's go upstairs, Lady Kinmarloch, and have a drink before we eat this wonderful goose."

Helen slid off the stool. She went to the large woman who was now stirring a pot. "Goodbye, Mrs. Mac." The woman turned and Helen hugged her, obviously not worried about the gravy stains on the apron.

After the embrace, the woman held Helen out at arm's length. "My lady, ye must come up here more often to the castle. Come and eat a meal with me. Ye are much too thin."

Helen looked at Jack and then back at the woman. "Now, Mrs. Mac, ye know I have always been lean like my mother and grandfather. And I widnae want to take advantage."

Mrs. Mac stared at Jack with a menace in her eye, as if daring him to contradict her. "If ye come here to eat, my lady, ye will eat *my* food. Naebody else's. 'Tis obvious I could stand to eat half portions myself so ye will eat from what is due me."

"Yes." Jack mustered his captain's voice. "You must come eat. And bring Mags." He would make sure Helen took something home tonight with her for the girl.

Helen shook her head, and Jack knew she wouldn't come and eat any of her meals here. Her pride. But at least she would get a good dinner tonight.

Helen led Jack up out of the cellars and underground rooms and back to the drawing room where he had paced, waiting for her.

"It's a good thing you know your way around. I'm lost."

"Aye." She looked around the room.

"Is it changed at all?"

"Nae."

"Is it hard to be in the castle again? I didn't think."

She shook her head. "Nae. 'Tis good to see the place."

"What will you drink?"

"Do ye have—could I have mulled wine?"

He called for the manservant and asked for mulled wine. Meanwhile, he poured her a small glass of sherry and took one himself.

"What is this?" She sniffed at it.

"Sherry wine. Try it."

She sipped.

The look on her face. Oh, the look on her face. It was the moment in the keep all over again when he had thought she was…not beautiful but something else.

Now she took another sip and another. And a gulp and the glass was almost empty. He brought the decanter to her and refilled her glass.

"Careful, Lady Kinmarloch, careful. The wine will go to your lovely brown-haired head and you will declare your love and throw yourself at me and then where will we be?"

She glared. "I'm a Scot, Jack Pike. I can handle a little wine. Whisky is our mother's milk up here, or havenae ye heard? And, rest easy. I willnae now, or ever, be throwing myself at ye."

Despite her scorn, he was glad to see she sipped the second glass more slowly. She had likely not eaten much today and she was so slight. She would feel the wine much more quickly than he did.

Helen took Jack up the wide stone stairs to the gallery and explained the portraits there. "I wish there was one of my mother but she was never countess and so wasnae painted. I dinnae know what she looked like. Grandfather says she was beautiful, but he said the same thing about me." She laughed. "The most recent painting is of my grandfather from fifty years ago. He must have been thirty."

Jack looked at the portrait of Malcolm MacNaughton, the Duke of Dunmore three dukes before him. His grandfather's cousin. Yes, the man was lean like Helen. Same blue eyes. And

Jack could see they had the same large nose with a delicate boniness down the center, the same large jaw.

"Do ye see any resemblance to yer master, Jack Pike?"

Jack looked closer. Maybe, just maybe, he himself had the same forehead as the former duke. The shelf of brow which looked much too heavy on Helen but suited a man.

He straightened up and shrugged. "Not really. John Mac-Naughton is much better looking."

"Is he as handsome as ye?"

He looked over at her. She was glancing at him sideways and her face was a little pink. Was Helen Boyd, Countess of Kinmarloch, flirting with him?

"Yes."

"Really?" She seemed disappointed.

"Why? Did you want the duke to be plain?"

"Aye," she blurted. Then she shook her head. "I dinnae care one way or the other."

A bell, signaling dinner.

He offered her his arm, and they went back down the stairs to their meal.

The goose was excellent. Helen had her mulled wine, and he had claret. She was careful, he noted, to cut her food neatly with her silver knife and fork, to take small bites, but she ate at a remarkable speed despite that.

And the sherry and the mulled wine softened her. She smiled when he complained about the profusion of names in Scotland which started with Mac and Mc.

"Ye havenae even heard the worst of it, Jack Pike. Ye know now that Mrs. Mac is the cook? Well, guess what we call the housekeeper of the castle? She is the *other* Mrs. Mac. They are both Mrs. MacDonald."

She laughed at his tales about his time in the navy. She especially liked the story about the time the ship cat jumped overboard after seeing a monstrously large rat, and he had swum out to get the wretched, clawing, ungrateful thing.

"Ye look like ye had an encounter with a cat yerself today, Jack Pike," she said and pointed at his neck with her dinner knife.

His shaving cuts. He put his hand to his neck. "Now, these might be scratches of passion from a lovely lass, Helen."

She flipped the knife in her hand so now it was oriented for stabbing rather than cutting.

"I'm joking, I'm joking. I'm obeying your orders. I promise. No lovely lasses."

She growled just a little but turned the knife in her hand again and sawed off a piece of goose.

Another glass of mulled wine and another slice of the goose breast later, Helen toyed with the stem of her goblet.

"Jack," she said. She was not looking at him but at some place in the middle of the table between them, her eyes a little hazed.

"Jack Pike," she said again.

"Helen Boyd."

"Ye never answered me yesterday."

"About what?"

"Is John MacNaughton married? Will he bring a duchess with him to Dunmore?"

Jack wiped his mouth and threw his napkin down. "He is not married."

"Oh." She was looking at him now. Her jaw jutted just a bit. "He is nae married?"

"No." Jack didn't bother to hide his irritation, but Helen didn't seem to notice.

"Is he engaged to be married?"

"No."

"Does he…will he…do ye know if…"

"What?"

"Is he very particular, do ye think?"

"Particular?"

"About his women."

"John MacNaughton rarely meets a woman he doesn't like."

She looked down. "Oh. He is a scoundrel, like ye."

"In London, they call us rakes."

"Rakes?"

"Short for rakehells. As we will wind up in hell and be raking the coals there."

The mulled wine must have had a very great effect on her because she giggled. Helen Boyd giggled.

Jack hated giggling. Such a vapid sound, indicating a tedious woman. A woman who offered no excitement in her love-making, a woman unable or unwilling to release despite the most valiant efforts of his tongue, his hand, his cock. A woman he would shed as soon as possible.

But a giggle coming from Helen was like a little spring bubbling up. A small gladsome noise. A harbinger of a bigger laugh to come.

"Aye, I can imagine ye in hell already with yer rake, Jack."

When she said that and giggled, he laughed, too, despite himself and his growing disappointment in her. He didn't like her questions about the duke, the duke's unmarried state, the duke's taste in women.

She hiccoughed and her face became serious. "But surely, when he is duke, yer master would settle down to one woman. A wife. He needs an heir."

Now Jack was more than disappointed. He was angry. He had thought Helen Boyd was something unusual. Something different. But just like every other woman, she was only interested in what she could get. And in this case, it was a duke. Yes, maybe he could excuse it partially because of her poverty. She likely hungered for security, a tight roof, something to eat besides groats.

But she had no right to want *him*. Even though she didn't know it was him.

He didn't mind her wanting Jack Pike, the charming, handsome, funny captain sitting in front of her. The man who had spent all day halting the clearances in the duchy and making sure there would be no more Dunmore sheep crossing her farmers' fields. The man who had given her sherry and mulled wine, who had loaned her a pound, who had stood up to Reeves. The man who had paid her flattering compliments that weren't true and flirted with her.

She *should* want Jack Pike.

But she didn't. She wanted some duke she had never seen. Whom she would likely cuckold as soon as she could find another man foolhardy enough to bed her.

Because, after all, breeches or not, she was a woman, wasn't she? And women were grasping. Fickle. Untrustworthy.

But he would show her. He would murder whatever dreams she held of being a duchess. Right now.

"Once he is named duke and if he decides to marry, Mac-Naughton will be shopping for a wife the way most lords do. In London. At balls. During the Season. He will have his pick of debutantes. The most beautiful daughters of the richest marquesses and earls. He will make a good match to a lovely and accomplished young lady of good breeding and wealth despite his duchy being not the richest and so far away from London. Unmarried dukes are much in demand."

"I see."

He looked at her face. The poor woman looked wretched now. All of the glow and fun and pleasure which had blossomed in her for the last two hours was gone.

Well done, Jack.

"Cheer up, Helen. You'll still have me." He winked.

Surprisingly, a little of her glow came back. "Aye," she said softly. "'Tis good to look on ye. I'm glad for that. I must take beauty where I can get it."

"But you are surrounded by beauty, Helen. Kinmarloch is beautiful."

"Aye." She sighed. "But I suppose 'tis like how it must for ye, looking in the mirror. Ye see it so often ye forget to enjoy it. Ye see only the neck scratches and are blind to the brown eyes, the bewitching smile, the cheekbones—"

He quirked an eyebrow. "Are you sure you're not throwing yourself at me now, Helen?"

"I am too tipsy to throw anything, Jack Pike. I must go."

She stood abruptly from her chair and swayed, and Jack had to make his way very quickly to her end of the table to grab hold of her.

Damn. She was so light but like steel under his hands. Her cheek made contact with the lapel of his tailcoat as he caught her. Her leg brushed his.

He should give her another glass of wine and take her upstairs and make free with her in her childhood home. He would enjoy himself. Her words about his looks meant she would enjoy him. And, after all, she was not under his protection, as a countess in her own right. And when Jack took Helen, he would work out a little piece of the anger he had for all the women who sought men not for themselves but for what they possessed.

It was a first-rate idea.

However, like all first-rate ideas, there were a host of repercussions. Jack fixed his mind on two. First, when he caught her, he had felt the knife—or was it a dirk?—strapped to her leg under her dress. Would she murder him as he fondled her? Second, he was fairly sure after pleasuring himself with Helen's body, every meal he had in the castle would be laced with poison or shards of glass thanks to the redoubtable Mrs. Mac.

Jack didn't want glass in his food. Or poison. Or a dirk in his already scarred chest.

He put Helen back in her chair.

"Sit there. You're going home in the carriage."

She made as if to stand again. "Nae, Mr. Pike, I widnae want to trouble ye—"

He pushed her down. "Jack. And shut up, Helen. I mean, Lady Kinmarloch. I am proxy for the purported next Duke of Dunmore so consider this the duke speaking. You are going home in the carriage. Sit. Stay."

She looked up at him, her eyes wide. "Aye, *mo luran*." She giggled.

He went and ordered the carriage to be made ready. Then he went down to the kitchens and found Mrs. Mac and told her to put the biggest ham in the larder in a basket and put the basket in the carriage along with several loaves of bread.

He came back upstairs from the kitchens and got Helen's coat from Macthingy, the manservant-cum-butler. The patched coat was very thin. Not suitable for nighttime, for March, for Scotland.

He led Helen to the carriage and put her in it and sat across from her.

"Ye need nae come all the way to Kinmarloch," she said and hiccoughed.

He found two lap blankets and put them over her. "I gave you the wine. And stuffed you with goose. I have to make sure you get to your keep. Safely."

She fell asleep on the short ride back.

He did not allow himself to look at her sleeping. He didn't know why, but he felt it would be a very dangerous thing to do.

NINE

Helen woke up a bit muzzy, her mouth dry. But she was warm even though she was alone on the pallet. "Mags." She sat up.

"Here, my lady." Mags was seated at the table, darning.

There was softness under Helen's hands. She looked down. Two heavy wool blankets covered her. And there was a meaty smell in the air. Fat frying. Could it be ham?

"Are ye well?" Mags asked.

"Aye. I think I drank too much wine at the castle."

"Aye. That's what Mr. Pike said when he carried ye in."

Blast. What a weakness to have been drunkenly asleep in front of him. And how disappointing not to have the memory of him carrying her out of the carriage, feeling his arms around her. She would have liked to have been able to hold that in her mind. His strength, his male scent, his handsome face and grin so close—because she was sure he would be grinning over the fact she had gotten drunk despite her claim she wouldn't. The memory of that almost-embrace by the beautiful Jack Pike would have been something to hug close and remember when she was tired and cold and alone.

She stood up in her nightdress. Wait. Had…had he seen her like this?

"I put ye in yer nightdress, my lady, after Mr. Pike left. Ye kept giggling in yer sleep."

"I will have to get these blankets back to him today."

"He said we should keep them."

Helen frowned at Mags. "I will return them today."

Mags put her darning down. "Are ye ready for breakfast?"

"What is it?"

"Ham."

"Where did the ham come from, Mags?"

"It came home with ye, last night. In a basket with bread."

"So it came from Mr. Pike."

"Nae. He said it came from Mrs. Mac. I knew she was yer friend so I have already cut off two slices and put them in the pan to fry." Mags' eyes were pleading. "Please, my lady, please. Dinnae make us give the ham back."

The aroma of the ham was stronger now, and Helen could hear a sizzle from the hearth. Mags never asked for anything. Ever. But Helen knew the ham was not from Mrs. Mac. The cook was generous, but she would never pilfer a whole ham—worth several weeks' wages, if not more—from the duchy, no matter how hungry Helen was or how thin she looked. Perhaps a small amount of meat, perhaps the bread, but never a whole ham.

Helen lied to herself. The ham was from Mrs. Mac. They would eat these two slices and then find a way to return the ham.

"We willnae give the ham back yet."

Mags scurried to take the pan off the fire and the slices were quickly eaten and very soon two more slices were in the pan. And then two more. But Helen made Mag eat those last two alone as she herself thirstily drank water. After all, she had feasted on goose and wine last night and had made no provision for poor Mags who had eaten groats.

Damn herself for not thinking about Mags. And damn Jack Pike for thinking of Mags. That was Helen's responsibility, and she must do better than a lecherous, flirtatious, beautiful Englishman.

"Oh, my lady." Mags' face was glowing and her mouth was full of the pink meat. "Is nae ham good? So very, very good."

"Aye. Now chew well and slowly. We want the ham to go down and stay down."

Mags chewed obediently but after she had swallowed, she said, "I willnae waste a morsel of this precious ham, I promise, my lady."

Helen opened her own mouth as she watched Mags take another bite. Then she closed it.

Aye. We willnae give the ham back yet.

Helen opened the door of the keep onto a sunny, warm morning. Unseasonably warm. She should start the shearing, and she had no help. Duncan, the blacksmith's son, was away, buying iron for his father's forge. But the lambs would come with the spring, and when the ewes made milk, their wool suffered. Best to shear now.

She went back into the keep and put on her breeches as Mags made her a ham sandwich. Helen wrapped it carefully in her only handkerchief and put it in her coat pocket. A rare treat to eat at midday.

She took a bucket and a rope, and she and Luran led the sheep out of the paddock and up into the foothills of the Benrancree mountains. There was a stream there which went down into her own deep loch where sheep had been known to drown. With luck, she might get all the sheep washed today in the stream, and she could shear them tomorrow after their fleeces had dried. Maybe Duncan would be back by then. And she could sell the wool in Cumdairessie and make enough to pay back the pound Jack Pike had lent her.

She got the rope around a ewe's neck and led it to the stream. The water was ice cold, as could be expected since it was melted snow. The ewe liked the cold water as little as Helen did, and it complained and tried to climb out of the stream bed. But she held it as fast as she could and used her bucket to scoop water up and over the sheep's back to loosen the filth and dried mud there.

After the first ewe, she was soaking wet and smeared with sticky yolk. Thank goodness the sun beat down on her and warmed her as she worked.

By midday, she had washed a dozen sheep.

She stood up and stretched her back.

"Ho there, boy, whose sheep are these and where are you taking them?"

It was Jack, standing ten yards above her on the far side of the stream, grinning at her. The sun hit his blond-brown hair and it glinted like gold. He was in a shirt and breeches just like she was, his coat slung over his shoulder.

But how magnificent he looked in his shirt and breeches. His wide shoulders, his narrow hips, that place where the tops of his legs folded into his torso, and the bulge there which she knew was his manhood.

She felt dizzy. She closed her eyes. She opened them. No, he was as heartbreakingly glorious as ever. Not that her heart was invested in the scoundrel. Not even a little bit.

"You look quite fetching, Helen. And not nearly as hungover as I would have expected."

He backed up a bit and took a flying leap over the stream, his boots slipping a little on the bank. But he didn't fall in the stream, and he laughed as she gave him a hand to help haul him up.

"Oh, oh. Nearly got a ducking myself. My lady, you are very wet."

She looked down. Her shirt was soaked and clinging to her breasts. Her nipples were clearly visible through the wet cloth. She had not worn a chemise or some other undergarment because she had thought she would be alone with Luran today. Quickly, she pulled at her shirt, moving it away from her body.

She looked at Jack, but he was not looking at her breasts. His eyes were fixed higher up, on her hair. Yes, what interest could her small breasts hold for him? She let go of her shirt and put her hands to her hair, brushing back some of the wettest bits which were hanging down around her face.

"I am washing sheep, Jack Pike. To shear tomorrow."

"Alone?"

"I have Luran."

He raised his eyebrows. "Luran is the dog's name?"

"Aye."

Jack reached out toward Helen's head. She held still and held her breath. He pulled a burr from her hair and threw it on the ground.

"The last time I checked, a dog can't wash sheep."

"'Tis his job to keep them from wandering."

Jack spread his coat over the boulder next to Helen's own coat.

"I should know about shearing sheep." He started rolling up his sleeves. "After all, the duchy has a lot of sheep. I should have some experience to report back to John MacNaughton."

"Ye should know about sheep?"

Good God, the man's forearms were things of beauty to match his face. Golden hair glinting in the sun. Long ropes of muscle. Veins popping into relief as the muscles in one forearm flexed when he rolled the sleeve on the other side.

What would it be like to run her hands over those arms?

To feel those surely soft hairs under her fingertips, to sense the power of that muscle?

"Yes."

Oh, he had said something to her. "Yes." But what had she said to him to provoke that "yes"?

"You're going to teach me how to wash a sheep, Helen."

"Yer going to get filthy, Jack Pike."

He leered. "I'm already filthy or hadn't you heard?"

"But that nice shirt." She gulped. "Those tight breeches."

"You've been looking at the tightness of my breeches?"

"Aye. Ye know I have. Is nae the reason for the tightness? So I and other women will look?"

He seemed taken aback. "Er, yes."

"And I've been looking at yer arms and yer hair, too."

"My hair?"

"'Tis the same color as mine when I was young."

"You're young now, Helen."

"Nae. I'm nae young, stupid man. The sun is high. Let's wash a sheep."

They started off with him holding the ewe, her scrubbing the fleece. He was not helpful at first, his boots sliding on the rocks, his hands scrabbling for purchase on the yolk-covered wool. Finally, he settled on being at the sheep's head, sitting on his buttocks in the stream with his legs splayed out, holding onto the rope around the neck of the sheep, and every once in a while using one of his hands to splash some water on the sheep's head.

"Ye dinnae need to do that, Jack. 'Tis the fleece back here that's important."

"But the sheep look so much better with their faces clean, don't they?"

That made her laugh. And his groans when he would sit back down in the icy water.

"My bollocks have climbed so far up into my body, Helen, I don't think they'll ever come down again."

They switched occasionally to give his "bits a chance to warm up," as he put it, but Jack did not scrub the fleeces as well as she did and she had to come behind him with her own hands to get the rest of the dirt off.

After ten sheep, his shirt was soaked and dirty and his sleeves were unrolled and flapping down and getting in his way.

He stood up. He stretched. He took his shirt off over his head.

Helen gasped. Silently, she hoped. The wet shirt had been dangerous enough, revealing the shape of his shoulders and his chest and his back.

But now...now. She trembled.

She looked away.

She heard his voice. "That's better."

"Aye," she mumbled and went to find another unwashed sheep.

It was both the best and worst afternoon of Helen's life. Just when she had almost become accustomed to Jack's handsome face, now she had to try to harden herself against the onslaught of his perfect, male body.

Because, of course, she found herself looking at that torso. Absorbing and memorizing every detail. How his little bit of blond chest hair darkened and curled when it was wet, lying sleekly over the rippling muscles of his chest as he wrestled with an unruly ewe. How his powerful shoulders framed that chest and the scar just below his left nipple, angling toward his hard, taut stomach. Even when he faced away from her, climbing out of the stream bed, hauling a bleating and now-clean ewe, his back was full of muscle under perfect, slightly golden skin. Golden muscle flexing in the sunlight with water beading on top of it, and the wet breeches clinging to his meaty, round buttocks…

How unfair that all that beauty should be concentrated in one person.

Yes, she saw how he preened for her. How he watched her face as her eyes couldn't help going to his body. She didn't mind that. He knew he was beautiful. He knew she thought the same. She had drunkenly said something of the sort to him at dinner, hadn't she?

And it was not Helen's way to hide her thoughts.

But…but he never looked at her. She knew her breasts, her nipples were apparent. The thin, wet shirt did nothing to hide them. So she knew he could see everything.

Not that there was much to see.

But there was something.

There was some proof she was a woman.

Look at me. Look at me, Jack.

But he didn't. He never looked below her face. Not even at her breeches as he had at their first meeting. And he made no noticeable effort to keep his eyes up. It was natural for him to ignore her.

She gritted her teeth. How she hated him.

And then the last sheep was done. He hauled it up to join the rest of the flock. She stood in the stream, panting. Exhausted. Covered in yolk. She climbed out of the stream bed and as she stood at the top of the bank, she slipped and he was there, one arm tightly around her waist, the other arm around her upper back. She teetered for a second and collapsed into him.

Her face was on his chest, her whole body pressed against him. He took two steps back, dragging her away from the edge of the bank.

His grip loosened but she did not shift away. She stayed there with her mouth, her cheek, her forehead on his chest.

And then his hands began to move, stroking her back. Long even strokes, all the way down to her bottom, where he cupped her cheeks lightly before beginning the long upward strokes, back toward her shoulder blades.

She trembled. His hands, his body, the exquisiteness of him. She could feel her center melting, an ache in her breasts and her nether regions which made her want to tear at the fall of his breeches and scream, "Take me!"

"Had a bit of a scare, eh?" he said. His chest thrummed with his low voice.

He was patronizing her, soothing her like a child when she was responding to his touch as a woman. And even as she longed to stay there, forever, against his body with his hands on her, it was too much. It hurt too much.

She stepped back and looked at him.

"I'm nae scared of anything."

He tilted his head, scrutinizing her face. "No, I don't think you are."

She went to the boulder and put on her coat. "Thank ye for yer help. I couldnae have finished today without ye."

He pulled on his shirt. "You're welcome. Thank you for the education in sheep."

She picked up her bucket and whistled for Luran who began to gather the sheep together.

"Goodbye, Jack Pike."

She walked down the hill with her sheep, Luran nagging at the stragglers with barks and running back and forth. She did not look back.

There was something in her coat pocket. She took it out. Her ham sandwich. She had forgotten to eat it.

I feasted on the vision that is Jack Pike, instead.

She laughed. She had to. How silly she was being. He was just a man, after all. And this was just a sandwich. And soon, he would be gone, back to London, just as the sandwich would soon be in Mags' belly. She would make sure of it. And when he and the sandwich had both vanished, all of her problems would still be in front of her to be solved. She needed to concentrate her mind on the problems, not on muscles and brown eyes and caressing hands.

TEN

"Good morning."

Jack could see his breath when he spoke. The sky was overcast and the air was much colder, and he was glad he wasn't going to be washing sheep in an icy stream halfway up a mountain today.

Helen's head popped up from where she was stooped, inspecting something on a sheep's foot. Jack put his forearms on the fence of the paddock and leaned forward, cracking his back. He was sore from yesterday's adventure in washing sheep, but he was well-rested, having first bathed upon his immediate return to Dunmore Castle and then fallen into his bed for ten hours of heavy sleep.

He grinned at Helen's obvious surprise.

"I'm here to learn about shearing."

She frowned and muttered something. Her head disappeared and she went back to doing whatever she had been doing before he interrupted her. Finally, she stood.

"Ye dinnae need to be here today. Duncan is coming to help."

"Duncan?"

At that moment, a giant of a young man came around the corner of the keep. He was surely the same height as Edmund Haskett, Earl of Longridge and Jack's friend from London, the tallest man Jack had ever seen. But Duncan had none of Edmund's heavy build. He was lean, like everyone else Jack had seen in Kinmarloch. And unlike Edmund's dark head, the young man's light-red hair was so bright Jack was tempted to put up his hand to shield his eyes. The young man came closer, and Jack saw a sprinkle of freckles across his nose and wide-set pale blue eyes.

Helen came out of the paddock. "Duncan Mackenzie, this is Mr. Pike from London. The purported new Duke of Dunmore's man. He's here to learn about shearing. He's useless but willing."

Jack smiled at Helen's barb. Useless but willing. Jack could make it the new MacNaughton clan motto.

He wasn't sure about this Duncan though. He looked younger than Helen, but the pair seemed to have an unspoken understanding of each other. A deep knowledge of what each of them needed in order to complete the job at hand. This spoke of long familiarity. And the way the young man concentrated on Helen, on her every word, her every gesture. Were these the looks of a lover?

Helen bumped Jack with her elbow. "Ye cannae shear. The fleeces are too valuable for me to let ye ruin one. But ye can hold the sheep for me as I shear and ye will be able to see what I do."

Duncan held his own sheep and he was swift and adept at moving the shears over the ewes' bodies. Helen was more careful, more deliberate.

Jack sensed she was tired from yesterday. Also, she was decidedly less interested in looking at him today since he had left his shirt and coat on. Or was that because Duncan was here?

They finished at long last, and the fleeces were rolled and piled in a cart.

"Duncan will take them to his father's forge until I can go to Cumdairessie."

"Why not hold them in the keep? Surely that would be more convenient?"

Helen grimaced. "Fleeces must be kept warm and dry."

Yes. Something needed to be done about that roof.

"Come have some dinner, Jack Pike."

They went into the keep and all of Jack's worries? Concerns? These words were too fraught. All of Jack's *thoughts* that Duncan might be Helen's man went out the window once the three of them entered the keep.

Duncan's eyes were glued on Mags. There was nothing else in the world for Duncan except Mags. Yes, Jack had thought Duncan had been closely watching Helen out of affection, but now he realized those had been the looks of a follower toward a leader. How could he have mistaken them for the gaze of a lover?

See how Duncan blushed as Mags handed him his bowl and his piece of bread. How Duncan asked every other minute if he could help her. How soft his voice was when he called her Margaret.

And if he was not mistaken, the shy Mags was smitten with the redheaded giant quite a bit herself.

It was sweet. Jack had never seen this kind of young love outside of the theater or a poem or a novel. Certainly, he had never experienced it.

Suddenly, he was jealous of Mags and Duncan. He, a rich man. Possibly a powerful man, in the future. A man who, in London at any rate, could charm his way into any woman's bed.

And it wasn't that he wanted Mags. Because he hadn't lied to Helen. To him, Mags was still a girl, much too young. But he wanted to be a young man, in love with a young woman, in a place where the accidental brush of a finger on the outside of a bowl of soup could make blood rise to his face.

But he had never had that and he never would.

Jack was halfway through his bowl of soup before he realized something was wrong with his meal.

Yes, the bread was the bread he had brought them two nights ago. It was stale but still good. Mags had toasted it. And the soup had the flavor of ham. And there were big chunks of potato in the soup. But there was no meat. None.

He raised his head, frowning.

"What's wrong, Jack?" Helen asked.

"Did you finish the ham already?"

Helen looked at Mags and then back at him. "Aye."

"Well, you are women with hearty appetites."

Duncan shook his head.

"No, Duncan? What do you mean, no?" Jack pressed the young man, but he kept his mouth clamped shut.

Helen sighed. "We shared it out. I meant to give the ham back because it was too much to accept, but then I thought again, I mean, I thought it might be best—

"Many people havenae had meat for a long time, Mr. Pike," Mags said in her soft way.

"So, everyone ate a slice of ham for dinner last night in Kinmarloch? Is that what you're telling me?"

"Well, half a slice anyway. We are nae so few as that. I hope yer nae angry, Jack. That we gave away yer gift."

No, he wasn't angry. How could he be angry at Helen's charity? But he wished she had been a little selfish and kept something back for herself.

Helen read his mind, staring into her soup bowl. "I kept the bread and the hambone for our soup. Rather piggish of me. Especially since I had a big ham breakfast yesterday."

Piggish? When most would have kept the whole ham with no thought for anyone else?

Helen looked him in the eyes. "I thank ye, Jack, for the ham. For Kinmarloch."

"Aye, thank ye," Mags echoed and Duncan chimed in with his own "thank ye."

"You're welcome."

Jack ate the rest of his soup, and it was almost as good as if it had ham in it. But he didn't take a second bowl. He would have to be careful here not to take more than he gave. Despite the widespread belief in the meanness of Scots, these people were too bloody generous, by half.

Eleven

Helen's horse threw a shoe while pulling the cart with the wool to Cumdairessie. But her horse showed no distress, and she managed to get to the wool buyer and sell her fleeces. It was not the price she had hoped for, not the kind of money to get her through the next winter. But there would be another set of fleeces later in the year. And she would never have the kind of money she really needed. The kind where she would know with certainty that all her people would be fed through the winter. The kind so that Mags could see a real doctor. The kind to fix the roof of the keep.

But she would pay back Jack Pike, and she would find a way to get more money. There was still the hope of the duke, no matter what Jack had said about the fine ladies in London. No matter that he had said the duke was good-looking. But, oh, how she wished John MacNaughton was the most deformed man in all of England. Then she might have a chance of him.

But maybe the duke would see the rightness of their union, as she did, and the advantages to him of having a wife who knew the land and the people. And maybe, despite being as handsome as Jack Pike had said he was, the duke was also kind-hearted and would take pity on her and not mind her looks.

Ha. She was going mad. Living in a dream world where handsome men were kind. Where beautiful men took off their shirts and held you against their bare, warm, muscled chests which smelled of wet sheep and stroked your back. Not because they thought you were scared, but because they wanted to touch you and hold you close.

An impossible world. A world which had no connection to the world she knew.

She idled, waiting outside the blacksmith's. The town, although it was the biggest for miles around, had no dedicated farrier. The fire burned hot in the forge, but no one was tending it. Why did her horse have to throw a shoe in Cumdairessie? If she had been in Kinmarloch, she could have taken the horse to Duncan's father, and the shoe would be back on in a flash.

She needed to get home.

She ducked into the public house, hoping to find the blacksmith there. The place was crowded, far more crowded than she had ever seen it before.

And then she heard that glorious laugh.

Jack Pike was sitting at a table, surrounded by men holding pints, his head thrown back. She watched him. Laughing. Talking. Drinking. The ale was flowing freely, and she saw men clapping Jack on the back and thanking him. Clearly, he was standing all of them to their pints today. No wonder the place was full. The blacksmith must be among these men somewhere.

Women were in the crowd, too, with some sitting at Jack's long table. And there were serving girls who brought the mugs of ale to the table. Often a few of them clustered around the group, needlessly. All the women looked at Jack just as Helen imagined she looked at him: slightly awestruck, flushed with excitement, unable to take their eyes away. She got closer and could hear Jack was telling jokes and stories. The same stories he had told her at dinner in the castle.

And over and over again, he found a way to say something flattering to each woman who came near him. A remark on the woman's fine eyes or her gay hair ribbon or her pink cheeks. Accompanied by a wicked grin or a wink or his eyes trailing over the woman's body.

It was his way, wasn't it? And it had some generosity to it because she could see it gave the women pleasure. And surely, he did not expect to bed all of them.

Or maybe he did.

Mmpf. She shrugged. She could probably get the horse back to the keep safely even with a missing shoe since the cart was empty and easy to pull. And she didn't fancy a blacksmith drunk on free pints laying hands on her only horse and injuring its hoof with his carelessness.

"My lady." Jack had seen her and gotten up from the table and made his way through the crowd to greet her.

"Jack Pike."

"Come have a drink with me."

"Nae, but thank ye. I must get back."

"There are some meat pies coming."

"I cannae."

"A countess can't eat and drink with an old sailor in a public house, eh?"

I cannae be the ugliest woman among many women at the table of Jack Pike. That would gut me.

She repeated herself. "I must get back."

He leaned and spoke in her ear so as to be heard over the ongoing raucous laughter and shouts. "That's a pretty dress,

Helen. I wonder why you didn't wear it when you came to dinner with me."

Under her unbuttoned coat, she was wearing her blue dress with the square cut neck. And, yes, it hung loosely on her as all her clothing did. But the dress had been tight when her grandfather had died so it hung less loosely than the other three she owned.

Jack went on. "You look much better in blue than brown."

It was the same as the fine eyes and the hair ribbon and the pink cheeks. There was no meaning to it. And he didn't really want to hear that the dress was worn so thin and patched in so many places she was surprised he could tell it was blue. And that there were sweat stains under the arms. And that no matter how many times she washed it, it smelled of sheep and smoke from a peat fire.

"I suppose 'tis a good thing God made my eyes blue, Jack Pike."

"Although I seem to remember you saying you had a fondness for a certain pair of brown eyes."

He winked and his brown eyes were sparkling at her and he was smiling. For a moment, the clamor of the public house died away. Then it surged back again, as noisy as ever.

"Aye. Enjoy yer meat pies," she mumbled and began to shove her way through the throng. She must escape.

She got out into the street, but Jack was behind her. Would the irksome man never leave her alone?

"I'll go back with you." He walked next to her.

"Ye shouldn't. Ye should go eat yer meat pies."

"Mrs. Mac stuffed me with rashers and eggs and scones this morning. I don't need the pies." He patted his flat stomach.

"But ye are in Cumdairessie. And ye have other appetites. 'Tis a good place to satisfy those, as I have already told ye."

He stopped walking. She turned to look at him. He was staring at her.

"You're telling me, Helen Boyd, that you would rather have me go back into that public house and eat my pies and drink my ale and bed a whore? Rather than have me escort the Countess of Kinmarloch back to her keep?"

I would rather have ye go far, far, far away from here, Jack Pike. Far away. Remove yer torso and yer laugh and yer cock and…yer man-self from my sight and my mind.

"If that's what ye feel ye must do."

"I'm my own man. I don't feel I must do anything."

"I thought ye were the duke's man."

"Well, the duke is not the duke yet. And he's not here. Jack Pike is operating under his own agency and he is escorting the Countess of Kinmarloch home. Now, where's your horse?"

Helen pointed with her chin down the street. "By the blacksmith's."

"Good. Let me go get my horse and we'll go."

"Ye should go back in and pay yer bill."

He waved his hand. "They know I'm good for it."

"Nae. Ye will go pay yer bill now. So the publican has money to buy meat to make more pies. To cut peat to keep the place warm. To pay those lasses who brought yer ale to ye."

He frowned and tilted his head. "Do you promise not to take off at a run and get away from me?"

"But yer so good at chasing women, Jack Pike."

"No, Helen Boyd." He grinned. "I'm good at catching them."

Their eyes were locked. He did not blink. It was like looking at the sun for Helen. She couldn't bear it. She looked away first.

"Aye. Go pay yer bill, go get yer horse. I willnae run away."

. . .

WHEN JACK LEARNED of the lost shoe, he insisted his horse pull the cart with him and Helen in it, her own horse tethered behind. Helen protested. His horse was a fancy mount from the stables of Dunmore.

"Yes, and he was barely being ridden before I got here. Let's make the horse do an honest day's work for once. And your horse looks like it could use the rest."

Yes, it was sad to see her scrawny, big-headed horse next to Jack's fine gelding. Likely as sad as it would be for a passing shepherd to see her sitting next to Jack Pike on the wooden seat in the front of the cart.

The cart made its way back along the rutted road to Kinmarloch, Jack commenting on the scenery, Helen naming the mountains surrounding them. It was good to sit next to him, not seeing him, only hearing his voice. It made her think that under other circumstances—ones where he was not a gorgeous rogue—they might have been friends. His ease made her heart easy, and she forgot her troubles for long minutes.

But, in time, the troubles came back to her. As they always did.

"Oh, I have yer money for ye, Jack Pike."

He waved his hand. "Pay me later."

"Nae. Ye made me take it. Now ye take it back. I have discharged my debt and sent the sixteen shillings off to Lord Reeves."

"You mean Lord Feces, right?" He grinned and took the pound coin and shoved it carelessly in his pocket. "That's the best news I've heard today."

"Have ye heard any other news today?" Maybe Jack had learned John MacNaughton was the duke now for certain and he was coming to Dunmore. Soon. Please.

"No. But even if I had, your news would still be the best. Here, I have an idea. When we get back, let me send the carriage for you and Mags to come and have dinner at the castle tonight. I heard tell Mrs. Mac is making lamb stew."

She laughed. "Nae, Jack. Whatever 'tis, it willnae be lamb stew. 'Tis too early for that. It will be mutton."

"Mutton?"

She looked at him. He was making a face. "Mutton is good, strong meat. If ye stay up here awhile longer, ye'll get a taste for it."

"Maybe." He started to say something else but then closed his mouth and fell silent.

She turned away again. "But ye will likely be going back to London soon?"

"Maybe."

"And ye will tell John MacNaughton about Dunmore?"

"Yes. I'll make sure he knows everything I know. And you shouldn't have any more trouble with Dunmore sheep going through Kinmarloch farms. The shepherds will be taking the flocks through the hills from now on."

She couldn't breathe.

"And if you do have trouble, you let me know. I'll give you my address in London."

One of her problems, solved, in an instant, by the man sitting beside her. She had said a few words to him on the matter several days ago and now, it had been done. He had taken care of it. And so, in a way, he had taken care of her. She was not accustomed to that. Tears pricked her eyes. She blinked.

She turned on the seat toward him, steeling herself to look at his perfect profile. "Thank ye. Yer a good man, Jack Pike."

He shifted uncomfortably and played with the reins in his hands. Suddenly, his face broke out into a sly grin. "No, I'm a scoundrel, remember?"

She grinned back. "A rakehell, ye mean?"

"Yes. A rakehell. And don't you forget it."

It started to rain. At first, just a patter. Jack gave her his hat to wear. But then there were buckets of rain.

She put the hat back on his head. "Ye must see to drive the cart!" she shouted over the downpour. He nodded, understanding her argument.

And the rain went on and on and on. Even the strong horse from the Dunmore stables was having a hard time in the mud. And it was a chilling rain that cut through Helen's coat and filled her with dread.

Finally, at long last, Kinmarloch and the keep. But there was no smoke from the chimney. Mags must be so cold. Helen jumped from the cart and pushed the door open.

"Mags!"

It was raining inside the keep. There were inches of water on the floor and big quarried stones and pieces of rotted beam. Helen splashed through the flood. "Mags!"

"Here, m-my lady."

Mags was sitting on a stool, under the table, bent over, her feet in the water. Helen crouched down. Mags' teeth were chattering and her lips looked blue. "The r-r-roof fell in, I think."

"Are ye hurt, Mags?"

"Nae. The roof d-d-dinnnae fall on me."

"Goddamn it." Jack waded over. "Let's get you out from under that table, brave Miss Mags." He lifted up the table easily. He picked up Mags in his arms. "There you go. You're safe now."

"Be careful of her leg, Jack."

"I am being careful. I'm being a hell of a lot more careful than you've been. Living in a leaking five-hundred-year-old hole. A deathtrap. Let's go."

He headed out of the keep, carrying Mags, and Helen followed behind him, fuming. Not careful? Her keep was a hole? And a deathtrap?

And then her anger turned to despair. Almost everything she and Mags owned had surely been ruined in the wet. They no longer had any shelter. Worst of all, Mags could have been killed. And this time, it was Helen's fault the girl had been in danger.

Jack put Mags in the cart and took off his coat and wrapped it around her.

Helen put her mouth to Jack's ear and spoke loudly. "Take us to the forge. To Duncan's father's house. They will give Mags and me a bed until the rain stops."

"No. Get in."

"The forge, Jack."

"It's foolishness, Helen. It's the same distance to the forge as it is to the castle. We are going to the castle and, at the very least, Mags is staying there until the goddamn roof on this goddamn keep is fixed. You can do what you like."

Luran twined around Helen's legs and yelped. She looked down at the dog. "Stay with the sheep." He ran off.

Helen got in the back of the cart next to Mags and put her arms around her.

Jack got up on the front seat and the cart began to move.

Helen put her mouth against Mags' wet hair. "I'm sorry, I'm sorry, I'm sorry."

Mags' teeth were still chattering. "D-d-dinnae be sorry, my lady. I've always wanted to be inside Dunmore Castle. 'Tis very grand?"

"Aye. 'Tis very grand."

"And warm?"

"Ye will be put in a warm room with a fire. And in a real bed with blankets. And ye will be given something hot to drink. Dinnae that sound good?"

"It s-s-sounds better than good. It sounds l-like ham."

TWELVE

The next day dawned warm but windy. The sky was a boundless, brilliant blue. Jack saw neither Helen nor Mags at breakfast, but he asked and was told they were eating together in Mags' room. He called in the steward Macsomething and told him work on the shepherds' hut in the far part of the duchy should halt today and all masons and carpenters and their supplies should be sent to the keep in Kinmarloch. The roof must be fixed. He would come himself later in the morning to survey the damage.

Then there was the arrival of the post for the first time since Jack had come to Dunmore. Had he really only been here a week? He opened a letter from London addressed to Captain Jack Pike, dated ten days after he had left London. It was from Phineas Edge, the Earl of Burchester.

Jack:

Reliable sources (id est, her lady's maid) say the Duchess of Dunmore's courses have come. You are the duke. Bring your well-favored self back down to London, Your

Grace. *The debutantes are not rioting yet, but they are close. It makes us lesser men shiver in fear and long for your return so you will make your choice and leave the rest of the field amenable to our more unwanted attentions.*

Lady Olivia Radcliffe, the daughter of the Earl of Titchfield, is newly out and, oh, Jack, what gorgeous children the two of you will have. Her beauty is unmatched. Even by yours. But you'll have some work to do, warming her up. Brrrr.

If you prefer something a little wilder, Miss Alice Danforth, George's sister, is still the source of a great deal of scandal and remains unspoken for. I can see the future trouble you two rascals might wreak together. The days of polite society would be numbered.

On the other extreme, there's her and George's friend, the Duke of Abingdon's daughter, Lady Phoebe Finch. She has a healthy pair of bosoms and good child-bearing hips. She's the nicest of girls, but I know you could bring out her naughty side. If you can get past George, that is.

Bad news on the heiress front. The youngest Lovelock daughter, the only one left unmarried, is apparently off to travel with her sister and her sister's husband, the Viscountess and Viscount Tregaron, for the unforeseen future. One has to wonder if it might be to hide something? About her? From her? Well, at seventeen, she was too young for you anyway, I think. And you don't need her money.

However, the ginger temptress Lady Ellen Stafford shows promise, and if I'm not wrong in my guess about what lies under her skirts, she has legs of glory. It would be something to be the man who gets to nestle down between those thighs and taste the quim framed by the maidenhair which matches the hair on her head.

And if you prefer a woman with experience in handling old codgers, which is what you are now, Lady

Lutton, the widow of the Earl of Lutton, has been at several balls. Oh, what a delectable, plump piece of flesh she is. Achingly sweet. Which is surprising, considering what a curmudgeon her first husband was.

Six of the seven Cavendish daughters are in town. There is word their father, old Middlewich, is ill, but they are determined to have a Season. The eldest, Lady Anne, is getting a little long in the tooth and a little desperate, they say. Her tongue is sharp, I know, but one wonders what it might feel like against one's cock, eh?

Anyway, I am sure each of the ladies above—and dozens more—would be ecstatic to have you compromise her as long as you also slip a ring on her finger. But you must be here in London to do that.

Unless, of course, you have already compromised some clan chieftain's daughter with breasts akin to Ben Nevis in size, a heart as warm as a glass of whisky, who looks on you with adoration and whispers in her lovely burr, "Och, Jack, I'd do anything to get yer caber up me."

Ha!

Oh, the Duke of Thornwick is looking around for a wife, too. He hasn't got a patch on you, in my opinion, and he certainly doesn't have your devilish charm or your legendary status in the bedchamber, but I am told the ladies think he is comely. You have some competition, you see, so don't dawdle.

All of London awaits you, John MacNaughton, Duke of Dunmore. Come home.

Yr. Friend,
Phineas Edge,
Earl of Burchester.

He crumpled the letter. Then he thought better of it and burned it in the grate of the breakfast room.

He couldn't go yet. He had work to do.

THE GROUND outside the keep was a churned mess of mud. Several men had scaled the outer walls and were straddled up there, looking at the damage, arguing amongst themselves about the best way to handle the roof.

And inside, puddles still stood on the floor, but they were drying. Up above, large pieces of blue sky showed.

Helen had insisted on coming with him. It was a sullen, angry Helen in a damp blue dress who stomped through the keep, picking up a pot here, a rag there, trying to find things she could rescue.

"It's not worth it, Helen."

She pressed her lips into a thin line and did not answer.

She had only said two words to him this morning so far. Literally. "I'm coming," she had snarled as she flung open the carriage door and climbed in.

Why was she angry at him? It wasn't his fault the blasted roof had fallen in.

I could have had the men fix the roof before they started on the hut.

But Helen was not his responsibility. Neither was Mags. They were of Kinmarloch, and he was the Duke of bloody Dunmore. Even though no one up here knew that yet.

He went outside the keep, into the sunshine and the wind, and waited for the verdict from the men up on top of the keep.

Helen went back and forth to the carriage, ferrying things she must be hoping she could dry out and save. He looked for tears but saw none. She was all fury. He did not volunteer to help her. Likely, she would have bitten off his head.

The man who had made himself in charge of the others climbed down and came to him at long last.

"Aye, we think the beams we had set aside for the hut will do. 'Tis nae easy thing to fix something this old. Ye would be better off just building a cottage beside it."

Helen heard this as she tucked one more pile of sodden garments into the carriage. Her back straightened.

"My lady," Jack said.

She turned. Her face was white. "I. Cannae. Say. Mister. Pike. Ye know I cannae say. I cannae pay. For. Any. Of. This." She gestured at the yard, the men, the keep.

Jack walked over to her and indicated with a jerk of his head that she should come around the other side of the carriage so they could speak privately.

"Let's put aside the question of payment." He leaned on the closed door of the carriage and folded his arms.

"That's easy for ye to do. 'Tis a privilege I cannae be afforded."

She wouldn't let him pay for this, that much was clear. Hell, the woman had barely accepted the loan of a pound, and she had paid it back as quickly as possible.

"Do you have something you could sell?" he asked.

She looked away.

"Let's say you had the money. Which would it be? Fix the keep or build a cottage?"

Her eyes came back to his. "The earls and countesses of Kinmarloch have always lived either in the castles of Kinmarloch or Dunmore. Always."

"Mags needs to live somewhere warm and dry and safe," he said in a low tone. He knew Mags was the way to get to Helen.

"So ye mean to set her up in a little love nest where ye have the privilege of coming and going when ye like?" she spat.

He wanted to seize her by the shoulders and shake her. But he restrained himself.

"I don't want Mags that way. Despite what you think, I am more than a cock and a pair of bollocks. Have no worries, all the women of Kinmarloch and Dunmore will be safe from me soon. I'm leaving, Helen. I'm returning to London. And I'm never coming back." He made that decision just then. "And I wonder at the sorry state of the men you have known all your life that you think I would take advantage."

She glowered at him defiantly. "I have known fine men. Good men. Better men than ye."

"Where are these better men, Helen, when you need them, eh? It looks like Jack Pike is the only one around."

Her shoulders hunched. In front of him, she visibly shrank. She looked defeated. But then she rallied and raised her chin.

"I think ye would take advantage, Jack Pike, because ye can. Ye could."

Yes, he could. He knew he could. He probably had, when he was younger. Wasn't that why he had designed his life in London the way he had? So that his bed would only be occupied by women who were married to other men. Women he could seduce solely with his charm, his looks, and his sexual prowess. Women who had no hope of his money. No hope of his providing for them in the future. No hope of even a piece of ostentatious jewelry, because how could they hide that from their husbands?

He had built a life where he could not use his money to take advantage. And where he would not be responsible for anything, except his own pleasure and the pleasure of the women he bedded.

He shrugged. "You're right. I could. But I won't."

His agreement with her, his tone of surrender changed her. Her face shifted. Now, all Jack could see was the portrait of her grandfather. She was a MacNaughton, through and through, more than he was, despite his last name and his title.

"So far, ye have only been good to me, to Mags, and to Kinmarloch. I am a spiteful bitch to think ill of ye and to accuse ye of such a thing. I hope ye know my words came from despair. And. Naething. Else." Her jaw jutted.

"Don't despair, Helen."

"I willnae. I dinnae."

He bowed. "I accept your apology."

"I do have something to sell." Helen pulled up her skirts.

Wait, what? Was she going to offer herself to him for money, here and now? Whore herself? Surely, not Helen Boyd. And hadn't she just accepted his word that he would not take advantage?

He was relieved when her skirts were arrested halfway up her thin thighs and her hand went to the dirk she had strapped there. He never thought he would be relieved to see a knife in the hand of someone who hated him, but he was. He hadn't wanted to lose his picture of Helen as an uncompromising countess, a woman above besmirching herself that way.

"'Tis very old. Carried by the Earl of Kinmarloch for centuries. Used against the English and others in battle. But I have the right to sell it."

She held it toward him, handle first. He took it carefully. Jewels glinted in the hilt.

"I'll buy it," he said abruptly. "It will more than cover the cost of what is needed to be done here."

Silently, she unstrapped the sheath from her thigh and handed it to him. As her skirts fell back down her legs again, Jack felt an odd pang. He had liked seeing the pale skin of her legs, the muscle from walking the hills, her knobby knees. But it was more than that. He liked that she had shown something of herself to him. Something private. Something that was more than her legs.

"So," he said, sheathing the dirk. "Which is it to be? Cottage or keep?"

Some deep war was being fought within her, Jack knew. But he was proud of her answer. Because it was both the right one and the one she didn't like.

"Cottage."

"Good."

"Aye."

"When your fortunes are better, you can get the keep fixed."

"It has stood for five centuries, Jack Pike. I suppose it can wait a dozen years or more for a new roof."

"Your children will live there, Helen."

He had meant it to be comforting. A sop to her pride. But it had been the wrong thing to say. She whirled and strode away from him.

"Where are you going?" he called after her.

A muffled answer came back to him. "Walking. Back. Now."

He watched her flapping thin coat and dirty blue dress dwindle in the distance for several long minutes and then went to tell the man in charge to build a cottage instead.

He lingered in the area for another hour or so, not wanting to pass her walking back while he was in the carriage. It was good he stayed because just as he had decided it was safe to leave since Helen must surely be back to the castle by now, the giant Duncan came at a dead run toward the keep, his long legs eating up the ground in huge gulps. Jack could not stop the young man before he flung himself through the doorway of the keep.

"Margaret! Mags!" Duncan roared.

Jack followed him and tried to catch one of his swinging arms.

"Careful, Duncan. Your voice might bring down more of the roof."

Duncan spun and towered over Jack. His freckles stood in stark relief against his white skin. His fists clenched at his sides. He had a look of horror which put Jack in mind of the face of the only man he had ever killed in hand-to-hand combat.

"Where is she? I heard—someone said—the roof—"

"Mags is safe at the castle, Duncan. She's fine."

Duncan collapsed, sinking onto his knees in a puddle, burying his face in his hands.

"I coudnae...I couldnae...I would die..."

"She's fine, I tell you, Duncan. Perfectly fine."

Duncan raised his head. "Aye." He got to his feet. Jack led him out of the keep, the giant staggering.

"I'm sure Mags will be glad to know you were concerned about her, but it wouldn't do for her to see you in such a state."

"Nae." Duncan wiped his nose with the back of one of his enormous hands.

"So, when you're calmer, come to Dunmore Castle and see her. This evening. I'll let her know you're coming, all right? To give her a little time to primp."

"To primp?"

"You know, to arrange her hair, change her dress." Although Mags might have no dry change of dress.

Duncan colored. "Oh, I am sure she would never do that on my account."

Jack laughed. "One of my friends in London is Lord Dagenham, one of the most dedicated gamblers who has ever lived. If it were him right now talking to you, he would make a bet with you that after I tell Mags you are coming, there will be quite a bit of primping. But I'm not him, so I won't bet you. Because it would be straight theft. I assure you Mags will spend a great deal of time improving her appearance before your arrival."

"She's always beautiful so she cannae improve her appearance."

"Yes. You should tell her that."

Duncan blushed an even deeper red. "I cannae say anything about how she looks."

"Why is that?"

"I cannae ask for her. I cannae provide for her until my father dies and I take over his forge. And although I want Mags, I also dinnae want my father to die."

"But surely you can say something nice to her without asking for her hand in marriage?"

"'Twould be forward."

"Be a little forward, Duncan. Just a little."

"What should I say to her, Jack Pike?"

Jack shook his head. "No, no, no. You must come up with your own compliment. But it should be easy, shouldn't it? After all, she has the face of an angel."

Duncan exhaled. "The face of an angel. Aye. Thank ye, Jack Pike."

THIRTEEN

Helen thought they were a strange group for dinner. The scoundrel with deep pockets. Her Mags, pink and glowing. The outsized Highlander fumbling with the unfamiliar fine silverware. And herself, the Countess of Kinmarloch in a dirty blue dress.

At least, the dress was fully dry. Finally. And the wretched brown dress had been salvaged out of the keep and was hanging upstairs in front of the fire in her room. She could wear it tomorrow. And her nightdress was drying as well.

She wiped her mouth with her napkin. "When do ye leave for London, Jack Pike?"

Mags' head, which had been angled toward Duncan, whipped around to look at Jack. "Nae. Yer nae leaving."

Jack shook his head. "I won't leave for several days yet. A week, maybe. I have things to do, I must make sure the cottage is well underway…" He glanced at Helen. "I don't plan to come back so I must soak up all I can of Scotland while I'm still here."

Mags gulped. "Nae coming back. But why must ye go?"

Helen thanked Mags silently for asking the question she herself wanted to ask but did not trust herself to.

"The new duke has been named. It will be John Mac-Naughton. He will be anxious to get my report. Hear my tales of the savages I have met. The sheep I have tamed." He chuckled and sipped his claret.

Hope woke up in Helen's chest.

"And do ye think the duke himself will come to Dunmore in the near future?"

"No." It was a blunt answer. "He will never come."

Helen's heart sank. It all seemed too much right now. The loss of her keep. The loss of her dirk. The duke not coming. Jack Pike going back to London. Although why that should upset her, she did not know. Hadn't she been wishing for him to leave just yesterday as they stood outside the public house in Cumdairessie?

That seemed a very long time ago.

Mags stared down at her plate. "And ye dinnae think ye will ever come back."

"Mr. Pike's life is in London, Mags," Helen said, leaning forward. "'Tis a long journey."

"But Mr. Pike likes long journeys. He was a sea captain. Dinnae ye like to travel, Mr. Pike?" Mags appealed to Jack.

He shrugged. "This was just a temporary arrangement. I have no real loyalty to the duke. I know him, but…"

There was a long silence.

Helen spoke first. "Well, it was very good of the new duke to have chosen ye to come. Ye have been the best gift to Dunmore a new duke could give. Sure, aren't all the ladies in love with ye already? And everyone else, for that matter. It reflects well on the duke."

"Well." Jack made a face. "Lord Feces isn't fond of me."

Mags looked confused. "Lord Feces?"

"Lord Reeves," Helen said.

A guttural laugh from Duncan which subsided when everyone else looked at him. His face reddened and he went back to eating, his fork and knife looking lost in his large hands.

Jack smiled. "And it might come as a shock, but I have not been pleasing to all the ladies I have met here." He looked at Helen.

"Ye have been." Helen cleared her throat. "Just some ladies dinnae like that ye are. Pleasing, that is. 'Tis nae reflection on ye. Only on them."

"And why would ladies not like something that is pleasing?"

"Perhaps—"

"Perhaps they are so contrary that they don't like being pleased?"

"Perhaps."

"Perhaps they don't like the feeling they get when they are pleased? That warm feeling that crawls down their spines and over their fronts—"

"Enough." She had to shut him up. The damned mind reader. "Ye will make me hate ye again, Jack Pike, and I am tired of hating ye. Let's call a pax."

Mags had been staring at each of them in turn during this exchange, her eyes wide.

"But ye have never hated Mr. Pike, my lady."

Jack sat back and smirked.

Helen took a deep breath. "That's right, Mags. I have never hated him. Why would I hate a man who would use his power to tease a poor, defenseless woman?"

"Defenseless?" The word erupted from Jack and he laughed. That glorious laugh. "You are nothing *but* defenses."

"Nae. I'm. Nae." The tears were close. But she kept them down. This was just a dinner conversation, after all.

"No, you're right. You are much more than that. You are the Countess of Kinmarloch—"

"—in her own right." This last was said by Jack and Mags and Duncan, all three together in one chorus.

She looked around the table. Mags and Duncan were serious. Jack wore his mischievous grin.

She straightened. "Aye. And nane of ye are ever to forget it."

"How could we when you remind us of it so often?" Jack popped a piece of bread in his mouth.

"When 'tis all ye have, ye might be guilty of being a bit repetitious, too."

He swallowed. "Like how I'm a scoundrel."

"Aye," she said. "Like how yer a scoundrel."

And then he laughed. And she laughed, too. And Mags and Duncan laughed as well, even though they couldn't possibly understand. But they were swept up by the magic of Jack Pike's laugh, just as she was.

Damn. She was going to miss that laugh. For a moment, just a moment, she didn't mind the warmth which crept over her spine and across her front when she sat at Jack Pike's table and laughed with him.

SHE WAS in the bedchamber of her girlhood. The *other* Mrs. Mac, the housekeeper, had put her there yesterday, not even asking if she would rather sleep somewhere else. But, in truth, if the *other* Mrs. Mac had asked, she would have said no, she wanted to be in this room.

Because so many hopes and dreams had been imagined in this bedchamber by a young girl whose grandfather had told her she was beautiful.

Her nightdress was dry. She put it on quickly and as she did so, she caught a glimpse of herself in the mirror which hung above the dressing table. She had not seen a mirror in over a year, not since the little one they had in the keep was broken by a small rock falling down. She should have known then that the place was not safe. She had been a fool about the keep.

But she had not missed having a mirror in the last year. Mags was good about telling her if her face was dirty, if her hair was disordered. She looked now in the mirror. At her jaw. Her nose. Her forehead. All still too big. Her brow, too heavy. She was still ugly. She thought about taking off her nightdress and looking at her body in the mirror.

No. She shuddered. She saw her own body with no mirror, often enough. She didn't want to see it as someone else might. As a man might. As the duke might. As Jack might. No, that was silly. Jack didn't see her that way.

But Jack did see her. In some ways, he saw her very well. Some parts of her. And maybe he might tell the duke about the good parts of her, the ones which had nothing to do with her body and her face.

She got into the bed.

There must be something else she could offer the duke besides her earldom, her title, her character. But the duke was down in London, surrounded by beautiful ladies. And Jack had said the duke had rarely met a woman he didn't like.

Rarely met a woman he didn't like.

She sat up. She did have something to offer the duke. She had no shame now. She had no pride. Well, she did, but she could let it go. She must let it go.

Those fine ladies in London, they would not be willing to do what she would. They would not be as desperate as she was. They would not be willing to whore themselves out before marriage.

But I am willing. If only I knew how.

Fourteen

She went to Jack Pike's room and woke him up. She was not coy. She did not know how to flirt, to hint, to hide what she wanted.

She asked him him to bed her. To undertake her training. So she could bed the duke and make him marry her.

And, yes, there would be the advantage that she would be bedded by *him*. A beautiful man. A man she wanted. A man she was hungry for in a way she had not known existed before she met him.

She did not hide her desire from him. That was not her way.

He was naked in the bed. And just to look at him and be this near to him. Oh, oh, oh. The ache he gave her. And then he touched her back, her leg, her breast, her other place. The place where she sought her own release the rare times she was alone in the keep. And he showed her his cock and put her hand on it. It aroused her to touch it. So hot and with velvet skin. But she was too angry and too rough, and he stopped her.

He kissed her. He kissed her again. And she was angry at

him because she wanted more kissing. But after she told him that, he kissed her more. And she was naked and he was lying on top of her and kissing her and she felt his hardness against her. He was harder than he had been before, and she thought she might have done that with her words and the kissing.

This was how a man and a woman fit together. No, no, not quite, but almost. Almost how they fit together. And her ache was unbearable.

"I love kissing you, Helen." A whisper in her ear. It wasn't love. She didn't expect love. Because how could he love her? That would have been foolishness. But he loved kissing her. And she didn't care if it was a lie or the truth because she loved hearing him say he loved kissing her. It was almost as good as kissing him. Because it was no lie that she loved kissing him. And to put her hands on his back and touch his muscles there as they kissed. To feel that hard pulsing thing between her legs as she pushed up against him, dying for the friction he might give her.

And then he was playing with her breasts with his tongue and his lips and his teeth. And she loved her small breasts for the first time because of the pleasure her breasts were giving her when he used his mouth on them. No woman with larger breasts could have ever felt more excitement than she was feeling at this moment.

Unhhh. She was groaning now and she didn't care if the whole castle heard her. Here, in Jack Pike's bed. But she knew no one could hear her. His bedchamber was…unhhh…far from the…other rooms. And castle…stone walls.

But she needed more. She needed more. She felt her cleft might fall off from the ache he was giving her as he made her nipples into shards of granite with his fierce, quick licks and nips. She writhed, she burned. It was the most wonderful agony in the world.

She took her hands from his upper back and put them on his head, in his hair.

"Oh, Jack. Please do that, but lower down."

He stopped suddenly. She raised her head. He looked angry.

What had she said that was wrong? Was what she had told him to do shameful? What could possibly be shameful to Jack Pike? But it must be. Otherwise, why would he be angry? But she had thought…she had seen…and she had thought that was something men did to women?

"You told me you were untouched, Helen."

There was a feral look about him now. A danger filled the room that had not been there before.

"Aye."

"How do you know about what men do with their mouths *lower down*? You didn't learn that from watching sheep."

"The blacksmith—"

"The blacksmith licked you between your legs?" He was pushing himself off her, away, and every moment the contact between their two bodies was lessening. Every part of his body had been against hers just seconds ago and now he was going away and she was going to die from need. Here. In Jack Pike's bed.

Her mind grasped at words through the haze of desire so she could make him understand.

"I saw the blacksmith up the side of the mountain with his head in his wife's lap, under her skirts. She was making little noises. I guessed what he was doing."

He relaxed back onto her. Thank God. Thank God. She held his broad shoulders so he couldn't go away again. Not while she was still in this state.

"I don't know what the blacksmith was doing under his wife's skirts, but I will promise you one thing, Helen."

Promise me that ye will keep touching me.

"Aye?"

"The noises you will make with my head in your lap will not be little ones."

He grinned at her. That devilish, seducing grin which made her so wet. And all she could think about was how it was going to feel when he did put his head in her lap.

"*Mo luran,*" she murmured. *My pretty boy.*

He slid down her body, kissing her ribs and her stomach, and her legs moved apart, allowing his torso to fit between them so that he was lying on the mattress.

And now he was kissing around her maidenhair. With any other man, she would have been embarrassed about having his face so close to that place. But not with Jack Pike. She would let him do anything he wanted. She had no shame about anything with him.

She was only aching need.

She felt his fingers touching her gently, spreading her. She moved her legs apart wider, drew her knees up higher.

"Unnh. Jack."

"You're lovely, Helen. Like a rosebud."

He kissed her then, in that wet, aching place. On her rosebud. She shuddered. And although it was dangerous and thrilling and made her want to grab his head and mash his face into her, she could tell the kiss had been as sweet as the words he had said. And it was good to know at least one part of her was lovely. She could not see it herself, so, this one time, she would take him at his word and allow herself to believe him.

And his tongue, it must be his tongue, touching her, her skin, her private lips, her opening. And he was so close, so close to where she needed him to be. But still he licked and kissed her in every other place than where she needed him.

"I need, Jack. I need."

She lifted her head and he was looking at her over the curls of her maidenhair, just the top part of his face visible, his eyebrows raised. He winked even as his tongue stroked her, made her wetter, wilder, a fraction of an inch closer to going…over…the…edge.

She put her head down. A devil. He was a devil, her pretty boy.

He stopped for a moment.

"What do you need, Helen?"

She raised her head. "I need…relief."

"Do you want me to give you relief now?

"Aye!" she howled.

"You don't want to enjoy this a while longer?"

She whimpered. "Aye."

"But I promised you relief, didn't I?"

"Aye," she sobbed.

"Don't worry. I'll give you relief. Lay your head back down."

She laid her head down. She felt his hands on her inner thighs, kneading her there.

"Relax, Helen, relax. I want you just to feel right now. Only feel. Relax these muscles."

She tried. She tried. Her legs slid down.

"Good," he said, his mouth so close to her that the rumble of his voice reverberated into her womb.

And then he gave her the contact she had been wanting and needing. His whole face on her. His stubble burrowing into her. His soft lips on her soft lips and his pulsing, throbbing tongue against her pulsing, throbbing place. And she kept his words in mind. *Relax* and *feel*.

She felt. Oh, yes, she felt. She felt she was nothing but that pulsing, throbbing place. Every other part of her had melted away and there was only that place and what he was doing to that place.

Her release came. Oh, my God, the waves of pleasure this

man and his tongue were bringing her. He splayed his hands over her pelvis and held her down as she bucked and thrashed. Oh, oh, oh, oh.

Oh.

As her body stilled, feeling clean and empty, her mind started up again. *I must remember nae to move so much if I ever experience this bliss again.* Because Jack had not been able to keep his mouth on her and she had been treated to his wet grin as she had moved helplessly on the bed, writhing with her own ecstasy.

"How was that, Helen Boyd, Countess of Kinmarloch?"

"Ye…know…how it was."

He clambered up the side of her, pulling the blanket over both of them.

Thank God. I won't have to look at my own protruding hip bones anymore.

One of which Jack Pike was caressing right now with his warm hand.

"I want you to tell me how it was."

She turned toward him and put her hand on his chest. She brushed the bit of hair there. She traced his scar with her fingertips. Her breath calmed, her heart slowed.

"Is that part of the pleasure for ye, Jack?"

"Yes."

She rolled onto her back and closed her eyes. "It was more than the perfect sunrise and the stars in the sky."

He chuckled. "So what I do with my tongue is better than how I look with my face?"

"Aye." She opened her eyes and looked at him. He didn't look angry. He was grinning. "Thank ye for my relief. I will never forget it."

"You're welcome."

"And now I am ready for my training."

He moved away from her slightly. "You already know how to kiss, Helen."

"I do?"

"Yes."

"Should I do anything differently when I kiss, Jack? Anything I could do better?"

"Not a thing."

"D-did you really love kissing me?" She couldn't believe herself. She was turning into Jack Pike. Angling for compliments. Wanting to hear those words again. And wanting to be kissed again.

"Yes, Helen. I did." He leaned in and kissed her. Slowly, deeply. She tasted herself on his lips and his tongue and she felt a strange satisfaction. That was her scent on Jack Pike's mouth. He pulled away and looked at her. There was no trace of a grin. "I do."

"Shall we rut now, Jack?

He didn't say anything. He just looked at her.

"Will ye show me how to give a man relief then? How to touch him?"

She hadn't looked at his cock as he had climbed up next to her. She couldn't feel it against her now. But it had been hard before, pushing into her when he lay on top of her.

"I think—" he said. She held her breath. "—you should go back to your own bed, Helen. Sleep."

She didn't understand. This went against everything she had ever heard about coupling. It was the man who must get pleasure. Whether or not the woman did—well, the woman's pleasure was unnecessary, surely? Wasn't that just one more unfairness put upon women along with childbearing and monthly courses and a lack of physical strength?

But she and Jack, they weren't coupling. Not really. He had said he would train her, teach her. Like she was a new sailor on his ship. She should not forget that. This was not like what other men and women did in bed together.

But didn't he need relief, too?

"I would like to make ye spend, Jack Pike."

"You're very sweet, Helen. Go back to your bed. The rest of your training can wait."

Sweet? Sweet? She was anything but sweet. Was the man mad?

She knew she should feel gratitude right now. The most beautiful man she had ever seen had kissed her mouth and her breasts and her private place and given her an ecstasy which would be burned into her body forever. He had paid attention to her in a way no one else ever had.

But she didn't feel gratitude. She felt anger. And a deep, deep grief. He had done nothing to hurt her, but she was hurt anyway.

He dinnae want me. Despite all he did to me, he dinnae want me doing anything to him. I dinnae arouse him. I'm ugly.

"Aye," she choked out. She got out of the bed and put her nightdress on. As she fled the room, she did not answer when he said, "Good night, Helen."

SHE WOKE LATE. She put on her brown dress. He was not downstairs. Not in the breakfast room nor the drawing room nor the Great Hall.

Mags was sitting in the morning room, looking at an illustrated book.

"These pictures are so pretty, my lady. See?"

"Have ye seen Mr. Pike this morning, Mags?"

"Nae. He left already, I was told."

Left. Gone to Cumdairessie, no doubt. To be with a beautiful woman who already knew what to do. One he wouldn't have to train, one who was not a burden.

"I was sorry to have missed him. Since he willnae be back," Mags went on, looking at Helen's face. "Aren't ye sorry, my lady?"

Helen felt a dread dragging at her chest. "What do ye mean, he willnae be back?"

"He's gone home to London."

She ran out of the morning room and ran upstairs and burst into the small bedchamber where Jack Pike had seen her naked body and touched her and kissed her and told her that he loved kissing her—twice—and made her spend with his tongue.

The room was empty. His clothes were gone.

She did not cry. She did not wail. She wanted to do those things, but she did not. After all, she was Helen Boyd, Countess of Kinmarloch.

In my own right.

She lay herself down on the bed and buried her face in the blanket. Stupid. Very stupid. Because the smell of him there made her want to cry even more over a man whom she had no right to cry over.

When she came back downstairs again, eyes dry but her lungs tight with no room for air in them, MacDougal gave her a letter with her name on it. And her title. And the words *in her own right* after her title.

Helen:

I am off back to London sooner than expected. My address is below and you are to write to me of any problems you have with Dunmore sheep on Kinmarloch land. Or really, any problems. You and Mags are to stay at Dunmore Castle until the cottage is finished.

If you have any need of money, you are to go to Mrs. Mac. I know you wouldn't take money from me so I have given it to her. It is what is extra from the value of the dirk, over and above the cost of the cottage. I don't want you getting into debt to a toad like Reeves again. And I want you and Mags to eat, is that understood?

Whatever you do, Helen, don't marry Reeves or a man like him, under any circumstances. If there ever comes a time when you feel you must do something like that, you are to write to me immediately so I can put a stop to it. I know you don't like doing what you are told, but you must listen to me on this.

And don't feel badly that the Duke of Dunmore will never come to Scotland. You are well shut of the scoundrel. He would never make a good husband.

Yr. Friend,
Captain Jack Pike.

PS I meant what I said about kissing you.

Fifteen

The postscript had been unwise.

Jack knew it as soon as he wrote it. But he did not scratch it out.

The kissing, and his appreciation of it, had seemed important to Helen. And he wanted to give her something besides the cottage and the money and his address.

He didn't really have anything else to give her, did he?

He had been sorely tempted to take something from her though, on that last night in Dunmore. Her virginity. He had wanted to climb on top of her or flip her over and plunge his cock into her rosebud. And until the very last moment, he had felt sure he would. He had had no compunction in the past when the woman was willing.

She had been willing. She had been asking. And she hadn't liked his refusal, his self-denial. She hadn't liked it one bit.

But there was no good way to explain to her why he would not rut with her or teach her how to make him spend with her hand or her mouth.

Because he didn't know the why of it himself. Or even why he had left Dunmore at dawn.

He was in his first bath since getting back to his house in London last night. He supposed his cousin's house was really his now. But he didn't want it. Let John MacNaughton stay here in the house that Jack Pike had built. Not in the town house of the Duchy of Dunmore.

He sank down into the steaming water. Let this hot water chase the chill of Scotland from his bones.

And besides, he must keep the house. It was the address Helen had. Captain Jack Pike's letters must find him, because he would not let her letters go unanswered. She had the ear of the duke, as long as he was duke.

He touched his member and his scrotum in the bath water. Yes, still there. But so much less demanding than in the past. He had sought his own release every night on his journey back from Scotland, but it had been by himself, alone, just as it had been in Dunmore. And his thoughts had been persistently haunted by a very particular woman. A strange woman who was…not beautiful.

His blood started to flow to his cock. He fondled himself in response.

He would think of other women now. Women in London. Marina. He would seek her out and break one of his own rules by going back to a former mistress. Or he would go to Nancy at Madame Flora's.

But those generous bodies would not stay in place in his imagination. They moved and squirmed and evaporated. He felt only a small, hard body underneath him, in his mind. A strong one. An unexpected one. One with breasts so small they were barely there. And yes, part of that smallness was from want, but her breasts would always be small, wouldn't they? The dresses she wore which were clearly relics from her days as the granddaughter of a duke had not been much bigger in the bodice than her body right now.

Her body right now. He tugged at himself almost as

fiercely as she had, his countess of the Highlands who was barely able to keep her savagery in check and who surely hated him now more than ever. Because of her unfinished training and her dashed hopes of the duke. Because she had received things from Jack Pike which she would resent forever. The money in trade for her dirk which lay on his dressing table right now. The stay at the castle and the food there. His mouth and his hands.

But not his cock. Oh, why, why not his cock? To be on top of her, looking at her face when he took her. That strength pushing up against him, her arms clutching at him. Why not his cock? When…it…would have…been…unh. Panting slightly, his face sweating, he released his seed into the bath water.

Good, he was done with that part of himself for the day. He would be able to clear his mind of Helen Boyd and think of something else.

He got out of the bath, the water now tepid. His valet came in and shaved him. He thought of Helen, pointing her dinner knife at the nicks on his neck where he had cut himself. Those were long-healed now.

His valet dressed him in tight-fitting breeches. The tight-fitting breeches designed to make Helen and other women look at his groin, his legs, his buttocks. As she had said next to that cold stream halfway up a mountain.

He went to his dressing table to get his watch to put in his waistcoat. The dirk lying there was a reproach of some kind. The rubies and emeralds and sapphires shining in the handle. He would get it appraised by someone expert in the matter and make sure he had not cheated Helen.

And then his breakfast. Ham. Big, thick, pink slices on his plate. An abundance. Enough to feed four people. Helen, Mags, Duncan, and himself laughing at a table.

He pushed the plate away. He wasn't hungry.

"You have a caller, Your Grace. The Duchess of Dunmore. I have shown her into the drawing room. Shall I say you are at home?"

Was he not to have twenty-four hours to himself in London before having to deal with Elizabeth? But time wouldn't necessarily make the encounter any easier. He got up from the table and went to the drawing room.

She turned from the window, dressed in black. She was as lovely as ever, wasn't she? Yes.

"Your Grace." He bowed.

"Your Grace." She curtsied. She met his eyes. "I suppose the news reached you wherever you had run away to. That I am not with child."

"Yes."

"You didn't come to me, Jack, as you said you would." A very soft reproach.

"No. I broke my word."

"Yes, you break your word just like everyone else. Just like me." She smiled and came toward him.

Wait. His knees weren't weak. His mouth wasn't dry. His cock wasn't hard. Had he become a stronger, better man in the intervening weeks? Was it because he was duke now? Did the title really confer that willpower?

No.

It was because of Scotland. It was because of Helen.

Because what was Elizabeth, after all, to him? Only a woman who had not deserved him. No, no, that was wrong. He likely had deserved her and the duplicity and the lies.

She was just a woman who had wanted a duke. As other women did. As another woman did.

She stood in front of him and her hand was reaching out to touch him. He caught it in his. Lightly. He wanted there to be no indication that there was passion in this room. Because there wasn't. Not on his side.

"I won't be bedding you, Elizabeth. And I won't be marrying you."

Startled violet eyes. The trill of a laugh. "Oh, Jack. Women like the chase, too, you know. You can't put me off that easily."

"Nonetheless, it's true." He released her hand and stepped away. "You're not welcome as a caller here. Ever again."

She betrayed herself with a single twitch above an eyelid. Then the appearance of a tendon in her neck. A sneer curling her full upper lip. "There will be things to discuss. Property. My dower. The town house."

"I will appoint someone to handle those things for me."

A clenching of her hands by her side. "You won't cheat me, Jack."

"No. I won't. Goodbye."

He left the room. "Show Her Grace out," he said to his butler.

He climbed the stairs, intending to go to his study and read his post. He wondered if Helen might write to him even if she didn't need to and how soon a letter might reach him.

No, she wouldn't write. She was too proud for that. He would be a fool to hope for a letter.

He stopped on the second flight of stairs, halted by a chest ache at the thought of Helen's pride, an ache which had been conspicuously absent when he had been in the drawing room with the woman who had broken his heart five years ago.

Or at least he thought she had.

He stood there and listened to the sounds of Elizabeth Hamilton MacNaughton leaving his house for the last time. Then he climbed the rest of the stairs, two at a time.

After he had attended to the letters which had come in the weeks he had been away, he would go find Phineas or Edmund in the club. Or George Danforth. He would make George teach him how to play chess. Or he would watch Sir Matthew Elliot doze off in a chair as he often did in the afternoon. Or he would seek out Will Dagenham in a gaming hell and play vingt-et-un with the viscount and Rhys Vaughan until dawn tomorrow morning.

He would surround himself with men. His men friends. He didn't need any other friends. Certainly, not a woman friend who ate him with her savage eyes and made his cock hard with her *mo luran* and told him he was like the stars on a summer night.

That was far too difficult a thing for him.

And too much responsibility.

Sixteen

J ack remembered now why he hadn't wanted to be duke. Because it was all difficulties and responsibilities.

"Come on, Jack, it's just like being the captain of a ship. But you're on land. And there's no excitement or danger."

Phineas' words helped him to remember that, of course, he knew how to lead, how to assess a situation and look for a solution. He was capable of making the hard decisions.

But being the Duke of Dunmore in London was not nearly as engaging as being Jack Pike, the duke's man, in Dunmore itself. Because here it was paper and numbers and dry men in spectacles and suits and the formality and the dullness of the House of Lords.

And the balls.

Oh, my God. The balls.

He had been to four already in just his first fortnight back. Him thinking the balls would fill his solitary nights and the women there would keep his mind off Helen. Phineas chivvying him into his satin breeches. George telling him he would be at the balls, too, chaperoning his sister Alice and to

watch out for the disgusting ratafia and under no circumstances was Jack to get anywhere near his sister. Or her friend
Lady Phoebe Finch. Edmund grunting he would go, too. Just
to look. And besides, there was nothing else to do.

He had met many debutantes at the balls, of course. He
had agreed with Phineas that Lady Olivia Radcliffe was beautiful but icy, that Miss Alice Danforth was a walking induce-
ment to scandal with her wicked ways, that Lady Phoebe
Finch would make someone a very good wife—but not him,
of course, not him, because after all, wasn't she meant for
George?—that Lady Ellen Stafford almost certainly did have
beautiful legs under her gown, that the widowed Lady Lutton
was sweet and plump and ripe for the picking, and that Lady
Anne Cavendish had a sharp tongue to match her wits.

He had liked speaking with Lady Anne the most, he
supposed. Despite being a duke's daughter, surely close to
thirty and still unmarried, Lady Anne had a spark and an
anger which reminded him of…well, she reminded him that
there were certain women in the world who were immune to
his charms. But her father had died five days ago and she had
gone back to Middlewich with her sisters. He had had no one
to spar with at the last ball he had attended.

At all the balls, he had danced. He had eaten midnight
suppers. And each time, he had gone home, rudely, long
before the breakfasts, wanting only to be alone, knowing his
thoughts would turn to Helen.

And he was home alone in the afternoon, sprawled on a
sofa in the front drawing room, in his oldest clothes,
unshaven, reading a report on the economic necessity of clearances in the Highlands of Scotland, when he heard a knock
and a burr-laden voice asking his butler, "If ye could please tell
me if this is Captain Jack Pike's house?"

A bounce off the sofa, five enormous strides, an elbow to
his butler's ribs shoving him out of the way, and he was faced

with Helen Boyd, Countess of Kinmarloch. And behind her a towering Highlander in full kilt with bright hair and freckles. And to the side of him, a seraph with hair of flame.

He ushered them into the house quickly, not allowing his butler to say anything, not wanting the words "Your Grace" to cross the man's lips. He got them into the drawing room and closed the door behind him.

Helen. He couldn't stop staring at her in her brown dress. She seemed so much smaller in his drawing room than she had been in his mind these last weeks. She also looked tired, but she had just taken a journey, hadn't she?

He forced himself to look at Mags and Duncan, to acknowledge them with a nod. The young people looked well. He turned his gaze back to Helen.

"What brings you to London, Lady Kinmarloch?"

"Besides the mail coach, Jack Pike?"

"Please sit. All of you. Please."

They did. Duncan and Mags drew away from Helen and went to sit in two chairs by a window. He sat next to Helen on one of the sofas and smelled cider and thought about a bed in a castle in the Highlands and two people lying naked in that bed and kissing. He touched her hand.

"No, really. Why are you here?" *Are you here to see me, Helen?*

She looked down at where his fingers rested on the back of her hand. She moved her hand away, into her own lap, and met his eyes. She didn't look tired any longer. She looked as fierce as ever.

"I need yer help, Jack Pike."

"Yes, of course. But you could have written. That would have been quicker."

"I needed to come myself."

"How can I help you?"

Helen took a deep breath. "I still think I should try to marry John MacNaughton, the Duke of Dunmore."

He held still. This was the moment to tell her. The truth. Here in London, how could he keep it hidden from her? It had been a close thing with his butler.

But she would despise him for it.

"I dinnae want to be any trouble. I only want an introduction. And I dinnae want ye to tell me 'tis foolishness when I know 'tis the best way to end my and Kinmarloch's troubles. I used the money ye gave Mrs. Mac to come down here. And I have enough left to buy a dress and get us some rooms. But I dinnae know anyone else here. So, if ye could tell me the least costly part of London where I might find rooms? And do any of yer women know of a good dressmaker?"

Her eyes searched his face and he held himself immobile, not wanting to betray anything to her.

She went on. "'Tis what fine men of means call a calculated risk. But I can tell from yer expression that ye think my calculations are very poor and I am very stupid to have wasted my bit of money and come here."

"No," he said slowly.

"And I would be lying if I didn't tell ye that I am a weak woman and I wanted to see ye again, Jack Pike."

You did come to London for me. Jack suddenly felt the room was too hot.

"Aye, I wanted to see ye one more time. To thank ye for everything ye did for me and Mags and Kinmarloch. And to thank ye for yer restraint when I had nane. On yer last night in Dunmore."

He cleared his throat. "And I would be lying, Helen, if I didn't tell you that I have regretted that restraint every day since I left the Highlands."

She stared, her eyes burning into him. Her jaw jutted.

Then, suddenly, she slumped and laughed. Not a real laugh. Some hollow, brave imitation of a laugh.

"Ye are the same as ever, Jack Pike. Are ye going to compliment my brown dress now? Are ye going to tell me that ye have been dreaming of my beautiful face and my large bosom? That ye love my kissing?"

"Don't mock me or yourself that way, Helen. It doesn't become you."

Her shoulders straightened, and she went rigid. "Aye. Nae much does. Become me." Her face was made of stone. "Thank ye, Jack Pike."

"For what?"

"For reminding me that I hate ye."

"You don't hate me."

"I dinnae know what else to call it."

He stood. "I'll help you get your rooms."

Helen rose, too. "And the introduction?"

He did not answer her. He felt in his pocket for his purse. Good. It was heavy.

"Stay here."

He went out into the hall and sent his butler away on an errand to another part of the house. Jack then ushered Helen and Duncan and Mags out of the house and into the street. He hefted the bag Helen had been carrying. Duncan carried another bag and a pack. Jack herded them away from the house as quickly as he could, given Mags' limp. He found a hack two streets away and got all of them into it. Duncan's knees scraped the opposite seat and he had to sit at an angle so that Mags and Helen had room.

"All three of you. Here. In London," Jack said, once the hack was underway.

"Aye," Helen looked away, out the window, at the street.

"I'm the honor guard." Duncan put his shoulders back which made his head brush against the ceiling of the carriage.

"The earl or the countess of Kinmarloch always travels with an honor guard," Helen said, still looking out the window, her voice flat.

"But, Mr. Pike, of course, a lady cannae travel unaccompanied with a man," Mags explained.

"So you, Mags, are chaperoning Helen, rather than the other way around?"

"Aye."

"I see."

They hadn't far to go. Jack had the Scots stay in the hack. He went into a building near where the new circus was being built. He found the man who leased rooms and asked for ones near the back, away from the noise of Piccadilly. He came back to the hack and got his charges out and into the building, Duncan eliciting stares from passersby on the pavement.

"You did bring some trousers, I hope, Duncan," Jack said as he followed the giant into the rooms.

"Aye."

"Wear them as much as possible. Your height alone attracts too much attention in London. Never mind the full kilt."

"Is there a reason we dinnae want to attract attention, Jack?" Helen was walking around the drawing room. No. Stomping. "Are we a secret? Is that why ye have bundled us off so fast? We might embarrass ye. In front of the people ye know in London, I suppose."

I don't want anyone to call me Your Grace in your presence, Helen. Not now. Not yet. Let me still be Jack Pike for you. For a little while longer. The man you want to hate. I'm not ready to be the man you really hate.

"No, of course not. I know you must be tired. I'll leave you all to get settled. I'm sure you want to bathe and that can be arranged. The price is included with the rooms."

"Get the stink of Scotland off us," Helen muttered.

Jack ignored her remark. "And coal and meals as well. I'll

go and make an appointment for tomorrow at the modiste for you, Helen."

"The what?"

"The dressmaker's."

"Oh." She mouthed the word. *Modiste.*

"I'll come early in the morning. Ten."

"Ten what?"

"Ten o'clock."

Mags and Duncan and Helen all glanced at each other. Helen shook her head. "Ten is nae early in the morning. Nae at this time of year. At the winter solstice, maybe."

"Ten is very early in the morning in London. At all times of the year."

"I can see I have a lot to learn about London ways. How much were the rooms?" Helen put her hand in her reticule.

Jack waved his hand. "We'll settle up later. I wondered if I might speak to you alone for a moment, Lady Kinmarloch?"

Helen looked at Mags and Duncan.

"I will go unpack ye and myself, my lady," Mags said and lowered her chin slightly at Duncan who picked up the bags and his pack easily and left the drawing room, trailing behind Mags.

Helen folded her arms in front of her chest and looked at Jack.

He took one step closer to her. "You are serious about marrying the Duke of Dunmore?"

"Aye."

"Have you thought about pursuing other matches? Besides the duke?

She frowned. "Ye know I have very specific reasons for marrying."

"I think you said wealth and power the last time I saw you. One or the other. Or both."

"'Tis to do with uniting the lands and the titles again. Ye know that."

"But you might meet someone else here. A man who would want to be your consort, would want to have a son who would be an earl or a daughter who would be a countess. Someone with money."

"Aye. But he widnae be a Scot."

"Neither is the Duke of Dunmore."

"His name is MacNaughton."

"That's the only Scottish thing about him," Jack said under his breath. "Think on it, Helen. It would be a shame to waste the trip and the dress."

"Ye mean to foist me off on someone else, then."

"It's not a question of foisting."

"What is it a question of, Jack Pike?"

"Of making sure you and Kinmarloch are taken care of."

Helen collapsed into one of the chairs. "Aye." Her voice was forlorn.

"Cheer up, Helen. You still have me."

But unlike the time he had teased her with those words at dinner in Dunmore Castle, when she was warm and tipsy with the mulled wine, she did not smile or soften as she gazed up at him.

"I dinnae think so," she said at last.

SEVENTEEN

Helen walked in circles in the drawing room. Duncan and Mags had gone off to sleep long ago, to their separate bedchambers. Three bedchambers in these rooms Jack had found for them. The cost would be high here in London, and she hoped she had enough money. On their way south, she and Mags had shared a bed as they did at home and Duncan had slept in bunks with coachmen or roughed it in the stables.

"This London bed dinnae fit me, my lady," Duncan had told her this afternoon after Jack had left.

"I'm sorry, Duncan—"

"But I'm used to that. I'll make up the bed on the floor. To sleep on a dry, wooden floor in such a warm room. In April. 'Tis a luxury I'm nae used to."

She did not think Mags would creep to Duncan's bed tonight or the other way around. But if they did, all the better. She knew there was love there. Let them have what they could. She did not begrudge them anything. Let them have the touches and the looks and the whispers and the kisses which she herself had never had.

Well, she had had kisses. One night of kisses which would have to last her lifetime.

Seeing Jack Pike again. It hadn't gone how she had imagined it would so many times in her head over the last weeks.

Yes, she must look to the future. She was here to woo the Duke of Dunmore. It was the only way to be free of need for her and her people. It was required of her. It was her duty. It was ingrained in her, that duty, from birth. That nagging, obstreperous, binding duty. It was her life's blood. Her purpose for being.

But she was also here because *he* was here. She would never have undertaken the trip to London unless she had known he was here, known she could find him because she had a scrap of paper with his address written on it, known she could lean on him even though she could not lean on anybody.

The moment of relief when she had first seen him again had quickly fled. She had thought he would be as he had been in Scotland. Laughing, flirting, playful, maddening. But, no. He had been serious. Worried. Anxious. Embarrassed that she had come to his house, even wanting to hide her from his servant. Dying to get her away from his house and into these rooms as quickly as possible.

But the ache and flush of arousal when she had first seen him standing in the door of his house—whiskers on his chin, shirt untucked from his trousers, hair sticking up as if he had just been lying down—had not faded. And when he had used his silky voice on her, the same voice he had used to compliment the women in the public house, when he had said he regretted not bedding her, the ache had become unbearable between her legs and in her chest, and she had been forced to dispel it as quickly as possible.

Because he didn't mean it. He couldn't.

She was a fool. She had told herself that many times

before. But as many times as she had told herself, she would always be a fool about him.

No matter. She might be a fool, but she was still the Countess of—somehow her title was not as comforting in London as it was at home.

But she was here now. In London. With a clear mission. The Duke of Dunmore.

And although he had not given her a warm welcome, Jack had been willing to help with the rooms, and tomorrow, the dress. He had not yet agreed to the introduction to the duke, but she would get that from him. And if not, she would find her own way to meet John MacNaughton, Duke of Dunmore.

She was sure she would not sleep tonight, but she must try. She must have her wits about her tomorrow. She must not look pale or drawn or have circles under her eyes.

She took three steps toward the hallway which would take her to her own bedchamber when there was a sudden rapping on the door. She looked at the mantel clock. It was just midnight. The knock came again. Faster, harder, more furious. Almost a pounding.

She opened the door.

It was him. Cravat askew. Sweat at his temples. The most beautiful man she had ever seen.

"Helen," he said. And he was grabbing her and kissing her. This was not like any of the other kisses he had given her in Dunmore in his bed. This was hard. Forceful. His body pushing into hers, pushing her back into the room. His tongue pushing into her mouth without warning. His hands a vise on her waist.

And she was grabbing him, his coat, his back, and pulling him into her, her tongue warring with his. She could not breathe, she could not think.

His hands were clutching at her breasts and his mouth was

on her throat and she was able to gasp out, "Do ye want to finish my training?"

The response was a growl. Followed by, "Fuck your training," into the curve of her neck.

He raised his head and laced his fingers into her hair and jerked her head back. "I want you, Helen. That's all. I want to fuck you. And I'm going to fuck you tonight if you're willing, and I'm not doing it to train you for another man. Is that clear? I'm doing it because Jack Pike wants you. That's the only reason. Is that all right?"

She shuddered. She could feel his hard length pressing against her and all she could think of was having it inside her.

"Aye," she managed to choke out. "Aye, that's all right."

"Good." And his mouth was on hers again. His hands were on her back, fumbling and grasping at her buttons, his thigh between her legs, pressing on that place. And she was shamelessly rubbing herself against him, riding his leg. There was wet heat pooling in her cleft and an ache there that was only bearable because she knew he would release it.

"Jack," she rasped. He pulled her dress down to her waist, only her chemise covering her top half. "Jack Pike, nae here. My bedchamber."

He picked her up, sweeping her into his arms. "Where?"

"The back, the right side."

She clung to him as he carried her down the hall, her arms around his neck, and she had a few seconds when she could look at him, at his face. Was it really possible this god wanted her, even if it was only for tonight?

He looked down at her. "You're not having second thoughts, are you, Helen?"

"Nae, *mo luran.*"

"Good."

"I-I'm having wicked thoughts."

His response was yet another growl and his head coming

down in an almost-lunge to tear at her mouth with his and then they were in her bedchamber where she had left the lamp burning. He fell on top of her on the bed and his mouth was roving over her chest, nipping and sucking at her breasts through her chemise.

"L-let me get my dress off."

He rolled off her and she got up from the bed and started pulling her brown woolen dress the rest of the way down, trying to be quick because he might change his mind and the ache, oh, the ache.

"I hate that dress, Helen." He was jerking at his cravat, unbuttoning his waistcoat. Only now did she realize he was wearing very fine clothes, far finer than any she had ever seen before in her life. He was dressed like a prince.

"After tomorrow, we are burning that dress." He threw his shoes in the corner.

"Aye." She pulled her chemise over her head.

His clothes were off. She had a glimpse of his muscled chest with its scar. His member, darker than the rest of his golden skin, large and pointing up toward his flat abdomen. He took one long step toward her and pulled her into him so their naked bodies could not be any closer, could not be crushed together any more tightly. She could feel his hard cock pushing at her own abdomen now, insistent. His hands were on the cheeks of her bottom and he was kissing her again. Wildly. Teeth clashing, his tongue deep inside her mouth. She went up on her toes and wrapped one leg around his thigh, trying to get her cleft closer to his cock, her mouth closer to his.

His hands were running up and down her back. Up and down. Just as they had been at the stream that day. But now it was because he wanted her. He wanted to be inside her.

"I'm ready, Jack," she managed to get out when his mouth went to her jaw, her throat, her shoulder. "I'm ready."

He lifted her by her haunches and took her to the bed again, lying half on her, half to the side of her on the mattress.

"I want you," he kissed her and rubbed the palm of his hand roughly over one of her breasts and she groaned, "to have enough kissing."

"Ah-aye."

"I want you," he kissed her with his tongue thrusting and took his finger to the seam of her cleft and rubbed her wetness there, "to have so much kissing that you beg me to stop kissing you and to fuck you."

"Aye," she trembled, "please. I beg ye."

"Say it, Countess of Kinmarloch. Say it."

"Please fuck me."

He rolled and knelt between her legs and pushed them farther apart. His cock protruded out, high, hard. So much larger than it had been when he had put her hand on it in Dunmore. And now he had his hand on it himself.

She came up on her elbows. "But maybe, Jack, maybe ye could do both? The kissing and the other? The *dàireadh*? At the same time?"

He leaned down and kissed her several times—short kisses with just his lips—and rubbed his cock in her cleft. She collapsed back onto the mattress as tremors ran through her body.

"You know it hurts for most women the first time, Helen?"

"Aye."

"And sometimes there's blood?" His cock was going over her place which needed touch and pressure and yes, sometimes roughness.

"Ah-aye."

"And you'll tell me if you want me to stop."

"I widnae tell ye that." She used his word so he would know she meant it. "Please. Fuck. Me."

She ran her hands over his chest and kept her eyes on his face as he looked down toward where his cock was stroking over her cleft. She felt the tip of him at her entrance.

"Aye, Jack, please."

He breached her. His eyes came up to hers. She nodded. He pushed in deeper. She felt pain and fullness. But the pain was nothing. She was a MacNaughton and this pain was nothing.

His face came closer to hers and he kissed her, his tongue probing her mouth, just as his cock went even deeper into her. And then he could not be any deeper and he was withdrawing and there was some pain with that, too, but not as much, and he was stroking into her again and kissing her again.

Her hands were on his shoulder blades, his smooth skin there. She lifted her hips to him, wanting more of him inside her. She still felt pain but she could not get enough of him inside her.

"Fuck me, Jack." *Take me, I surrender.*

He groaned and began stroking into her more quickly.

"Aye," she said. Her hands went to his buttocks, pulling him into her.

"Yes," he said.

"Jack, Jack."

"Helen." His lips brushed hers. "Helen."

She brought her legs up, spreading herself wider, her heels digging in beneath her hands on his buttocks. So he could not stop. He could not leave.

There was no pain now, only want. Only a deep, driving, primal need to take him in. To have him fill that emptiness she had not known was there until she met him.

She could hear her wetness as he moved in and out. The slap of his skin against hers. His grunts. Her own pressured breathing.

He went onto his elbows. His abdomen against hers, his

chest rubbing against her breasts, even as he stroked in and out and kissed her.

She groaned into his mouth.

He leaned to one side, putting all his weight on one arm and moved his other hand between them, his fingers sliding over her maidenhair and into her wet folds. He found the right place and rubbed her there, above where he was pumping his cock.

"Feel, Helen," he commanded her. "Feel me."

"I…I…Jack. Jack!"

It came on so quickly. She could not hold it back. The waves of ecstasy rolled over her body and she felt herself clenching around him. Her upper body curled with the contractions of the muscles of her groin, and her head came up, hitting his forehead with hers.

He moved his hand away from her cleft.

"Good, Helen."

"Jack." She looked at his face. He was sweating. His eyes were unseeing. His movements became wilder. He was thrusting into her violently now. Like she was just a vessel for him.

His body pulled away from hers and she was empty and he had his hand on himself and he was gasping and she couldn't see but she was sure he was spilling onto the sheets between her legs.

She heard her own heart thumping. His panting.

"Damn." An abrupt curse from him, his head down. She couldn't see his face. He moved from between her legs and collapsed onto the bed beside her. She stayed still at first, lying on her back. Then she turned her head to see him.

"Goddamn it." He rubbed his face with his hands and shook his head. Finally, he took his hands from his face, but he didn't look at her. He looked up, at the underside of the canopy of the bed.

No parts of their bodies were touching now. Not even an accidental brush of his hand.

He was so far away. He had been so close, and now he was so far away. Even though it was only inches. She turned her own head to look at the underside of the canopy, too. She felt a dirk in her guts, twisting.

Dinnae get soft now.

His voice. "That wasn't supposed to happen—"

"Ye had better go."

"Yes." He sat up. "I'm sorry, Helen—"

"Now."

He stood and began to dress. She didn't move. She couldn't. She breathed and was surprised to find she still needed air even though she was dead.

His shoes were on and now his tailcoat. He held his cravat in his hand.

"Helen," he said.

She reached and found a sheet and pulled it over her, hiding her body from him. "Good night, Jack Pike. I'll see ye. Tomorrow morning. Dinnae. Worry."

She turned over, her back to him, and waited for him to leave.

A sigh. Footsteps. The door clicked shut.

And then she wept.

Eighteen

"No! It's wrong, I tell you. Damn it." Jack ran his hands through his hair, wanting to rip it out.

Helen stood in front of him, drowning in some ungodly pink dress with bows and ruffles. Ruffles!

"This dress is already made up and with a few quick alterations, it could be taken away today as requested. And it is what the debutantes are wearing, Captain Pike."

"She's not some bloody debutante."

"Are you a widow, Mrs. Boyd? I didn't understand."

Jack stood. "She's the Countess of Kinmarloch, in her own right. She is *my lady*, to you."

The modiste Mrs. Allen looked from Helen to Jack and back to Helen again. She curtsied. "Yes, I see that now. My lady."

"'Tis a very nice dress, Jack. And if this is what other women are wearing, surely 'tis fine." Helen's eyes were worried, anxious, trying to placate him. He didn't like that. He didn't want her to placate him. He wanted her to fight with him.

"You're not to wear what other women wear, Helen. And

I thought," he rounded on Mrs. Allen, "someone else might see that." He turned back to Helen. "And that dress is a horror on you. Take it off."

Helen's worried eyes turned fierce. Her jaw jutted.

That's better. Hate me.

She turned and stomped back into the closed-off dressing area at the back where a seamstress waited to assist her. The shop had been shut to the public this morning at his request.

Mrs. Allen spoke. "I am a little uncomfortable with this arrangement, Your Grace."

He answered in a barely voiced whisper, "I told you not to call me that."

"She can't hear us, I assure you."

"Nonetheless, I am Captain Pike, Mrs. Allen. Or Mr. Pike."

"Yes, Captain Pike."

"Thank you for doing this. The appointment, everything."

"You know you can have what you like from me and from the shop."

He waved his hand as if to brush her words away.

"Tell me, Captain Pike," Mrs. Allen said carefully, "what you envision for the countess."

"I don't know. But not that."

"What color have you seen her in that you like?"

"Blue."

"What kind of blue?"

"I don't know. Blue blue."

"The color of the lady's eyes?"

"I don't know. No, I do. The color of the sky on a perfectly clear spring day. After it has rained the day before. And it's windy. Have you ever been to Scotland?"

"No. But I spent one summer when I was young in York-shire. I think I know what you mean. It's not a harsh blue…"

"No…"

"But it's not fair to call it a soft blue either. Because it's so full of color."

"Yes. And the dress is not to have…" He gestured with his hands around his neck and chest.

"Too much decoration."

"Yes," he grunted.

"But the lady is quite slender. Everywhere. A few ruffles give the illusion of fullness."

"I don't want illusion."

"But the lady might."

Jack paused. "Ask her."

"I will. And I still don't quite understand. Is the dress to be a ballgown, an afternoon dress, what?"

Jack didn't know. Helen thought she was buying the dress to meet the Duke of Dunmore. How had Helen imagined meeting the duke? At a ball? At a private appointment at his house because she was his neighbor and it would be a meeting between two nobles whose lands adjoined? During a stroll or a carriage ride in Hyde Park?

She would never have occasion to wear a ballgown in Scotland. But nonsensically, Jack wanted her to have a ballgown. One thing fit for a countess.

"I don't want you to tell the lady but make a ballgown. And a spring day dress. And a warm woolen one for winter with long sleeves. She will pay for a small part of the spring one. A very small part. I will pay for the rest. She's not to know this."

"This is indelicate, but I know you will forgive me. I noticed the lady does not wear stays. She does not need them, of course, given her figure, but if she goes to a ball, it would be noticed by her partner during a waltz."

Jack thought of the debutantes he had waltzed with recently. His hand on rounded waists. The thickness of the stays under his hand, so unlike the feel of Helen's waist when he had supported her at the table when she was drunk, or when she had almost fallen into the stream, or when he gone to her last night and seized her as soon as he had seen her, unable to do or think of anything besides possessing her and her body.

He had first gone to another ball last night. He had already accepted the invitation. The Duke of Dunmore was expected. He had thought the ball would serve as other balls had, to distract him and keep him from thinking about Helen. That dancing and flirting would keep him from brooding about how he might find a way to tell her he was John MacNaughton without making her hate him more. Or about how he might fix her situation without seeming to be the one to fix it. Or about how his heart had been in his mouth when he had seen her on his doorstep and how he had only thought of her body under his when he had sat next to her on the sofa.

But the music, the heavily scented air, the laughter and vacuous conversation were intolerable. His cravat strangled him. He could barely recognize the faces around him. His mind and his emotions would not bend to his will, and he could only think of Helen, less than a mile away in her worn muslin nightdress, her hair in a plait.

He would go to her right now and tell her he was the duke. That would stop this. She would hate him thoroughly and she would go home, and he could go back to his new life in London as the Duke of Dunmore.

He left the ball even before the midnight supper, sending his carriage home, walking quickly through the streets in his dress clothes, headed toward her rooms. And then she opened the door and he saw her and he only felt desire. Ravening desire. Nothing else.

There was wild, savage need with her in her bedchamber. He tried to slow himself. To put himself in her place. But he couldn't. Not for long. And she didn't shy away from his crude language, his brutal thrusts at the end.

But after he took her, after he released, he felt the heavy burden of his deception and a crushing responsibility he didn't want.

Walking home, he wondered what his reception would be when he came at ten o'clock in the morning to take her to the modiste.

She was unchanged. Fierce. Bristling. She met his eyes. She answered she was well and she hoped he was well and all of them had eaten breakfast. She took the hack with him to Mrs. Allen's shop, intent on getting her dress. She made no mention of their tryst when they were in the carriage alone, Mags and Duncan having stayed behind. Instead, she looked out the window and asked him what a London modiste's shop would be like, what would be expected of her, how much her dress might cost.

Her dress.

"Yes, stays," he told Mrs. Allen. "Have them made and whatever other underthings she might need."

"Chemises and petticoats. Some silk, some more practical?"

"Yes." Gruff.

"And she will need shoes and hose and gloves, of course."

"Yes, yes. Arrange for it. And she needs a dress today. An additional one. The simplest one you can find. Not that pink thing. But she can't leave here wearing what she came in with." Which was the brown dress he had promised her last night they would burn. Together.

"Yes, Captain Pike."

"I'll come back." He left while Helen was still in the back of the shop, likely cursing him under her breath. He walked down to the Thames and looked at the boats out on the water.

He pushed a cobblestone into the water with his toe. *Plunk.* Detritus floated by. The river stank of sewage.

A far cry from a mountain stream in Kinmarloch.

Or from his own beloved, vast, briny ocean. He should never have resigned his commission at the end of the wars. Of course, he was already a lost man by then, Elizabeth having married his cousin Norman. But the loss of his ship, his men, his purpose—now he could see he had unthinkingly compounded the wound.

When he should have been busy, he had been idling. When he should have been concerned with the lives of his men, he had been only concerned with himself.

He was a wastrel. The worst kind. Because what he had wasted was himself, his manhood, even as he thought he was proving his manhood by copulating with woman after woman. Seducing them away from their husbands' beds only to prove the point that all women were faithless, cuckolding whores.

Like his mother. Who, even while his father had still been alive, had surely lain with his future stepfather. And had gone on having lovers even after she had become Lady Pike, until she had died from influenza.

Like Elizabeth, who had bedded his cousin while betrothed to him.

Like Helen, who had not stopped Jack Pike from taking her last night.

It wasn't the same, he told himself. Helen had made no promises. She wasn't betraying anyone. She wasn't engaged to the Duke of Dunmore.

But she wanted to be.

When he returned to Mrs. Allen's shop, Helen had been fitted out in a sprigged muslin dress, the material a white field with small blue flowers on it, and a matching blue spencer. It

was not the right blue—too dark—but it was a vast improve-
ment over the brown.

"We were able to alter the dress and the spencer quickly,
Captain Pike," Mrs. Allen said. "They had been meant for
someone else, but she won't be coming to get them for two
more weeks so we will make copies."

"'Tis two dresses, Jack," Helen said when they left, a
paper-wrapped parcel under her arm. Her voice was harsh,
choked by some emotion he couldn't place. "The one she is
making and this one. With the jacket. I cannae afford it."

"Don't worry about the cost. She owes me a favor."

"Is she one of yer women?"

"No."

"Do ye take yer women there for dresses?"

He shook his head. Mrs. Allen's shop hadn't been fancy
enough for Elizabeth. It wasn't on Bond Street. It wasn't French.
And Jack had never given presents to his married mistresses.

"Mrs. Allen is the widow of a man who served under me. I
set her up in the shop."

A hand on his forearm, squeezing tightly. "Thank ye."

He looked at her face, pointed toward the oncoming
pedestrians. Her forehead, that broad forehead, not furrowed
with rage for once. That strong nose. Because it was strong,
wasn't it? Not too big, as he had first thought it. It was right
for her face. And now he admired the fine bone that defined
her nose and made it as uncompromising and rugged as the
Benrancree mountains. That nose he had bumped with his
own as he had sought her mouth last night, again and again.
Giving her the kisses she wanted along with his cock.

Her hand was off his arm now and she was stepping away
from him, into the street to avoid a group of tradesmen. Wait,
shouldn't he have been on the outside?

And there were horses and a carriage coming and he was

weaving and grabbing and pulling her out of the way, jerking her into him and onto the safety of the pavement. Her body against his.

He looked around the street, not at her, he couldn't look at her, and he saw an alley and he dragged her into it and pushed her against the wall there and kissed her.

God help him, he kissed her. He kissed her cider-flavored mouth and pressed his groin against her and crushed her into the bricks of the wall of that alleyway. He didn't notice if she was kissing him back, if she was pushing or pulling him away.

He grabbed her arm and took her back out onto the pavement, walking quickly, tugging her to his side.

Her voice, out of breath. "Aren't ye going the wrong way?"

"We're not going back to the rooms."

"I told Mags and Duncan—"

"They'll be fine."

She fell silent, trying to match his swift pace.

NINETEEN

A shabby place, an inn, half a street away. Mrs. Allen's shop was, as Elizabeth had pointed out years ago, only a good one, not a fine one. It was not in the best part of London.

He would not be recognized.

Even when they got into the inn bedchamber and Jack locked the door behind them, Helen said nothing. She put her parcel down on a chair and shrugged her way out of her new spencer. As she turned away from Jack to hang the jacket on the back of a chair, he came up behind her and unbuttoned her new dress. His cock pushed at the fall of his trousers, reaching toward her. Her own hands reached back and clutched the sides of his thighs, pulling him closer. He undressed her and backed away and undressed himself. She did not go to the bed but stood, watching him take off his clothes. Not hiding her body but not presenting it either. Just letting him see her, like she was standing in her own keep, fully dressed, holding a cup of hot water to her lips, thanking him for listening to her.

When he was naked as well, she went to the bed and pulled

down the coarse blanket and rough sheets and got in. He followed her, sliding in next to her, taking her in his arms. She felt so much smaller here in the bed than she had looked moments ago as she had watched him undress.

She kissed him. His mouth, his jaw, his neck. He rolled on top of her. She spread her legs. His cock rubbed her cleft and she was as wet as she had been last night.

She winced.

"You're sore."

"Aye. Just a little. It dinnae matter. Please, Jack."

"No, Helen. I want it to be good for you."

"'Tis good for me. Please."

"Let me put my mouth on you. Like I did before."

"Aye."

And so he got to see her rosebud again, but this time in daylight, spread wide and glistening for him in all its glory. Yes, in this sordid bed, in this sordid room, in this sordid inn. But there was nothing sordid about tasting her again, sipping from her like she was a cup of ambrosia, rubbing his cheeks against her inner thighs, running his hands up her concave abdomen to her nipples which he caressed and pinched as she moaned wordlessly and her flower became fuller and redder and wetter and he ground his own hardness into the mattress.

And then he couldn't wait any longer. She had demanded nothing from him since he had slid down the bed between her legs. But her arousal, the smell of her, her sounds—he couldn't hold himself back from bringing her to her climax.

But unlike in Dunmore, she held still and did not flail when the moment came. He knew she was having her release from her clenching and her quivering and the change in her breathing and her sounds and her wetness.

She spoke while his tongue was still on her. "Dinnae...stop."

He continued, and in seconds, she was building to a

release again. He softened his tongue now against her little nub of hardness. Playing with it. Toying with it. Sucking on it, kissing it. Then lapping at it furiously. A gush of sweet liquid and the quivering and still she did not move off his mouth. He couldn't see her face, only her body in front of him, flat, her small breasts and nipples.

"Keep…going."

She was his countess and he was her vassal and he would keep going until his lady had had her fill. Or his tongue gave out. He was rougher now, using his teeth on her, his tongue penetrating her opening, her soreness forgotten by him.

This last time, she thrashed as she had in Dunmore, ripping herself away from his mouth since he had not thought to hold her down, so still and quiescent she had been for her last two climaxes.

He waited until her thrashing stopped. But no further commands came from his liege lady. He came up beside her, his head on the pillow next to hers. He stroked her abdomen and breasts and looked again at her profile, drinking her in. She turned to him and kissed him, licking his lips and tongue, eating herself off of him.

He felt her hand on his cock. His aching, throbbing cock.

"No, Helen."

"Ye will tell me what to do, Jack Pike, and I will heed ye." She pushed herself off of his chest and slid down his body.

He didn't stop her. He didn't want to stop her.

He watched her. She held him delicately, like he himself was a flower, almost certainly remembering his words in his bedchamber in Dunmore Castle. Gentler hands.

Her fingers ran over him, exploring him. She touched the veins along the sides of his shaft. She felt the seam and the ridges around the head. Her hands went to his scrotum and cupped him there. She kissed the slit that was beaded with a drop of his own arousal and then kissed everywhere her fingers had gone.

"Ye must tell me, Jack. Tell me how to give ye relief."

Her touches and kisses had been agonizing. They had pushed his need higher than ever, driving him to thoughts of seizing her head and savagely pushing her down on him, using her mouth without her participation.

"If I tell you what to do, Helen…" He did not recognize his own voice, it was so strangled. So rough with desire.

"Aye?"

"It will not be training."

"Nae."

He put his hand under her chin, holding her jaw, turning her head toward his, forcing her eyes off his cock. Doing his best to meet her fierce gaze with his own authority.

"It will be a lover telling a lover what he likes."

"Aye. Tell me what ye like."

"Hold my cock like a staff. Firmly."

He took his hand away from her chin and she turned back to his cock and wrapped her hand around it. She crouched by his side, bent over him, and he ran his hand over her back.

Maybe there was a bit more flesh overlying her muscles than there had been in Dunmore? Maybe her stay at the castle and eating Mrs. Mac's food had done some good?

"Now move your hand up and down."

He felt her calluses as he had in Dunmore and they were just as arousing as before.

"Again." *Oh, my God.* He worked to control his voice. "You can lick the shaft so there is wetness there for the rubbing. To make it smoother."

Her warm tongue, the same dark pink as her nipples, joined her hand on his shaft and she was licking and rubbing him simultaneously.

"I like that, Helen." He touched her hair even as the desire in his body demanded he clench a fistful of it. *Like* was too weak of a word, but he did not want to dilute the word he had used for kissing her with praise for what she was doing to his cock.

"You can take me in your mouth, if you want to. But don't let your teeth touch."

She kept stroking him as she raised her face and grinned, showing her teeth, teasing him. "I think I felt yer teeth on me."

"And was that good?" He hadn't thought twice about what he had done to a woman in a dozen years. If that. Hadn't he always been cocksure? Confident he was giving a woman what she needed?

Until now.

She growled. "Good is nae the right word. But I will tell ye, as a lover, I liked it." She looked down at her hand, stroking him relentlessly now. Then she engulfed him with her warm mouth, her tongue swirling first over his tip and his ridges and then over his shaft. Still her hand moved up and down.

"Oh, my God, Helen. Yes."

Her lips loosened for a moment, and he thought she was smiling. Then her mouth was following her hand so that as her mouth withdrew, her hand came up his shaft and as she took him in her mouth again, as deeply as she could, her hand went all the way down to the hair he had at the base of his cock.

The grip of his pleasure was overpowering, almost impossible to withstand. He clutched at speech. "That's it, Helen. That's…good."

Barely were the words out of his mouth, when he felt the heaviness in his testicles, the tingle in his spine that told him he was about to spend. He didn't have time to warn her and he didn't want to. Because he wanted her mouth and her hand to stay where they were.

I'm a selfish beast. Forgive me, Helen.

He released, thrusting upwards, surely choking her. He

was too consumed with his own ecstasy to see how she reacted. He pumped and he pulsed for what he thought was a very long time, but she did not pull away.

His words were gone but he grabbed her hand and took it off of his shaft. Still, she kept her mouth on him, her tongue and lips gliding over him slowly, gently.

Finally, he managed to say, "That's all, Helen."

She let his cock slide from her mouth. "Ye can tell me to keep going, like I did for ye."

"Men don't work that way."

She frowned.

"I don't work that way."

The frown relaxed. "I hope ye got some enjoyment from that."

"I did."

Her eyes went to his cock again, only at three-quarters-mast now. She sat back on her small haunches and wiped her mouth. "That was both harder and easier than I thought it would be."

He reached down and pulled her up the bed. She did not resist. He settled her body against his, his arms around her.

He tried to summon the right words. But his mind protested.

Be still. Wait. Don't run your mouth yet. You don't know what's in her head right now. Just hold her. Do what you should have done last night, you imbecile.

He occupied his mouth by kissing her forehead. Long, slow, lazy kisses where he kept his lips against her skin for half a minute at a time, her warm breath sliding over his chest.

He felt her body become more pliable, relaxing against his incrementally.

She was asleep, worn-out. He shifted slightly to pull the sheet and blanket over them, and she only sighed and nestled more closely into him.

Yes. Let her sleep. She carried a burden few other women did and that few other women would be capable of carrying. And unlike other female rulers, she had no help. Or very little help, he amended, thinking of Mags and Duncan.

He couldn't carry her burden for her. That was impossible. But he could let her sleep.

She slept for an hour or so, and Jack felt completely at peace during that time, holding her and holding still.

She wasn't angry when she woke, but she was anxious. Wanting to dress quickly and get back to Mags and Duncan. Not wanting to lie in his arms and let him enjoy himself with her again, as he had hoped she might. She wouldn't even allow kisses on her lips and innocent caresses of her back. She likely knew what it would lead to. And she exerted her will with a barked "Stop, Jack Pike," and he complied like she was an admiral and he was a midshipman. He didn't want to ruin what had passed between them.

But once dressed, she hesitated. She shoved her parcel at him. "Here. I think ye wanted to do something with this."

He ripped the paper. It was her brown dress. He grinned. She grinned back, and he was back in her keep again, in front of the fire, her taking his pound coin from him and telling him he was easier to look at than Reeves.

He was sorely tempted to take her back to the bed despite the fact she had refused him just minutes ago.

He lit the coals in the grate in the room and threw the parcel in it. They stood in front of the grate together. He reached out for her hand as they watched the flames, and she laced her fingers with his.

But outside the inn, on the pavement, she didn't take his arm. He was looking up and down the street, searching for a hack so they could get back to the rooms as quickly as possible to assuage her worry about Mags and Duncan, when he heard his name.

"Jack!"

It was Phineas, bright as a button, eyes dancing, a grin on his face.

Jack spoke quickly. "The Countess of Kinmarloch, this is the Earl of Burchester. Phin, you call me Jack, but Lady Kinmarloch likes to call me Jack Pike. Both names. It's a peculiarity of hers. Or it's a Scottish thing. But in those parts, I'm known as Jack Pike." He raised his eyebrows at Phineas meaningfully, hoping Helen wouldn't see him. And she didn't. She was curtsying even as Phineas was bowing. Phineas tucked his chin to Jack and Jack hoped that meant Phineas understood. He was Jack Pike. Not His Grace, the Duke of Dunmore. Not John MacNaughton.

"Very pleased to meet you, Lady Kinmarloch."

"And I am pleased to meet ye, Lord Burchester."

A hack was coming down the street, and Jack waved it down frantically.

"We have to go, Phin. I'll see you at the club." He helped Helen into the carriage and sat across from her, wanting to see her face, wanting to make sure she had not thought the oddly worded introduction too odd.

She folded her hands in her lap. "I was glad to meet someone ye know, Jack Pike. An earl. An important man. I thought ye might be ashamed of me. But maybe my new dress helps."

"I would never be ashamed of you, Helen. And a countess in her own right has the same precedence as an earl. You are an important woman."

"Yesterday, at yer house. I thought ye wanted to get rid of me." A little pain leaked out there.

"I have a reputation, and a proper lady wouldn't call at my house, even with an honor guard and a chaperone. I didn't want anyone to think less of you."

"As they might if they saw me coming out of an inn with ye?"

"Phineas will be discreet."

She mouthed the name *Phineas*, learning it. She smoothed her dress. "I widnae want the duke to hear of anything improper."

There it was. She had done it. Jack was glad, for a moment, that at least he had not been the one to ruin it.

And then he was angry. At her. For reminding him she was like every other woman, wanting a title and money rather than a man. He said nothing else to her for the rest of the ride back.

She also said nothing. After all, she had erected the wall between them by mentioning the duke. She must want it there.

TWENTY

The dressmaker's—no, the modiste's—overwhelmed Helen. She had not known there were so many different kinds of dresses and so many different kinds of cloth for making dresses. And she had worn her brown woolen dress into that place full of ivory silks, cream brocades. Yellows, blues, greens.

Jack didn't like the pink dress. She thought it was pretty. Of course, she wasn't pretty in it. She wouldn't be pretty in anything, but the dress seemed like something a princess might wear. And surely a countess?

But Jack liked the simpler dress Mrs. Allen eventually found for her. So much so that he kissed her in the street and took her to an inn and made love to her with his mouth. And then she did the same for him.

Of course, she knew it wasn't really the new dress. He took the dress off of her, didn't he? And last night, when it had been so heated between them and she had thought he would ravish her right there in the drawing room, she had been in her brown dress. Which they burned in the grate of the bedchamber at the inn. Good riddance.

In a way, she felt closer to him as they stood watching the dress burn than she had felt when they had been in the bed together. Because she couldn't believe she was touching and kissing and receiving so much pleasure from a man who was still the most handsome man she had ever seen, even after seeing so many new faces on her journey.

She couldn't believe he wanted her.

But she could believe Jack and her destroying something they both hated. Like the brown dress.

It was a puzzle. What was he doing with her? It wasn't just male need. Surely, there were plenty of women available to him for that, here in London. Beautiful women. Feminine women. Much less difficult women.

Maybe it was a jab or some spite directed at John Mac-Naughton. To despoil the woman who hoped to marry the Duke of Dunmore. To be able to laugh about it behind the duke's back if the duke did marry Helen.

But she couldn't think that ill of Jack. He was not a bad man. His greatest sin so far in her acquaintance with him was that he made her want to do bad things. With him.

In the room at the inn, he told her what they were doing had nothing to do with her training. Nothing to do with teaching her to seduce the duke. And he had said the same thing the night before.

And she was fine with that. Because, of course, she wanted Jack Pike for his own sake. She had wanted him from the first moment she had seen him getting off his horse in the cold rain just over the border of Kinmarloch.

But suddenly, this was all becoming too much about Jack. Which dress he liked. What he wanted done to his cock. How much her thoughts were consumed by him.

If she had been a different woman, not the Countess of Kinmarloch, she would have been happy to have it be all about him.

She didn't care too much about clothing. She could dress to please Jack Pike, even though seeing the pink dress whisked away had given her a twinge in her chest.

She would do anything to his cock he wanted. She had liked giving him a release with her mouth, feeling that power over him. But if he wanted something else done to his cock, that was fine, too. Because the important thing was he wanted *her* to do it.

But being in London was not about Jack Pike. Or about her. It was about Kinmarloch. She must remember what she was trying to do. She was here to save lives and livelihoods. She was here for duty's sake and it was what she had been born to do. She hadn't been born to wear a pretty dress and pleasure Jack Pike.

If only she had been.

Back at the rooms, Jack silently followed her up the stairs. She didn't know why he bothered accompanying her since he wasn't talking to her.

She opened the door onto an empty drawing room.

"Mags? Duncan?" Calling at first, then shouting, then running from room to room.

They were not here. They were on the streets of London. Alone. Two innocent bairns from Kinmarloch. She saw Duncan being beaten and impressed into the army, Mags kidnapped to work in a brothel.

Thank God, Jack had followed her up the stairs.

"Jack. They're nae here!" She threw herself at him, clutched at him.

"Helen, hush. They likely went out to see something of the city."

"But I told them to stay here."

"They're young. They're in London for the first time. Of course, they went out. Although if I were a young man with a redheaded girl," Jack raised his eyebrows, "I would have stayed in, myself."

"Stop," gasped Helen. "Yer nae helping."

"Helen. Duncan is, what? Twenty? One and twenty? He's a grown man. A very protective, very large, grown man even a drunk would think twice about crossing. I grant you he knows nothing about city ways—wait, check his room."

"For what?"

"His kilt."

"'Tis there. Lying on the bed."

"Then they're fine. As long as he's wearing trousers and they didn't take much money with them in case of pickpockets, then they're fine."

"They didn't take any money with them. They don't have any. I have all the money. What if they need money? To pay a ruffian or a bribe of some kind?"

"A bribe? Helen, calm down. You're being ridiculous."

"Aye, fine, then ridicule me. But tell me where I should go to find them!"

"You should sit here and wait for them to come back."

"They could be lost, Jack. They dinnae know London."

"You don't know London either but you knew enough to point out when I was going the wrong way."

"Aye, but—"

"Just wait, Helen."

"Will ye, please, Jack, please, will ye wait with me? Please? I cannae bear it."

Although she was frantic with worry, Helen couldn't help noticing this was the first time since she had assumed her title that she had someone to soothe her when she was anxious. Arms to hold her, a chest to burrow into, a voice in her ear shushing her.

And she wondered how she would survive if she never had it again.

Just as ye have been surviving all along, Helen Boyd. Dinnae get soft now.

The relief, oh, the relief, followed quickly by rage, when the young pair came back a quarter of an hour later. Mags, tearful and apologizing for worrying Helen. Duncan, stoic and silent under the barrage of Helen's ire.

After Jack had left, saying he would call tomorrow, and Duncan had gone to his room, Mags sat on the drawing room sofa and explained.

"I am so sorry, my lady. We dinnae mean to worry ye. Ye were gone so long and…and…Duncan is nae used to being idle and shut up inside. And we've been—I mean, we had naething else to do so we were kissing and I wanted to go on kissing, but Duncan said it was too hard to stop and we had to stop because he cannae ask for me and it would be wrong, and I said we should go out so we widnae be tempted to do the kissing anymore, and we walked all around and it was so different and we liked seeing all the shop windows and the people. We dinnae realize how late it was. Please dinnae be angry at Duncan. 'Tis my fault."

Helen sat next to Mags and stroked her hair. "I got angry because I was so scared, Mags." She hugged the girl. "It made me think about—" She pulled away and held Mags at arm's length. "Yer here and yer safe and ye willnae go wandering again." Mags nodded. "And I will apologize to Duncan for being such a harridan. I've been thinking if I manage to become the Duchess of Dunmore, maybe there might be a job for Duncan as a farrier in the duke's stables."

"Really?" Mags' eyes lit up.

"Dinnae say anything to him yet."

"I willnae. Did ye meet the duke today? Yer dress is so fine. Look at the little flowers on it."

"Nae, I dinnae."

"Oh, I was hoping ye were gone so long because Mr. Pike had taken ye to meet him."

"Nae yet."

"Ye will meet him and he will see yer pretty dress and fall in love with ye and ask ye to marry him."

It was all so simple for Mags. She loved a man and he loved her and as soon as he was able, he would marry her. And they would have children and grow old together. There was none of this business of being in love with one man and marrying another.

No, that wasn't right. Helen wasn't in love with Jack. She mustn't think that. She was bedding Jack. There was a difference. But bedding one man and wanting to marry another man was complicated enough. Even if the other man was as-of-yet unseen and unspoken with.

She might not feel an attraction to the duke. She might never love the duke. But if he were willing to save her earldom and to keep her and every soul she loved from want, John MacNaughton would have her body, her loyalty, her attention for the rest of his life. And a fair imitation of love. She owed him that.

The duke need not have brown eyes and a wicked grin and a handsome chest.

But it would help.

TWENTY-ONE

"The Countess of Kinmarloch, eh?" Phineas grinned. "Is she the third cousin you mentioned?"

"Yes." Jack was curt.

Phineas had called after dinner, just as Jack had known he would. The earl's curiosity would not have let him stay away. The two men were closeted in Jack's study.

"And she doesn't know you're the duke?"

"No."

"Mmmm." Phineas stretched out, cradling his glass of whisky. "The two of you coming out of an inn in the middle of the afternoon. And I noted the lady's cheeks had a pinkness to them. That rosy I've-just-been-fucked-by-Jack-Pike color."

"Shut it about the lady, Phin."

Phineas raised his eyebrows. "Well, all right, I'll talk about you. You had a look about you."

"What look?"

"Rather a guilty look. Never seen that on your face before, Jack. You must be friends with her husband."

"She doesn't have a husband. It's not a courtesy title. She's a countess in her own right."

"No husband?"

"None."

"Jack." Phineas shook his head. "Jack, Jack, Jack. What happened to you up in Scotland? An unmarried woman? Has the apocalypse come and no one has made me aware of it?"

Jack gritted his teeth. "Don't worry. I'm never going to Scotland again."

"Because you didn't like it?"

He hadn't told Phineas his real feelings. That he had loved the wildness, the roughness, the brutality of the Highlands and Dunmore, specifically. That he had felt like he was on the ocean again, captain of his own ship, navigating beautiful but dangerous waters. That it had felt more like home than any other piece of land ever had.

But he had ruined it, now. He could never go back. He could explain away his pretense to the people of Dunmore. He could never explain it to Helen.

"You loved it up there." Phineas leaned forward. "I can see it. I always knew you were more Scottish than you let on."

Jack rubbed his jaw. "It's... difficult."

"The best things are."

"Aye."

Phineas laughed. "Oh, it's *aye* now, is it? The MacNaughton in you is rising to the top. Well, it's a great tribute to you to have a countess chase you clear across the island of Britain."

Jack got up and paced. "She's here because she wants to marry the Duke of Dunmore. She's not here for Jack Pike."

"Oh."

"She has some fool idea she can woo the duke or seduce him and get him to marry her."

"Well, she's halfway there, isn't she?"

"What?"

"Since you're the duke. She's clearly seduced you."

"Women don't seduce me. It's the other way around," Jack growled.

"Really? Even in this case? I mean, she's not your type, Jack. She must have seduced you."

"What do you mean?"

"She's very nice, I'm sure, but she's not pretty. Not very much woman there. She must have other talents, eh?"

Jack found himself holding Phineas by the lapels of his tailcoat, having pulled him up out of his chair.

"Calm down, Jack. Don't spill the whisky." Phineas held the glass to his mouth and drained it. "Now my glass is empty. You can go ahead and thrash me, if you wish."

Jack released him with a snarl, almost throwing Phineas back into the chair. He stalked to the far corner of the room but Phineas' voice followed him.

"She's unmarried. She's plain. You feel guilty about her. You're very sensitive about her. Mmm. If I didn't know better, I would say you loved her."

Jack whirled around, his fists at his side. "Don't throw that word around, Phin."

"I'm not. I don't. I've never declared love myself, as you know. Love is for other men. But you've had a sea change, Jack. And it's not just because you're a duke now."

Jack couldn't think. Because it was unthinkable. Phineas went to him and put his hand on Jack's shoulder.

"You'll tell me if you need help, right? Not that I know anything about love or whatever this is."

"Yes." Jack got the word out.

"Don't mess about." Phineas clapped Jack on the shoulder, gave him a stern look he could not maintain and which transmuted into a grin, and left.

Jack collapsed into a chair.

Don't mess about. When it was all one big mess.

. . .

In the morning, Jack went back to the river and made some arrangements. Then he went to the rooms on Piccadilly.

"Am I to have an introduction to the duke today, Jack Pike?" Helen asked him after they had greeted each other. She wore her new dress.

"No." He went on before she could protest. "You need to wait for your dresses to be finished."

"Dresses?" A look of panic mixed with suspicion on her face.

Jack cursed himself. He couldn't even keep track of the simple lies now. "Your new dress. I thought we'd all go out. I'll show you a bit of London. All of you."

Yes, let Duncan and Mags chaperone them. Today, there would be no sneaking into an inn, no stolen kisses in an alleyway. Let him see the not-beautiful Helen in the cruel light of day with her clothes on, without his cock hard. There would be no question of love then.

Mags' face flushed pink with excitement. Duncan grinned. Yes, and let him give a little pleasure for once to someone besides himself and the women he bedded.

"What's this?" Helen asked when they got to the riverbank.

"It's a boat, Helen."

Jack got in the boat and had Duncan get in. They handed down Mags together. Helen stayed on the little jetty, looking down at them. Her jaw jutted.

Jack reached his hand up. "Get in."

"I've never been in a boat before."

"Not even in your own loch?"

"Nae."

"Are you scared?"

She straightened. "Nae." She took his and Duncan's hands and got in the boat. She got to a seat as soon as she could and sat, crouched, both hands clasping the side of the boat.

"Where are we going, Mr. Pike?" Mags asked as Jack took off his coat and rolled up his sleeves.

"If we go upriver, we could see some fancy houses. But I'd like to take you downriver, toward the sea." Jack cast off the boat and sat down to the oars.

"Will we see the sea?" Mags asked.

"That's too far for today."

Duncan was behind him with Mags in the bow. Jack faced Helen sitting alone in the stern. "Helen, you'll have to be my look-out. Tell me about the boats I can't see behind me."

Jack got them a little way out into the river. Helen still gripped the side of the boat, peering everywhere, warning Jack of boats which were far off and that he would never bump into. "Just the boats that are close, Helen."

He tried to point out buildings of interest. "That's Somerset House. Where the Navy Board is."

"Oh, 'tis so grand. It looks like it would be a king's house. Dinnae ye think so, my lady?" Mags called out.

"Aye."

With Helen's warning, Jack got the boat out of the path of a crossing wherry. He was pleased to see Helen's grip was a little less white-knuckled than it had been before.

He rowed easily but he knew he wasn't as accustomed to rowing as he had once been.

"I hope you're watching me, Duncan. I'll handle the oars while we're in this crowded bit of the river, but once we get away, past the bridge, I'll have you take over for a while."

"Aye."

Jack pointed out St. Paul's Cathedral, the high dome visible despite the building not being all that close to the river.

"All right. We're coming near the bridge now." He pulled the boat to the Three Cranes stairs. "All three of you will get out here and go up to Thames Street and walk to your right and then come back down to the river at the Billingsgate stairs and dock, right? You should be able to smell the fish market there."

Helen's mouth moved, forming the word *Billingsgate*. Then she spoke out loud. "Why will we nae be going under the bridge with ye?"

"The piers make the water go very fast underneath them. The watermen call it *shooting the bridge*." Jack chuckled and handed his coat up to Duncan. "Take that and the hamper, too. After all, I can swim and our luncheon and the coat can't."

"Dinnae do anything dangerous, Jack. We dinnae need to go farther. We can turn around and go back." Helen's face was white as she looked down on him from the wharf.

"Don't worry. I've done this hundreds of times. It's not high or low tide. I'm a navy man so I'll be fine as long as there are no French frigates waiting with cannons to blast me. Just meet me on the other side."

Jack made it under the bridge and through the piers easily, his oars up at the crucial moment, a little swoosh and a rush, and he was on the other side. He rowed to the Billingsgate dock and waited. A long time. Damn, had they gotten lost? He remembered his counsel to Helen yesterday and told himself the same thing. Just wait.

Finally, he saw Duncan's bright hair. Then, the two women, Helen helping Mags down the stairs as Duncan hovered a step below, holding the hamper.

"Took you long enough," he grumbled when they reached the boat.

"'Tis only been a few minutes, Jack," Helen said menacingly as Duncan handed down the hamper and coat and joined Jack in the boat.

"I'm sorry, 'tis my fault, Mr. Pike. My leg," Mags said as he and Duncan lifted her down.

"Nonsense, Mags." Helen deliberately ignored Jack's hand

and took only Duncan's as she scrambled into the boat. "Mr. Pike is just an impatient wretch who is so used to travel by water that he cannae remember how long it takes to walk anywhere. Especially in London."

Yes, Jack had not remembered about Mags' limp. And now he had made her feel badly about it when he had wanted to give her a day of fun. He made a mess of everything.

"No apologies necessary, Miss Mags. It's just as Lady Kinmarloch says. I am an impatient wretch. No, Duncan, I'll still do a bit more rowing. I've got a taste for it now. Brings back my youth."

Let me pay for my lack of care somehow.

He pointed out the Tower of London. "Where Mary, Queen of Scots, was imprisoned."

Helen shook her head. "Nae, Jack, ye've got it wrong. I dinnae know about a lot of things, but the history of Scotland is the one thing I do know. She was never there."

"She wasn't?" Funny, Jack had always pictured her there every time he went by the Tower. The Scottish queen, imprisoned for years by her cousin, the queen of England, then executed. It had reminded him of the bloodthirsty and power-hungry nature of women. Especially women named Elizabeth.

He stopped at the King James stairs, feeling wrung out, and had them all switch around. Now, the two women sat in the bow, and he sat where Helen had, facing Duncan at the oars so he could advise the young man. He'd let the giant row them all the way to Greenwich.

Duncan's strokes were sloppy at first. But powerful. And much bigger than Jack's.

Jack's back, his flanks, his arms ached. Damn. He hated getting old.

But he caught Helen's gaze in the boat as Duncan bent to the oars. She was looking at him as she had in Scotland. Eating him with her eyes. He straightened up. He wasn't old yet. He grinned and winked at her. Her look did not change. His mind went to her mouth sliding over his cock, her body underneath his in her bed. He shifted in his seat and finally, he had to be the one to look away.

He got Duncan to take them closer to the south bank of the river. Mags oohed and aahed over the spectacle of the Royal Hospital for Seamen at Greenwich.

"It's for retired sailors. Designed by the same man as St. Paul's. Sir Christopher Wren."

"Och. The king and the Prince Regent must value the navy highly to pay for such a grand place for sailors to go. Mr. Pike, if ye never marry, will that be where ye will live when yer old?"

"Maybe." Jack wouldn't, of course, because of his wealth, how insulated he was against misfortune. And now his title. But the three of them didn't know that.

Helen said nothing until Jack directed Duncan to pull the boat up to a small dock far downriver from the Royal Hospital, on the north bank, a wooded spot.

"Can we do this?" she asked, suspiciously. "Who owns this land?"

Jack had been prepared to lie. He had lied about so much already. He was going to say the land belonged to a friend of his and he had permission to be here.

"I do, Helen."

He wanted her to know it was his. It was a large piece on the river with some beautiful woods still standing, a good aspect at the top of a hill where a house could face south toward the river. He had bought the land after capturing his first French ships as a captain. While on shore leave, he had come out here many times with architects and builders to discuss the various views, the potential size of the house, the possible gardens, the lawn that might come down from the house to the river.

He had even brought Elizabeth out here once, telling her she must see it since he was going to build the house for her, for their future family together. She had suffered through the trip, insisted they take a carriage, and then complained about the condition of the roads.

He had lost his temper, one of the few times he ever had with her. He remembered he had sworn at her.

"If you had let me bring you by boat, Elizabeth, you wouldn't be whining about the damned roads."

"Once you build the house, are we to travel by boat every time we want to go to London? We wouldn't have our own carriage once we got there. This is not fashionable." She had sniffed. "You should have bought land in Richmond."

"You wouldn't be going every day to London."

Elizabeth had said nothing more, but he could tell by her silence that she thought it a very poor site for building and she had, indeed, planned to go to London every day to buy things and to visit other ladies. After all, she was the greatest beauty of the *ton* and a viscount's daughter. Yes, she had no dowry, but she was still condescending to marry a navy man. Yes, a handsome one, one with good prospects as a captain, the stepson of a baronet. But only third in line, at that time, for a dukedom and unlikely ever to have the title himself with a young, healthy cousin above him in the rank of succession, sure to have a lot of sons, each one of which would push Jack Pike further and further down until it would have taken a plague for him to have a chance of being duke.

But it hadn't taken a plague. Just an overly-hasty swallow of a poorly-chewed breakfast and a barren bitch of a duchess.

"Ye own this land, Jack Pike?" Helen's eyes were wide. "Right by the river. Sure, ye must like that. Is there a house?"

"No."

"Aye, it would be a pity to lose these trees. So many of them."

Hundreds upon hundreds of trees must have been cleared from Dunmore, along with the farmers, when his cousin had decided to turn Dunmore land into sheep pastures. It was like Helen to notice the trees and think of them as something to safeguard rather than as something which might block a view or shade a lawn.

He tied up the boat and was the last one out of it, bringing his coat and the hamper with him. "I thought we would have a picnic."

Duncan and Mags were already walking along the bank, Mags leaning on Duncan's arm maybe more than she needed to, laughing gaily and affectionately.

Helen said in a low voice, "'Twas very good and clever of ye to think of this way for us to see the city and parts surrounding. Because of Mags."

Jack had not thought of Mags. He had wanted to be on the river because it wouldn't have done to walk them around on the streets of London where he was sure to see someone who knew him and who would address him as Your Grace.

He mumbled and looked away at the river. He hated to have Helen ascribe a noble motive to his actions when they had only been self-serving. In a way, it was worse than when she had thought him an unfettered lecher in Scotland. At least that had some truth to it.

"I dinnae know ye were so rich, Jack Pike. Do ye own that grand London house as well? And live there all by yerself?"

"Yes. Does it change how you see me? Make me more attractive?"

"As if ye could be." She snorted and he grinned. Then she smiled a little, too. "Nae, it dinnae change ye. Ye are so easy about money, I should have known. But to have yer looks and wealth, too. I'm surprised yer nae married already."

Jack thought she was flirting with him after her compliment. "What's to say I'm not?" he said teasingly and laughed and stepped off the dock onto land.

He didn't hear her laugh, and suddenly, he noticed she was not walking alongside him.

He turned around and she was still standing on the little dock. What was that expression on her face? Was it horror? She suddenly turned and vomited into the water.

"Helen—" He rushed back to her side but she held her arm up, holding him off as she gagged and spat.

"Nae." It was a strangled word. She wasn't looking at him but down at the water as if she thought she would vomit again. "Tell me yer nae married, Jack Pike. Please tell me yer nae married."

"I'm not."

She finally raised her head.

"Ye promise?"

"Yes, I'm not married. I was joking."

She wiped her mouth with the back of her hand and squinted her half-moon eyes at him and searched his face.

"I think something from breakfast disagreed with me. I'm nae used to all this rich food. And the boat ride. But I feel better now. I hope ye have something in that basket so I can rinse my mouth."

"Yes."

They walked off the dock together, her following him, him looking over his shoulder to make sure she was all right. Her face was pale but her gait was steady. She stared back at him, her jaw tight, her brow heavy.

He had not known someone could vomit out of jealousy. And he had not pegged her as a jealous type, wanting him to be wifeless, even as she pursued the duke. He shook his head. He didn't know her. Not at all.

They joined Mags and Duncan and found a sunny clearing on the bank where they could sit.

But Helen did not sit when Jack offered her his hand and
Duncan helped Mags lower herself to the ground.

"My dress."

"Yes." He spread his coat out for her and she sat on it,
cautiously, holding her skirts up against her legs so they
wouldn't touch the ground.

Helen rinsed her mouth with the small beer but declined
the sandwiches. "I'll wait until we get back."

Now Jack only wanted to get Helen alone. To take her
into these woods he owned, to show them to her and the view
at the top of the hill just as he had shown her his chest by the
side of a mountain stream. And then he wanted to find a way
to strip her dress off her and to cover and contain her with his
own body. His possessive, savage countess.

He stood and held his hand out to Helen. "I'll show you
the rest of the property," he said, not caring that he was being
rude to Mags and Duncan.

But Helen did not take his hand. She stayed where she
was, hugging her legs. "I'll stay here with Mags. Show
Duncan."

So, the two men went off into the woods, Jack feeling
disgruntled. And he knew Duncan must feel the same. The
men separated from their women.

Jack made mention of the better air out here, far from the
city.

Duncan huffed. "Aye," he said, clearly thinking the air of
Kinmarloch was much better. And it was. Jack knew that.

They got to the top of the hill, and Jack said he had
thought of building a house here.

"Aye."

"When you left Scotland, how was work going on the
cottage next to the keep?"

"The walls were going up. I must thank ye, Jack Pike."

"Why?"

"For finding a way to get Margaret a snug place to sleep. Since I cannae."

Jack waved his hand, again embarrassed by being thought he was a better man than he was. Because for him, the cottage was for Helen. And she had traded her dirk for it.

"It's Lady Kinmarloch's doing, not mine."

"Aye. We owe her so much. My Margaret widnae be here."

Jack looked at Duncan's face. The giant was staring down the hill, trying to see the place where they had left Mags and Helen.

"What do you mean?"

"My lady was the one who got Margaret out of the fire."

What Helen had said on Jack's first day in Dunmore. The village that had been burned by the Duke of Dunmore's men. The sick girl in one of the cottages, not evacuated because that part of the village was in Kinmarloch and the people there had been given no warning. The girl who had lived but whose leg had been burned.

Jack cleared his throat. "Helen rescued Mags."

"Aye. 'Twas terrible."

"Tell me what happened."

"There was nae time. People were crazed and running and screaming. I dinnae know Margaret well. She was just thirteen and I was sixteen, thinking myself a man. She was a child to me, then. Word of the fire spread to our forge, and my father and I got to the village just as my lady came up on her horse from her keep. She was trying to calm the people, to count them, to make them collect their families together. Then someone remembered Margaret, feverish in her aunt's cottage. I dinnae know why, but the rest of us dinnae move. But my lady ran like the devil himself was behind her and went into that cottage, the roof aflame, and dragged Margaret out."

There was a long silence.

"When it should have been me. Or any of the able men there. So, I will do anything for the Countess of Kinmarloch."

Jack looked at Duncan and the young man was looking at him with a look Jack knew well. The look of a soldier for his enemy.

"Margaret sleeps heavy and is an innocent. But I have ears and I know what passed between ye and my lady two nights ago." Duncan's hands hung loosely at his sides but his body was poised and tense. "My lady can do as she likes. If she wants ye, that is her right. She is a countess and shouldnae be deprived just because there is nae man good enough for her to wed in Kinmarloch. But I am still her honor guard, even here. Even in London."

"Yes."

"Just so ye know."

There was a silence.

"Is the Duke of Dunmore good enough for her, Jack Pike?"

Jack took a deep breath. "No."

"I dinnae think so. How could he be? But she is set on him. And willing for the rest of us. She dinnae care about herself." Now a smile twitched Duncan's mouth and his body relaxed. "So, I am glad, for once, she has taken something for herself. Something more than a hambone."

"What's that?"

"Ye, Jack Pike."

TWENTY-TWO

Helen brought her knees up to her chest and looked at the river and the boats going by. She had not cast up her accounts since she was a child.

But she had never considered that Jack Pike might be married. Those had been terrible moments, standing on the dock, when she had thought he could be.

She shuddered.

She didn't want to own him. She never could. He had had many women, and after her, he would have many more.

But a marriage. A promise made in a church. She would have been part of his breaking a vow. That might be the way in decadent London, but it was not her way, not the way in Kinmarloch.

And she hated that she did not know if, in the heat of passion, she would have thought twice about bedding him.

No. She straightened her back, sitting on the riverbank with Mags. She wouldn't have bedded him if she had known he was married. She would have gone elsewhere for her training despite the havoc of lust he wrought on her body. She had a mind and a soul and she could control her desire. She was the Countess of Kinmarloch.

"Are ye all right, my lady?"

"Aye. 'Tis very pleasant here, isn't it, Mags?"

"I like to see the boats."

"I do, too."

Jack and Duncan came back after a while. Something was changed about both of them. Jack was thoughtful. Duncan seemed clear of some worry Helen had not sensed earlier.

Helen took Jack's hand to stand and twisted to look at the back of her dress. No grass stains, no dirt. She noticed Jack looking, too. She thought of his look at her bottom in her breeches when she had met him and first known how much a woman could want a man.

Not the thoughts that belonged at a picnic.

"Are ye to row us back upriver? Sure, willnae it be a strain?" she asked.

"No," Jack said. "I'll just row us back to the hospital. I arranged to leave the boat there. We'll take a ferry back to London."

"I'll row us back to the hospital, Jack Pike," Duncan said.

Helen expected some argument from Jack, but he grinned instead. "The honor guard will be allowed to do the honors. Especially since we'll be going against the flow of the river. I'm already worried about how I'll feel tomorrow."

Jack said the ferry they boarded at the wharf by the hospital was a barge. Duncan watched the watermen plying their oars, as if to see how he might improve his own rowing. Jack spoke with the men, asking about the tide, had they been in the navy. Oh, what ship? And Jack made the watermen aware they should watch their coarse language.

"There are ladies present," Jack said and caught Helen's eye. Their joke together.

But she did not let her gaze linger on his face or his body. She looked at the water and the buildings on the shore and listened to his voice and his laugh.

It had been a good day, one she would always remember. Seeing London from the water, watching Jack Pike row a boat as he must have when he was young, picnicking on the land he owned.

But it had been a wasted day, too.

She could feel her tie to her duty growing more and more strained under the weight of her desire for Jack Pike. She was here for the Duke of Dunmore, and she didn't want to wait any longer. She wanted it done with, like pulling out a loose tooth. When she was a child, she hadn't liked the feeling of a tooth wobbling in her mouth, her tongue incessantly worrying it. And her patience had not improved with age.

Tomorrow, she would find a way to the duke's house without Jack. This dress was surely good enough.

JACK HAD LEFT the trio in their rooms, saying he would call tomorrow afternoon. And he had meant it when he departed from them. He needed to get home. He needed time, by himself, away from them all and everyone else. He needed to settle himself, find a solution to the predicament of Helen and Kinmarloch. But mostly Helen.

Why then did he find himself pounding on the door to the rooms again at midnight?

Helen answered the door as before, but in her worn night-dress this time, her eyes blinking with sleep, her hair loose around her shoulders. She drew him in by his arm and called him *mo luran* and kissed him tenderly. She took him to her bedchamber and undressed him, her hands sliding over his waistcoat, his trousers, his shirt.

"Are you still sore, Helen?"

"Nae. I dinnae think so."

He made agonizingly slow love to her that night. All parts of their bodies touching, his hands on her hair and her face, with either his mouth on hers or his face right above hers, looking at her. She released several times while he was inside her without the use of his hand, and he watched her face as she did so. He thought he had never seen anything in his life as gratifying as his savage countess responding to his cock and rising to a boil and tipping over and simmering for long seconds, contracting around him, gripping his back with her hands. And then her hands would fall away and she was soft and hazed and sated until she wasn't any more and her mouth on his and her hands and her eyes and her sounds told him she was, once again, reaching that same boil as before.

Finally, inevitably, he couldn't bear it any longer and he pulled his shaft out of her and with a few strokes of her hand, he released. Her grip had been rough but not too fierce, giving him exactly what he needed to end his long, drawn-out torture.

He wanted to sleep then, holding her close.

But she whispered in his ear, "I'm sorry, Jack. I cannae let Mags find ye here in the morning. I must pretend to be an example to her and Duncan."

"Do you think they're doing what we're doing, right now?"

"She likely wants to be lying in his arms, but I dinnae think so. Duncan widnae permit it. Nae yet."

"He wants to be married to her first."

"Aye. The young people are better at denying themselves than we are."

"Are you regretting we haven't denied ourselves, Helen?"

She kissed him. "*Mo luran*, I would find it impossible to

deny myself when ye touch me. It would be like doing without air to breathe or water to drink."

What was unsaid lay heavy between them. That unlike Mags and Duncan, Helen and Jack would not be marrying. It was this unsanctified bed or none at all.

TWENTY-THREE

Helen got up early and washed her face with cold water. She arranged her hair carefully. She put on her new dress and spencer. Her boots had gouges and stains, but she hoped no one would look at her feet. She spat on the leather of the boots and rubbed at the toes.

She tapped on Duncan's bedchamber door. "Stay here with Mags. I'll be back before midday."

A thud. The door opened a crack. "Ye should have yer honor guard on the streets of London."

"Nae, Duncan. For this, I must go alone."

"Aye, my lady."

She walked out onto Piccadilly. It was early, far too early to make a call on anyone. But she would use the hours to find out where the Duke of Dunmore lived. West of here, back toward Jack's house, and north, there was Mayfair. She knew that was where many peers and wealthy people lived. She would go there and ask questions and find the duke's house.

She looked at faces as she walked. So many pretty women, even though none were fine ladies, but likely servants or women who did other work. A few, like her, were coarse and ill-featured. And the men, about their business, some hand-some, some not. But still none who could compare to Jack Pike.

Up past the fine shops on Bond Street, the gowns and suits of clothing and jewelry gleaming in the windows. She began to ask passers-by.

"Do ye know the Duke of Dunmore's house?" Shaking heads or disdainful looks with no answer.

Finally, a young woman, perhaps a lady's maid, anxious, clutching two large bags, pointed with her chin. "Grosvenor Square." She gave Helen the number. And then the woman was off, looking behind her, frightened.

Helen found the house. It was grand. Far grander than Jack's house and that had been the finest house she had ever seen. Dunmore Castle was large and imposing, a hulking mass of stone, but it did not have the fancy detail of these London houses with their delicately wrought railings, enormous windows, painted doors.

She idled, waiting, circling the large square for hours until she knew from the church bells that it was well past ten o'clock. She steeled herself. She rapped on the door.

A butler answered.

"I am the Countess of Kinmarloch, and I am here to see the Duke of Dunmore."

A suitable bow. "This is the house of the Duchess of Dun-more, my lady."

Helen despaired. The Duke of Dunmore had already married. Jack must know of the marriage and it was why he wouldn't take her to meet the duke. She was too late, and he was shielding her from the knowledge that she had wasted her money in coming to London.

And then a bubbling joy. She could not marry the Duke of Dunmore because he was already married and she was free to bed Jack Pike. Forever.

Despair again. She would never be free to bed Jack Pike forever. Her duty was to Kinmarloch.

Finally, she made some sense of the butler's words. This was not the house of the duke, only the duchess. Why would they have separate houses?

"John MacNaughton dinnae live here?"

"No, my lady."

Some activity behind the butler and a musical voice asked, "Who is it, Gibbs?"

The butler turned away. "A lady, Your Grace. She says she is the Countess of Kinmarloch. Looking for John MacNaughton, the Duke of Dunmore."

A fluting laugh. "Oh, yes, women are coming out for the new duke in full-force. And so early in the morning. Have her come in so I can see the candidate."

Helen was ushered through the door by the butler. There, in the hall of this fine London house, she was confronted by Jack Pike's counterpart in beauty even though this lady was his opposite in every way. Short where he was tall. Soft and curving where he was hard and muscular. Dark-haired and fair-skinned where he was blond-brown and golden. Full, pouty, luxurious lips to his sculpted ones. Round, kissable cheeks to his angular cheekbones.

Feminine where he was masculine.

She saw Jack and this woman next to each other in her mind's eye, and her breath was taken away.

"Yer Grace." She stumbled over the words and curtsied.

The beauty surveyed her. "Scottish, of course. I should have known when Gibbs said Kinmarloch. Come into the drawing room, Lady Kinmarloch."

Seated across from the duchess, Helen noted for the first time the color of her elegant dress. Black. Mourning. Most ladies did not marry while mourning, at least not in Scotland. Even if it were a distant relation who had died.

It came to her, then. She knew the house number had seemed familiar.

"Are ye the widow of Norman MacNaughton, the previous Duke of Dunmore?" It was a brusque question. *But that is my way.*

Startled violet eyes. A beautiful and sad smile. "I am."

John MacNaughton might still be unmarried. He likely was. Helen should feel hope, but she did not.

"My condolences to ye, Yer Grace."

"Thank you, Lady Kinmarloch."

"I wrote many letters to ye and yer late husband."

"Did you? I don't recall."

"I asked for some help. Kinmarloch is surrounded by Dunmore as ye probably know—"

"I don't actually." The duchess let out another beautiful laugh. "I know nothing of the place. Sadly, yes. But it's so far, and everything of significance is in London."

"Aye, but the—"

"And one gets so many letters asking for help. So many charities. So many musical societies and literary societies wanting endorsements or letters of support or, most vulgarly, money. Did you come to my house to ask for help? Is that why you're looking for the current duke?"

The duchess did not need to know why Helen wanted to see John MacNaughton. "Do ye know where His Grace lives? Is his house near here?"

Lady Dunmore studied Helen again. "I have only your word you are who you say you are."

"Aye, that is true, but—"

"And the current Duke of Dunmore is a very private man. Not welcoming to unexpected callers. But he is a very particular friend of mine. An intimate friend, one might say." The duchess stood.

Helen recognized her time with the duchess was over. She stood as well.

Again, the laugh. Like a bird singing. "I will tell the duke about you, I promise. He will write to you in—what was it? Kinmarloch?"

"Aye, thank ye, Your Grace, but I am in London—"

"And if you are in need of shoes," the duchess shuddered as her gaze went to Helen's boots, "I'll have my butler give you the name of his cobbler."

In less than a minute, Helen was out the door, clutching a scrap of paper with a shoemaker's address written on it, walking away from the house of the Duchess of Dunmore. Tears held back but head down and eyes on her boots, worn and scratched by the stones of Kinmarloch, now moving quickly over the cobblestones of London.

She had been barking mad to think she could ever be a duchess. Why hadn't Jack told her there were women in the world who looked like that? Why hadn't he been honest and laughed in her face when she had crept into his bedchamber and told him her hopes of a duke?

He had pitied her. That's what everything had been. Pity. He had made himself her consolation, knowing she would fail.

She went back to the rooms.

"We're going back home tomorrow," she said to Mags and Duncan. "I know there's nae much to pack, but pack what ye have. And nae a word to Jack Pike. I'll tell him myself."

JACK HAD SPENT his morning reading the same line over and over again in the report on clearances he had abandoned the afternoon Helen had come to his door. Finally, he threw the pamphlet down. All his thoughts were of her, constantly. What she might be doing right now. What he might say to her, what he might do to her the next time he saw her. And, yes, what she, in turn, would say about this report which laid out the hard facts about letting farms stay in the barren Highlands.

He was disturbed by the mood that met him when he went to the rooms in the early afternoon.

Does Helen know I'm the duke? Is that why she won't look at me?

But the young people also seemed melancholic and apprehensive.

"Duncan, take Mags out. Here's some money, buy some sweets." Helen put coins in Duncan's hand. "Stay close."

"Oh, my lady, may I use my part of the money for something else?" Mags asked. She glanced at Duncan. "There is a hair ribbon I saw in a shop window. With pictures of flowers in the weave. Little ones, like yer dress. I dinnae know the cost—"

Duncan grunted. "Ye will have my part of the money, too."

Jack went into his purse and took out some coins and gave them to Duncan. "Payment for saving my back yesterday. Get the sweets, as well. Or get two hair ribbons." He looked at Helen, expecting a glare at his indulgence, but she was looking away.

She knows.

He prepared himself for a drubbing. An excoriation. A tempest. But when the door shut behind Mags and Duncan, he heard "*Mo luran*," and she was next to him.

Her hands came to his face and she ran the tips of her fingers over his cheeks, his jaw, his lips. "So beautiful. My sunrise. My stars."

He felt the blood rise to his face, not only because of her words but also out of relief. She wouldn't be whispering sweet things to him and touching his face this way if she knew he was Dunmore. Something else must be wrong. Something that had nothing to do with him.

"Does it still hurt here," he put his hand on her breastbone, "when you look at me, Helen?"

"Aye, worse than ever. Does it still make ye hard when I tell ye that?" She brushed the back of her hand against his groin, fleetingly.

"I should stay away every morning if that's what it takes to get you to appreciate me." He caught her other hand and kissed her palm, her calluses. "Did you send Mags and Duncan away so I could ravish you, Helen?"

"I sent them away so I could look at ye."

"They could have stayed if all you wanted to do was look."

"They couldnae have stayed for what looking at ye leads me to do." Her hand grasped him through his trousers. "To look at ye and touch ye at the same time, Jack Pike. There cannae be any greater delight for me on this earth."

He felt himself engorge under her strong, rubbing hand. He pushed a tendril of hair behind her ear. "There could be, Helen, there could be."

"How is that, *mo luran*?"

"I could be without clothes. And you could be, too."

"Aye."

A graze of his lips against hers. "And I could kiss you."

"Aye."

He put a hand to one of her breasts. "And I could touch you here while you touch me."

"Aye."

"Or here." He grabbed a cheek of her bottom. "Or here." He moved his hand from her breast to her mound.

"Aye."

He stroked her cleft through her dress. "Or I could be inside you."

Her voice was hoarse when she said, "Dinnae make me dampen my new dress with what ye do to me. Take me to the bed, Jack Pike."

Once in the bedchamber, they undressed themselves swiftly, efficiently. She stepped to him and ran her hands up and down his arms. "Ye are so handsome everywhere that I forgot about yer arms. How I looked at them when I first saw ye roll up the sleeves of yer shirt."

"At the stream? With the sheep?"

"Aye." She stepped back, and her eyes went over his body. "There are too many things to remember about ye. I fear they will all slip away."

"Then you'll just have to remind yourself by undressing me again."

"Aye."

He stepped toward her but she held her hand out.

"Nae." She came forward and with just the tip of her dark-pink tongue, she slowly licked the scar on his chest, from bottom to top. She suckled briefly on his left nipple where the scar ended and then sank to her knees in front of him. She took his cock in her hand and stroked him.

"I want to taste ye."

She put him in her mouth. Her warm, wet tongue licking over his entire shaft. He groaned. He put his hands in her hair. She looked up at him, moving her head forward and back, one hand chasing her mouth on his member, her calluses rubbing him, the other hand clutching his thigh.

"Helen."

When he said her name, she took him as deep as she could into her throat and he saw tears in her eyes.

Now he *had* to be inside her, this wild woman who swallowed him whole with her eyes and her mouth. He lifted her under her arms and took her to the bed. He got between her legs and her arms went up over her head as he grabbed her thighs just under the buttocks and lifted her pelvis to his so he was kneeling upright, pulling her onto his achingly hard member, slick from her mouth. She gasped as he plunged into her, but she did not reach for him. She kept her arms above her head and watched him.

"Jack? Can I do that?"

He didn't understand her. He was overcome by the sensation building inside him as he held her and took her and moved her and himself at the same time.

"Can the woman be on her knees like ye? Atop the man?"

From somewhere deep in his haze of animal need, he grunted an incoherent "Yes."

"Let me, Jack. Let me be atop ye." She tried to sit up, pulling away from him. He reluctantly let go of her legs and slid out of her. Groaning, he traded places with her on the bed and caught a glimpse of her rosebud as she swung one slender thigh over him. She held his cock and very slowly sat down until he was entirely sheathed by her.

Jack had never minded this position. In fact, he liked lying back and having a lady perched on top of him, riding him, pleasing him, showing him what she was willing to do for him.

But with Helen, as in everything, this was different.

At first, she just writhed and undulated, keeping him deep inside her, her hands stroking over his abdomen, her eyes on his chest and his face. He was intensely aware this was for her pleasure, not for his.

"Do I feel good inside you, Helen?"

"Aye," she gasped, her eyes burning. "Different. This way."

He couldn't stay passive any longer. He sat up and clutched her buttocks and ground into her with his hips, matching her movement with his. He captured one of her small breasts in his mouth and sucked there and then bit down on the nipple and pulled back.

"Oh," she said. He did the same thing to the other breast. "Oh, Jack." Her arms were on his shoulders, her head thrown back. He returned to the first breast and spent more time suckling and licking before biting. Back and forth he went even as she moved her narrow hips sinuously, hungrily over his shaft.

He let go of her and lay back. He put his hand to her mound and found her hardness with his thumb.

"Oh," she said.

His hand chased her as she rose up on him for the first time and came back down. Then she began to set a rhythm of rising and falling, her legs flexing. At first slowly, then more quickly, more powerfully, her small bottom slapping against him every time she sat down. He could not keep his thumb on her so he moved his hands to her hip bones and held her there.

Her brown hair had tumbled down, her face had flushed pink. He felt he was about to come, but she had not released yet.

"Are you close, Helen?"

"Aye. I've been close ever since I put yer cock in my mouth."

As if her words were a spark set to a fuse, her upper body quivered, her thighs trembled, and her walls clenched around him. She stopped moving up and down. Her mouth hung open. Her eyes were vague, not fierce. Her shoulders slumped and her head bowed.

He jerked himself up, roughly lifted her off his cock and set her on his thighs. He stroked himself and gasped, releasing his seed up and onto her abdomen.

"Oh," she said.

He lay back and held out his arms. "Come here, Helen Boyd."

She collapsed onto his chest, with no concern about his stickiness on her body. He wrapped his arms around her and they lay together, unmoving, for long minutes.

In time, she spoke. "We're leaving tomorrow."

Nausea swept over Jack. This was what he had felt when

he had come into the rooms. The *something else* that was wrong.

"No. Why?"

He lifted up her shoulders to see her face. But she rolled off him and lay on her side, her back to him.

"I got a look at a real duchess today."

He rolled too and cupped her body with his, her buttocks against his groin, her back against his chest. "Who? Which one?"

"The Duchess of Dunmore."

Fear joined nausea in Jack's belly. Helen had met Elizabeth or seen her. Had the two women talked? Had the fact Jack Pike was also John MacNaughton been mentioned?

Calm down, Jack. You have to stop getting spooked. Helen wouldn't be able to hide if she knew you were the duke. She doesn't have your talent for lying and deception.

"Have ye met her or seen her, Jack? She is a goddess."

Jack mumbled something that could have been yes or no.

"When there are women in the world like that, a duke would never pick me. In fact, when there are women in the world like that, I wonder why ye are spending so much time in my bed. Do ye feel sorry for me?"

He rested his chin on her shoulder and spoke next to her ear. "Helen, I don't know if you realize this or not, but a man's cock doesn't get hard because he feels sorry for someone."

"Does it need a reason to get hard?" She shifted so her back was on the mattress and she looked up at him.

"Yes."

She ran one finger over his lips. "It dinnae just need a few words about a man's handsomeness? A sunrise and some stars?"

He snugged an arm around her waist. "Let me put it this

way. I would rather bed you than the Duchess of Dunmore any day."

A flush rose from her breasts to her face, tinting her red.

"But…I'm so ugly, Jack."

"Helen." He kissed her mouth but she didn't kiss him back. He pulled his head away and looked at her. Her nose, her jaw, her skin, her brow, her eyes, her mouth. "You're not ugly."

"Plain, then."

"You're not."

"I am nae beautiful."

"I don't even know what that means when I look at you. You're more than beautiful."

"Och, Jack. Yer losing yer touch. Dinnae ye know every woman wants to be called beautiful?"

"All right, you're beautiful."

"I dinnae believe ye."

"I like looking at you, Helen. I like touching you. What is that, if not beauty?"

She shook her head. He gripped her chin and forced her to look at him.

"You're a thistle, Helen. Tough and spiky and able to flourish in a rocky, brutal place. You draw blood with your prickers. But a thistle also has a flower. A rich, purple, majestic flower, like a crown."

She stared at him. He didn't know what that look meant. He was relieved when she finally laughed. "That's very good, Jack. How long have ye been practicing that?"

"I didn't practice it."

"Dinnae sulk like a child. I widnae be angry if ye had practiced it." A small tremble of her lower lip. "Thank ye, Jack Pike. I know that compliment is for me, and only me. Yer nae calling yer London women thistles."

"Stay, Helen. Don't go. Don't leave London, not yet."

"Ye know why I came."

"Yes."

"Is there any reason to believe, in yer mind, that I have a chance of getting a husband here?"

The moment stretched. "Not the Duke of Dunmore. Maybe another man."

"Aye."

"I'll help you. I promise I will."

"Haven't ye done so much already?"

He had done nothing but get her some rooms and some clothes, show her the river, use her body for his own desire, and lie to her. Done nothing of worth compared to this woman who would do everything for the people she loved. Marry a man she had never met. Run into a burning building, starve herself, literally work herself to the bone.

He ran his hand now over those bones. Her hipbones, her ribs, her shoulders, her face, one finger on that uncompromising bone in her nose.

"Stay, Helen."

She looked up at him, eyes not fierce or adoring, but something else.

Lost.

"Aye, *mo luran*."

TWENTY-FOUR

Jack and Phineas' boots crunched on a gravel footpath in Hyde Park. Jack had gone into their club and dragged Phineas out, not wanting to discuss the matter indoors where too many ears were peeled for salacious stories and gossip. And as they had walked through the late afternoon sunshine toward the park, Jack had told Phineas. Everything.

"Why don't you come clean and marry her, Jack?"

"I've told you before. I'm never getting married."

"That's sounding a little thin. You went to balls. You were making the motions of looking for a duchess."

"I was trying to forget Helen at the time."

"Elizabeth is the one you should forget."

Jack bit down on his tongue before answering. "I've forgotten her. Elizabeth is *not* the reason I'm never getting married."

"Really?"

"Well, it's not just Elizabeth. It's my mother. It's the women I've been with since Elizabeth."

"You don't want to get married because you don't want to be cuckolded."

Jack shrugged. Yes, he didn't want to be cuckolded, but it was more than that. Marriage was a whole host of things he had shied away from for years. Obligation. Responsibility. Although he had both of those things now with his title, whether he wanted them or not. And, truth to tell, of all the women he had ever bedded, Helen was the least likely ever to constitute a burden. He was far more likely to be a burden to her.

So it wasn't duty he feared. He didn't want...oh, fuck it. He didn't want to care. He didn't want to care enough to feel betrayal. Agony. Loss. Grief. But he could barely say that to himself. He could never say it to Phineas.

"You do know, don't you, that most men are never cuckolded?" Phineas asked.

"That's not been my experience."

"With the exception of your mother, Jack, you've chosen all these women. All these unfaithful women. It sounds like this woman, this countess, has chosen you. It's a good start."

"She didn't choose me. I practically forced myself on her."

"She came to your bedchamber in Scotland and asked you to bed her, you old salt. Sounds like she did the choosing, all right. You probably wouldn't have given her a second thought if she hadn't come to you when you were so deprived of a warm place to put your cock. If she hadn't come to you in Scotland for what, you said? Her training. I must remember that." Phineas chuckled. "Her training in how to bed you even though she didn't know it was you. You were vulnerable to her wiles."

"She doesn't have wiles, Phin."

"What does she have?"

"She has will. Tenacity. A strength, a—"

"It sounds like you're buying horseflesh, not thinking of a wife."

Jack bristled. "That's the whole point. I'm not thinking of a wife."

There was more he had been going to say about Helen to Phineas. How she could be both so unyielding and so soft, and he felt it was a privilege to be the one to see that softness. How she expected more of him, just as his best commanding officers had, and how she made him yearn to meet those expectations, be that better man. How she challenged him and forced him to see that his money and his power didn't have to weigh him down, but could free him.

And how she made him feel.

Not alone.

"You don't think it's a bad sign she asked me to bed her so she could seduce another man?"

"The other man, being you? But as the Duke of Dunmore."

"Right."

"She doesn't care about the other man."

"Exactly. She cares about his title, what he'll do for her—"

"Wait, wait, wait. I thought you said she wanted to marry Dunmore for Kinmarloch. That she would do anything for her people. That she gave away a ham, rescued a child, *et cetera*. She wants to marry Dunmore for them."

"Exactly."

Phineas was silent for a long time. A strangely long time. The Earl of Burchester was the most loquacious man in London. It made Jack even more uncomfortable.

Phineas finally spoke. "I see. You don't want to marry her because you know you'll never be the most important thing in her life. Kinmarloch will always come before you."

"That's ridiculous."

"Is it? It sounds like a perfectly reasonable objection to me. I fully intend to be the foremost thing in the future Lady Burchester's life. Although, mmmm." Phineas laid a finger over his mouth and tapped thoughtfully. "Children. Those pesky creatures. I hear mothers are devoted to them. Well, I'll just have to remind her constantly how important her husband's cock is to her. After all, it's the thing that will give her the children. And it will be there long after the baby birds have flown the nest. Perhaps not in working order, but it'll be there."

"I would appreciate some gravity right now. I should have gone to George. Or Edmund."

"No, no, no. Look at me. I'm grave, I'm serious. Let's think this through. Does Helen the woman give a damn about the Duke of Dunmore and his title? No. It's the Countess of Kinmarloch who wants him. There are three questions here. First, does Helen Boyd want you? Let's hope, yes. It certainly sounds like she can't get enough of you and you of her. Second, can you live with the fact she will always be a countess first and a wife second and she would sacrifice Jack Pike in a heartbeat for Kinmarloch?"

Jack remembered how Duncan had looked at Helen when they had sheared the sheep. How he had watched her so closely Jack had thought Duncan might be Helen's lover. Duncan's looks at Helen had been akin to the way his own sailors had looked at Jack when he was captain. Helen was the captain of Kinmarloch. And a captain would do anything for his ship and his men. The ship and her sailors came first.

"Third, do you love her?"

Love. The word, the idea had been in Jack's mind ever since Phineas had raised the notion two days ago. His initial reaction had been, no, of course not, never, no, impossible.

Jack had thought he loved Elizabeth years ago, when really, he just had been enamored with her face and her body. The woman he had thought he loved didn't exist. It had all been illusion and deception. So he had never loved. Not that kind of love. Love of friends, yes. Love of his ship and his men, yes.

But he wouldn't, couldn't love any woman. And certainly not a thistle.

But he did love kissing Helen. That had never been a lie. And he loved how she looked at him and how she made her raw desire known to him. He loved her body, under his, on top of his, against his. But that was just lust.

And once he told her he had deceived her for so long, she wouldn't let him near her again. Not the woman who ripped him open with her ferocious honesty.

She would hate him. Genuinely hate him. Loathe him. Despise him. And he would deserve that.

Maybe he didn't want to marry not because he feared his wife would betray him, but because he couldn't face disappointing his wife. Scratch that. He couldn't face disappointing Helen.

"Phin, I don't know how I'm ever going to tell her John MacNaughton is the same man as—"

"Jack Pike."

Jack looked behind him. Lord Feces, dressed in a flowered waistcoat and a tailcoat with overly puffed sleeves to make himself look bigger, carrying a walking stick.

Jack swallowed the bile rising in his throat and bowed. "Lord Reeves." He turned to Phineas. "Lord Burchester, this is Lord Reeves, a greater baron in the Highlands. We met when I was recently there on behalf of the Duke of Dunmore."

Reeves made a deep bow to Phineas. "My lord." He didn't look at Jack or acknowledge him any further. "It's an honor to meet you, Lord Burchester."

Phineas looked at Jack and then bowed to Reeves. "Likewise, I'm sure."

Reeves' answering smile was akin to a sneer. "London is so full of lords. I find myself meeting them, right and left. Even just here, in the late afternoon, strolling in the park. So many important men. So many introductions."

"Well, welcome to London, Lord Reeves." Phineas moved as if to walk on, but Reeves kept speaking.

"But I am here in London to meet young ladies, of course. And one finds it difficult to procure invitations to balls. I was sad to miss Lady Huxley's ball last week. However, I have gotten an invitation to the Earl of Titchfield's ball. His daughter Lady Olivia Radcliffe is out and I hear she is unparalleled in beauty and grace. Tell me, do you know the size of her dowry?"

Phineas blinked. "I don't, Lord Reeves. Good day to you." He turned as if to go and Jack began to turn as well.

"Ah, but it's comforting to know if I can't find a Lady Reeves this Season, I still have my Scottish lass to fall back on."

Mags? Was Reeves talking about Mags? When Jack had met the man in Helen's keep, he had said something about Mags being the only attractive woman around, hadn't he? And he had wanted to see her.

Jack's fists tightened. He would drive the carriage himself to Gretna Green and get Mags and Duncan married before the end of the Season. He would get Duncan a position in the duchy, whatever post Helen thought would be best for him. Duncan would have the means to marry Mags.

"I'm speaking of Lady Kinmarloch, of course." Reeves turned his gaze to Jack for the first time since accosting him. "You know her, Jack Pike. I believe that is where I met you, where you were so impolite, in her shithole of a keep. I see your manners are better in London."

Jack's eyes narrowed as he hissed, "You think you could marry Lady Kinmarloch?"

"She's practically consented to it. She doesn't have much choice, after all." Reeves shrugged. "And it would be some-thing to have a son who would be an earl, even if it's of Kinmarloch. An earl, like you, Lord Burchester. One could put up with the countess' coarse manners and speech, I suppose. It's the face that would be difficult. But the land would be valuable once I cleared it of farms and farmers."

Jack saw red. He had thought such a thing was hyperbole, but it was not. He was slightly aware of being pushed and Phineas saying, "Mr. Pike and I have an important issue to discuss, so good day to you, Lord Reeves," and an iron grip on his upper arm leading him at a fast clip up the gravel path.

"Steady now, Jack. Steady."

"That man—"

"Let's get away from here." Phineas led Jack to the edge of the park and waved down a hack. He told the driver to take them to Jack's house. Jack's heart was still pounding, his breath short.

"Well, that was unpleasant," Phineas said, as the carriage started moving.

"Unpleasant? The man is a—"

"Vulgarian? Yes."

"I was going to say something far fouler. You shouldn't have kept me from striking him."

"You weren't going to strike him, Jack. You were going to beat him to a bloody pulp. In Hyde Park, in front of witnesses."

Jack took a deep breath. "Yes."

"But I want you to use your rage to concentrate your mind on your problem."

"My problem?"

"Your Helen Boyd problem. It sounds like Lord Reeves is a potential solution."

"Phin, you can't mean to say she should marry that despicable man? And he plans to clear Kinmarloch. She would never marry him for that reason alone."

"Jack. Helen Boyd will either marry or she won't. What do you think?"

"She must have money to live."

"Will she accept money without marriage?"

"Set her up as my mistress? She'll bed me but she won't take my money. I'm lying to her as it is about what everything costs. And if she never has a legitimate child, her title will go extinct. She won't allow that to happen."

"So, she will marry."

"Yes, she must, she says."

"So, she will either marry you or another man. Which is it to be?"

Jack groaned. "I don't like either of those choices."

"But you have choices, Jack. Unlike the countess. After all, she must wait for a proposal."

Jack shook his head.

"Well, my advice is to tell her you're the duke and propose to her. Simple."

"She would hate me."

"You're still Jack Pike. She wouldn't hate you for long. Just pull out your charm."

"She doesn't like my charm."

"No, Jack. She doesn't like that she likes your charm. There's a difference."

Jack sat back. Phineas was misguided. Phineas didn't know Helen.

But Jack's course was clear.

Helen must marry. Jack wouldn't marry. Therefore, Helen would marry someone else.

But not Reeves. Jack would protect her and Kinmarloch from that.

And he would start by making it clear to Helen she could have no hope of marrying John MacNaughton, the Duke of Dunmore. Then, Jack Pike would find her another husband.

Twenty-Five

He told her she was beautiful, more than beautiful. She didn't believe him, lying in bed with him, naked, his seed still on her skin.

What he said had no meaning. It was the fine eyes and the hair ribbon and the pink cheeks and her dirty blue dress. It was just his way.

But then he called her a thistle.

She believed that.

It didn't matter, in that moment, if she was beautiful or not. She felt beautiful. As she had when her grandfather had told her she was. And everything came rushing at her. His own beauty and how he had shared it with her in this bed. His care for her in Kinmarloch by stopping the invasion of the Dunmore sheep. And the cottage being built right now and how he had managed it without damaging her dignity. How he had wanted to show her his land yesterday.

And how he had seen her just now. As she truly was. A thistle.

She looked into his eyes.

I love you, Jack Pike. I love you for seeing that I'm a thistle.

But she didn't think she saw love looking back at her. Care, desire, concern, but not love. So she laughed and accused him of rehearsing his compliment and the moment passed.

But I still love him even though he doesn't love me.

Jack came at midnight. Helen hadn't known if he would. He hadn't said he would. And after all, they had just coupled that afternoon, when he had convinced her to stay in London and told her she was a thistle and made her realize she loved him.

She bathed and brushed her hair in the hopes he would come to her again.

She opened the door just as his first knock was finished. She had been waiting for him and didn't care if he knew it. Didn't care if he knew she wanted him, knew she was yearning for him. It was the one thing he had always known about her, wasn't it? That she desired him. She could show that to him even if she couldn't show her love.

He kissed her as if he hadn't just kissed her hours before. As if they had had a long separation. A deep, fervent kiss that aroused her heart as much as her body.

I made him realize today our time together is growing short. Because I will either leave or find a man to marry.

He picked her up as he had the first night he had come to the rooms. He carried her to her bedchamber. The lamp was not lit. He undressed her and himself in the dark and lay down next to her and touched her gently. Soon her breath was ragged, wanting him inside her. Why did that ache for him not lessen? Why did it come back again and again? Why could she never have her fill of this man?

"I want to light the lamp. I want to see ye, *mo luran*."

He whispered, "Let's stay in the dark, Helen. Don't leave

the bed. Let's pretend we've fallen asleep together and woken up together, in the middle of the night."

"Why did we wake up?"

"Maybe you heard a sound?"

"I heard a sound and woke ye up?"

"Yes."

"Do ye want me to be frightened?"

"No, I never want that." He laughed. "I would never believe that of you."

"So, I kiss ye awake." She found his face in the dark with her hands and kissed his lips with her fingers still next to his mouth. "And I say to ye that I heard a sound."

"Yes, and I say 'What sound was that, Helen?'"

"Thunder?"

"Oh, a storm is coming? I like that. A storm with my countess. But maybe I better shield your body with mine." He got on top of her.

"Aye, Jack. Ye better do that."

"Is the rain coming down, Helen?"

"Nae yet, just far-off rolling thunder."

He moved against her. Pressing his hardness into her maidenhair. She trembled and ran her hands up and down his back. She knew this skin and these muscles now by feel.

"Do you want to go back to sleep, Helen?" He was still pretending they had woken up together. His warm breath on her face.

"Nae. I want *dàireadh*. Can I say that?"

"You can say anything you like. But I especially don't mind that. Because that's what I want, too."

And then he was inside her, stroking in and out of her, his mouth either on her breasts or on her own mouth. She came to her peak as he was kissing her and she felt her moans reverberate in his throat as she put her hand blindly around his neck. Soon after that, he was releasing outside of her. He lay on top of her afterward.

"You don't mind, do you, Helen?"

"Nae. Ye must shield me from the rain."

"Yes."

"I dinnae miss the lamp, Jack. I thought I would."

"You didn't miss seeing my handsome face?"

She put her hand to where his head was turned into the angle of her neck and shoulder and felt his cheek, his jaw. "Always, *mo luran*. But yer cock provides ample compensation."

The glorious Jack Pike laugh. Not as full-throated as usual since it was night.

It had been strange what he wanted. To pretend to wake up from sleep together. As if they had some domestic arrangement. As if they were husband and wife. It had added to the tenderness of their coupling, she thought. But now it twisted at her heart.

"Helen?"

"Aye?"

"What's the worst thing you've ever done?"

"The worst?"

"Yes."

"I froze my grandfather."

She felt him lift his head from her shoulder. "What?"

"He died three weeks before I was to be one and twenty. I was frightened. I know ye think that impossible, but I was. I was nae of age and widnae have my own sovereignty. I dinnae know who would be in charge of me for those three weeks. And I quaked at what might happen. So I talked to those I knew best in the castle, and we took his body out to a shed and left him there until the day after my birthday. It was January. The body dinnae spoil in the cold. Then we brought him in and thawed him and made his death known. I was made

Countess of Kinmarloch, and I left the castle and moved into the keep."

"You moved into the keep in January?"

"Aye. It dinnae leak as badly back then. And I stayed warm shoveling out the sheep dung."

"The sheep shit."

"Aye."

"Helen. There's a lady present."

She had been running her fingers up and down his spine and now she gave his buttock a small spank. "That's why I said dung, Jack."

"Ow. And that's the worst thing you've ever done?"

"'Tis a crime. So, aye."

"You didn't hurt anyone with the worst thing you've done. So that may be the best worst thing I've ever heard of."

A silence. Did he want her to ask him what was the worst thing he had ever done? She had opened her mouth and was about to ask when he spoke.

"The Duke of Dunmore is not in London, presently."

Suddenly, he felt heavy. She shifted under him.

He went on. "But I've written to him. About you."

"Ye have?"

"So you may get a letter from him."

"I thought ye felt I dinnae have a chance?"

"Maybe I was wrong. Maybe I said that for other reasons. Not noble ones."

"Oh."

He rolled off of her. "So we shall see."

"Aye."

She was glad of the dark then.

If only she had known, back in Kinmarloch.

If only she'd known that coupling, for her, would become more than bodies and need and the relief of her ache and the means to get what she must have. More than seeing physical beauty and wanting it for herself.

It would become love.

And there was no place in her life for her love for Jack Pike.

Twenty-Six

The letter came to Helen the next day. Jack must have written to the duke days ago for a letter to arrive so quickly.

To the Countess of Kinmarloch.
My lady:

Please forgive my writing to you as if I know you already. I am away from London at present. However, Captain Jack Pike has written to tell me you are in London and you desire an introduction.

I know my predecessor did not administer the duchy as your grandfather would have done. I am anxious to hear from you what his wishes might have been, what he would do if he were duke now. I also want to hear more about the difficulties in the Highlands, specifically Dunmore and Kinmarloch. I would like things to be better than they are now. I know you can help me.

Please write to me via Captain Pike who will see I get

your letter. At this time, I do not plan to return to London in the immediate future.

Captain Pike has told me in his letter much about you and Kinmarloch. He says you are a woman of great fortitude and honor and you have the best interests of your people in your heart, at all times. These are qualities that speak to me, very deeply.

I feel I should be blunt with you, to spare you time and expense. Captain Pike hinted you might have expectations of a marriage with me. But I will not marry. I am purported to be a scoundrel, and I would never be a good husband. I would only disappoint, and I am sure you will find a man much more worthy of you.

Please answer this letter and know you can be open and honest with me. I like frankness. I assure you there is no need for politics or etiquette in your correspondence with me. You need not hide your wishes or motives. I am like you, in that I only wish for what is best for the Highlands.

> *Yrs. Sincerely,*
> *John MacNaughton,*
> *Duke of Dunmore*

Helen read the letter many times. She went out and found a shop and bought paper and a pen and ink and pounce and sealing wax. She came back to the rooms and sat at the secretary in the drawing room and thought for a long time. Then she wrote her reply, carefully, in her poor, scratching script.

To the Duke of Dunmore.
My lord duke:

Thank you, Your Grace, for your letter. I hope you will

forgive any errors that follow. My education is lacking in many things and I am not as well-read as I would like.

I thank you for your concern for my time and expense. I am sure you are much less of a scoundrel than you think you are but it is not my place to try to change your opinion of yourself. If you know you will be happy without a wife, then I am glad for you.

I will be pleased to undertake your education about the Highlands. The most pressing item is the need to stop the clearances. Captain Pike has already undertaken this in Dunmore, and I hope you will continue his practice. The issue is a difficult one. The people wish to stay on the land, but the land does not support them. However, I believe, with time and money and care, new livelihoods could be found that do not uproot the people from the land they have lived on for centuries and they should have the right to live on forever, as it is part of dùthchas, the ancient Scottish clan right.

I am happy you wish to hear about my grandfather and that you already care about the people of Dunmore.

Please write with any questions you might have. I hope this correspondence will be of use to you. I only wish to help you fulfill your own duty as the Duke of Dunmore. I am sure you will.

> *Yrs. Sincerely,*
> *Helen Boyd,*
> *Countess of Kinmarloch*

She sent Duncan and Mags to their separate bedchambers when Jack came to the rooms at noon. She did not want the pair to hear what she had to say. But she wanted Mags and Duncan there, close by, to shore up her weakness, to remove temptation.

Before Jack could touch her or kiss her, she put her arm out in front of her, keeping him away, pressing the letter into his chest. He looked at the outside of the sealed letter before he tucked into a pocket inside his coat.

"He's written to you?"

"Aye."

"I hope it was an encouraging letter."

"Nae. The duke dinnae plan to marry. But I thank ye for speaking so well of me. I think ye praised me too highly."

"I didn't. I couldn't." Then, "I'm sorry, Helen."

"Jack."

"Yes?"

"I..." He was as beautiful as ever. "I. Cannae. Be. Yer lover. Anymore. Jack. Pike."

"Why is that? What changed between last night and today?"

Ye made me feel beautiful. And I'm in love with ye. And I know now that everything forward from those two things will only tear my heart out.

"I am going to see if I can find another man to marry me. As ye suggested."

I willnae be a bother to ye any longer.

"You're going to try to get yourself compromised, is that it?"

"Nae. I have realized that widnae be honorable. I am going to be forthright with what I hope for. As I was with ye."

"Yes, you were always forthright. With me."

Until now, Jack Pike. I cannae tell ye what is in my heart the way I could tell ye what was in my loins.

Jack patted the pocket which held the letter. "Do you intend to tell the duke about us?"

"If he had offered to marry me, I would have told him I was a woman of experience. But I widnae have told him it was ye."

"So last night was our last time together?"

He came toward her now, reaching for her, but she backed away.

"Aye, but please. Dinnae make this more difficult for me. I hope...I hope ye will think well of me."

He got hold of a piece of her hair that had fallen down. He rubbed it in his fingers.

"And I hope you will think wickedly of me, Helen Boyd."

"If I can control my thoughts, I willnae think of ye at all."

He leaned forward and whispered in her ear. "What if you can't control your thoughts?"

She stepped away, well clear of him. "Then I'll control my deeds."

Jack looked at the floor. "I hope you get what you want, Helen."

I cannae. I want ye. "Aye."

He raised his head. "Mrs. Allen says your dresses are ready to be fitted."

She did not correct his use of the word *dresses* instead of *dress*. Hadn't she always known he would give her both more than she deserved and less than she wanted?

TWENTY-SEVEN

J ack watched Helen look at her reflection in the mirror. She had on the winter dress. Not quite the right blue. The dress covered her completely, stopping just shy of her chin and coming down over her wrists. He came closer and felt the material of her sleeve. It was thick and soft.

Mrs. Allen went to fetch more pins. Helen hissed down at him from the small platform she stood on, "Jack, three. I dinnae need three more dresses."

"They're already made for you, Helen. You have to take them. It's a favor owed me, as I said." He wanted to put his arm around her waist, touch her bottom through the dress, feel how warm she would be in it.

He folded his arms across his chest, tucking his hands into his armpits, and stepped away.

His letter was meant to divert her attention away from the Duke of Dunmore, not away from Jack Pike. It had not even occurred to him she would break it off with him. If anything, he had thought she would turn to him for comfort after the letter. Comfort that would end with the two of them tangled together in a bed. But, instead, something in the letter had made her decide their coupling should stop.

Why, oh, why had he dictated that letter to Phineas in his study yesterday evening after their excursion to Hyde Park? Because if he hadn't, he would be stealing a grope or a kiss right now. And, after the fitting of her dresses, they could have gone to the inn again, delaying the inevitable future while they moved against each other, their mouths and groins locked together.

The next dress was the one suitable for spring. Light blue with a little white lace that looked like clouds along the square neckline and at the ends of the elbow sleeves. Again, the urge came to touch her, to run his fingers around the neckline where the lace was and feel her smooth skin there.

Helen's cheeks were pink. She touched the lace herself. Then she caught his eye in the mirror and scowled and shook her head.

Finally, the ballgown in the blue Jack had requested, a blue of the sky over Scotland on that rarest of things, a clear spring day. Silk fell in a column to pool at Helen's feet. The smallest bit of gold cording under her breasts. The sleeves just fluttering wisps of silk.

"Jack," she whispered when she saw herself in the mirror.

He turned to Mrs. Allen. "You did well."

He turned back to Helen. He had no urge to touch her in this dress. This was a dress for looking at her in. And for another man to take off of her. Not him.

Besides, I still prefer her in muddy breeches. Or her muslin nightdress.

They walked away from Mrs. Allen's, back toward the rooms, in the opposite direction of the inn where he longed to take her right now.

"Jack, that last dress, 'tis a dress for a queen. I cannae wear it."

"It's a ballgown."

"Am I going to a ball?"

"It's where lords go to meet ladies who might become their wives. And for ladies to meet husbands. That's what you're here for, you said. Why you're in London."

"Aye."

"The dresses will be delivered tomorrow. I'll have Phin get you an invitation to a ball for tomorrow night."

"Phin?"

"Phineas. The Earl of Burchester, whom you met."

"Aye. But won't I need a chaperone?"

He hadn't thought of that. "I'll find you one."

"Will the duke be there, do ye think?"

"No. He must have told you he doesn't plan to return to London any time soon."

"And will ye be there?"

"Jack Pike is not a lord."

"But surely, with yer money, ye could get an invitation, too."

"I'm not looking for a wife."

They walked the rest of the way back to the rooms in silence.

In the drawing room, Duncan helped Jack move the furniture to the periphery to create a large, open space. Mags sat in a chair in the corner, her eyes shining.

"Do you know how to dance, Helen?" Jack asked.

"Aye, but it has been a long time since I did so."

"What dances do you know?"

"I know the Scotch reel, of course. The country dance, the cotillion."

"Show me."

Helen looked around the room, her cheeks pink again. "There is nae music and I have nae partner."

"Duncan?" Jack asked.

But Duncan shook his head as he answered, "I dinnae know how to do this kind of dancing."

"I'll be your partner, Helen." Jack bowed.

Helen stared at him, eyes fierce. "There is nae music."

"I'll hum."

And so he danced with Helen as he went *bum bum bum* under his breath and instructed her to turn that way or to skip this way. She needed reminding of certain figures, but they came back to her quickly. She was a lively, surprisingly graceful dancer, and he thought she forgot herself a few times. She became the girl who had grown up in the castle of Dunmore.

Duncan leaned against the wall, grinning. He must not know Jack Pike would never come to Helen Boyd's bedchamber again. Mags was clapping and giggling, watching closely.

"You have to learn the quadrille, Helen." He taught it to her. She picked it up easily.

"And now the waltz." He came close to her and put his hand on her waist. She pulled away from him.

"In this dance, the gentleman puts his hand on the lady's waist and stands very close to her."

"Oh."

She let him seat his hand on her waist again, but she held her body rigidly and would not meet his eyes.

She still wore no stays since the ones for her ballgown were at Mrs. Allen's shop. So her waist under his hand felt much the same as before. Perhaps slightly more flesh here than when he had felt it first in Dunmore. But it was the same waist he had felt here in London. Delicate, yet strong. Taut and quivering right now. So alive.

He took her hand in his other one.

"Your left hand goes on my shoulder, Helen."

She reached up, her arm over his. Her eyes were suspicious

when she looked at his face briefly before she turned her head away.

She could not learn the waltz. She stumbled and jerked and did not turn with him as he directed.

Finally, she broke away, her face red. "I willnae do the waltz at the ball, Jack Pike."

"All right."

"And...and I think I will go rest now."

She fled the drawing room. Every fiber of his being wanted to follow her to her bedchamber, close the door, and be with her. In any way she might permit. Sitting on the edge of the bed with her. Looking at her. An arm around her. The side of his leg against hers.

Jack walked back to his house, his shoulders hunched. Despite Phineas' warning, he had made a mess of it, hadn't he?

TWENTY-EIGHT

T he next day, Helen went to the windows of either her bedchamber or the drawing room every few minutes. She knew she wouldn't see Jack approach the building from these back rooms, but she couldn't go out on the street to look for him, could she?

And it would have been foolish since he never came.

Not that she should want him to come. She should want to spare herself that cruelty. But she didn't.

The dresses were delivered to the rooms as promised, along with chemises, petticoats, gloves, slippers, hose, a little golden shawl for her shoulders. Mags was consumed with touching and looking at each piece, wanting to point out to Helen the fine stitchery, the softness of the silk chemises, the little heels on the satin slippers.

Helen had not worn slippers in five years. She put them on and stumbled. What foolish things these heels were. They made her so unsteady. Would she be able to dance in them?

She must.

In the course of a single day, her time in London had gone from the greatest adventure of her life to a round of duty. A list of *musts*. She must wear stays and she must wear a ball-gown and she must dance in heeled slippers and she must go to a ball and she must find a husband.

She must do all these things and not mind that she was dead.

The *musts* were her life in Kinmarloch, too. But she didn't mind them there. Partly because in Kinmarloch, the *musts* were about survival. Food, heat, shelter, sheep. And partly because she was paid back for her obligation by being able to see her people, her lands, her mountains, her loch. Here, in London, with Jack gone, only Mags and Duncan reminded her why she was still going through the motions of being alive.

She bathed. She dressed, Mags lacing the stays for her.

"Keep them as loose as possible."

"Aye, my lady."

Mags arranged Helen's hair, fussing that she did not know the styles of London.

"'Tis fine, I'm sure, Mags. Dinnae worry."

Another delivery, two boxes. One small, one not-so-small. And an unsealed note in a hand she recognized from the letter Jack Pike had left her at the castle. The letter she had read a thousand times and the postscript she had read a million times: *PS I meant what I said about kissing you.*

This note said:

Not a gift, a loan. My mother's. Good luck.
J. Pike
PS (turn this over)

Her heart was in her throat, beating wildly. She turned the note over.

The other, well, it's just been sitting on my dressing table.

You hold on to it for me. It belongs with the Countess of Kinmarloch, not Jack Pike.

The not-so-small box held her dirk and its sheath.

The small box contained a sapphire necklace and two hair combs encrusted with the same jewels.

Mags then had to take Helen's hair all down again so as to nest the combs in her curls, despite Helen's protests she didn't need them, she didn't want them.

"Yer nae going to wear Mr. Pike's jewelry?"

"He willnae know."

"Please, my lady. Let me put the pretty combs in yer hair."

She could at least make Mags happy in this. She sat in the chair and Mags brushed and repinned and coiled her hair and then coaxed Helen to put the necklace on.

"Do ye want to see yerself in the mirror, my lady?"

She looked at herself in the mirror for Mags' sake. She swallowed. "Thank ye. Ye did a wonderful job. I am a real countess."

"Aye, my lady."

She was the same Helen. The same face. The same body. The same ugly. In a way, she looked worse because the clothes and the jewelry were so fine.

She was pacing the drawing room when Phineas Edge, the Earl of Burchester, came for her. It was night, now. The earl was kind and praised her dress and hair. He was courtly both to Mags and to Duncan who had put on the full kilt to welcome him.

Mags hugged her goodbye. "Good luck, my lady."

"Aye. Good luck, my lady," Duncan echoed.

Jack's friend with the silver hair chuckled. "Lady Kinmarloch doesn't need luck. She is enchanting."

The earl held out his arm. Helen now saw he was dressed in clothes identical to the ones Jack had been wearing her first night in London, the night he had come to these rooms and told her he wanted her.

Jack must have been at a ball himself that night, in those satin breeches and dancing shoes and elegant tailcoat. He had been at a ball in the London Season, a ball meant to introduce gentlemen and ladies to each other so there might be courtship and eventually, marriage.

He had told her just yesterday he was not looking for a wife.

But he had gone to a ball. He did want a wife.

Just not me.

And still she breathed and still her heart beat, even though in that moment, she died all over again.

"Your chaperone is waiting in my carriage, Lady Kinmarloch. Shall we go?"

"Aye, thank ye, my lord."

Down the stairs on Phineas' arm, into his fancy carriage with a coat of arms painted on the door.

"Lady Kinmarloch, this is Lady Fitzhugh."

Helen nodded. Lady Fitzhugh was a plump, middle-aged woman with a pleasant smile.

"I have known Lord Burchester since he was a boy. He was a rascal, even then, so do be careful of yourself around him, the naughty man." She spoke as if Phineas were not there, seated across from her. "But it's just like him to be kind enough to ask me along tonight. He knew I was at loose ends because I usually help chaperone my deceased husband's cousin's daughters, the Cavendish girls. But their father, the Duke of Middlewich, has died and their drunken brother, such a disgrace, has been made duke. Poor girls. Their entire Season has been canceled now. And poor me. I do like going to the balls and seeing the dancing and the gowns and hearing the music. It makes me feel quite young again. This is your first ball, isn't it, Lady Kinmarloch? I don't want you to worry about a thing. Your gown is unusual but quite lovely, and Lord Burchester and I will make sure you have a good time and meet plenty of gentlemen and have plenty of dances."

Helen let the woman's words wash over her. *All I must do in this carriage is nod.*

It was a very short ride and she was out of the carriage into the cool spring night and into the front hall of a large house that was hot with the breath and the bodies of other people. She was glad to shed her little golden shawl.

Beyond the hall, a large room full of people. Talking, laughing.

The talking paused. A resounding voice. "The Countess of Kinmarloch."

In my own right. She straightened and walked into the ballroom. She did her best to relax her brow, her jaw. She was very aware of the eyes on her. And then Phineas was also announced as the Earl of Burchester, and he was at her elbow and taking her to meet their hostess, Lady Titchfield, and her daughter, Lady Olivia Radcliffe.

Helen was glad now she had met the Duchess of Dunmore. Because it had partially prepared her for meeting Lady Olivia Radcliffe.

Partially.

Lady Olivia was more beautiful than Jack Pike, and until that moment, Helen had not thought such a thing possible.

Each component of her appearance was dazzling in and of itself, and her features combined in such a way that the whole was overwhelming. Blonde curls. The biggest and bluest of eyes, fringed with dark lashes. Perfect cream skin tinted with just a bit of pink on her cheeks. A perfect posture, nose, figure. Lady Olivia Radcliffe made the Duchess of Dunmore look tawdry with her beauty mark and her full lips and her slightly too large bosom for her height.

Lady Olivia's eyes sparkled as she drew Helen aside and

whispered, "I love your ballgown, Lady Kinmarloch. You must tell me who made it. Is it a Madame Beauchamp?"

Helen stroked the front of the dress, the fine silk slipping under her gloved hands. "Nae, Lady Olivia. Mrs. Allen made it."

"Mrs. Allen. I'll remember that." A beautiful and gracious smile. And then Lady Olivia turned to Phineas and her manner changed. Her face froze in a haughty look and her voice was ice as she curtsied and accepted his greeting which was accompanied by his own warm chuckle and grin.

She dinnae like Phineas. How can she dislike him?

But Helen saw Lady Olivia have the same frigid reaction to every other gentleman who approached her, while giving real smiles to the ladies.

She dinnae like men, for some reason.

Phineas wandered off, and Lady Fitzhugh took Helen around to make the acquaintance of various matrons and debutantes.

Helen met Lady Phoebe Finch, the youngest daughter of the Duke of Abingdon. Lady Phoebe smiled and curtsied politely, but Helen could see that the young woman's mind was elsewhere and her eyes were flitting constantly toward the entrance to the ballroom.

A tall, slender woman with reddish-brown hair and a matching reddish-brown gown rushed up to the short, buxom Lady Phoebe.

"Oh, Alice, good, you're here." Lady Phoebe clasped the other woman's hands. "And so that means George is here?"

The other woman rolled her eyes but then grinned. "Of course, Bumblephee. Where else would he be if you're here and I'm here?"

The tall woman was then introduced to Helen as Miss Danforth.

"Sister of Lord Danforth and the wildest debutante of the

nineteenth century, without exception," Lady Fitzhugh whispered into Helen's ear as they moved away from Lady Phoebe and Miss Danforth.

Faces, names, ballgowns blurred together as Lady Fitzhugh gave out names and titles and Helen curtsied and curtsied.

Finally, Lady Fitzhugh drew Helen aside, gesturing to a footman bearing a tray to approach them as she did so.

"I mustn't let you get too overwhelmed with meeting other ladies, Lady Kinmarloch." Lady Fitzhugh took two glasses from the footman's tray. "Here, dear, sip this lemonade. We must reserve some of your energy for the the gentlemen. Lord Burchester is finding partners for you. He'll bring them to Lady Titchfield to have them introduced to you. You will dance so many dances tonight."

"Thank ye, Lady Fitzhugh."

But it was Phineas who was Helen's partner for the first dance, a quadrille. Throughout the dance, he chatted to her about the room, the other guests. He was just as talkative as Lady Fitzhugh. But when the dance was over, he returned her to her chaperone with a worried look and crossed the ballroom to mix with a group of gentlemen.

Helen saw subtle looks cast her way from the men after Phineas approached them. Appraisals from across the room. Heads shaken, *no*. And Phineas was moving on to another cluster of gentlemen.

Helen made her spine into a rod of iron.

She turned to Lady Fitzhugh. "Ye mentioned the young ladies ye usually chaperone. They dinnae come to balls while in mourning then?"

"Oh, no, my dear. That wouldn't do at all. In fact, there has been a great deal of scandal recently since the Duchess of Dunmore is in mourning but has been having dinners in her home and accepting invitations for house parties. Her husband died recently, you know."

"Aye."

"Of course, you must know that since Dunmore is also in Scotland. I have to tell you," Lady Fitzhugh shook her head, "Miss Elizabeth Hamilton never understood propriety. That was her name before she married the duke. And I never liked her. She was engaged to another man first, a very handsome man, a navy captain who was making a name for himself, and she broke it off quite cruelly and married Norman MacNaughton days later, just before his father died. When it was certain he would be the next Duke of Dunmore. Everyone said she had seduced her husband while still engaged to the other man. Oh, what was that man's name? Jack Pitt."

"Pike," Helen said, the sapphire necklace suddenly a weight around her throat.

"Yes, that's it, but since his cousin died, he now goes by his fath—"

"Lady Kinmarloch."

Reeves stood in front of her, giving her a slight bow. She was startled. Like her, he didn't belong here. Then she remembered his plan of coming to London to look for a wife.

"Lord Reeves." She curtsied. She realized she did not know Lady Fitzhugh's precedence. "Uh, Lady Fitzhugh, this is Lord Reeves. From the Highlands."

The two exchanged a bow and a curtsy as gentlemen and ladies began to assemble at the center of the ballroom floor.

A sneer. "I see you have no partner. May I have this dance, Lady Kinmarloch?"

Helen panicked. "I-I-I dinnae waltz, Lord Reeves."

"It's not a waltz, Lady Kinmarloch," Lady Fitzhugh said, "it's, oh dear, I believe it's a country dance. And since you know Lord Reeves already, you need not wait for an introduction from Lady Titchfield." Lady Fitzhugh smiled and nodded.

Helen found herself on Reeves' arm, being led away from Lady Fitzhugh.

"I was surprised to see you here, Lady Kinmarloch. I did not think you had funds for travel like this."

"I…"

"Dressed in silk and wearing jewels, you almost look presentable."

The dance started and Helen was saved for a moment from having to say anything. It was not like her not to be able to think of something to say. But she was occupied by thoughts of a younger Jack Pike, his heart broken by a raven-haired beauty with a laugh like a bird singing.

"You do not compare to the other ladies here but it's possible to see you might make a wife," Reeves said as one of the figures of the dance brought him close to her.

"Where is your tongue, Lady Kinmarloch?" he asked a minute later, during another figure.

"In my mouth, Lord Reeves, where it belongs."

"I can think of somewhere else your tongue could be."

"My tongue would sooner be in hell."

Lord Reeves laughed. "You're both fiery and clearly wanton tonight, Lady Kinmarloch. I was suggesting that after the dance, I might fetch you one of the ices. That was all. But I am glad to see how your mind works."

"Ye were nae suggesting that."

"You think I was suggesting an unnatural act?"

Every act with ye would be unnatural.

The dance was over. She curtsied, he bowed. She took his arm reluctantly, glad of her gloves so no part of her skin was touching him. She assumed he would lead her back to Lady Fitzhugh as Phineas had done. But her mind was in a welter and she did not pay attention to which direction they walked.

She was surprised to find herself pushed out of the noise

of the ballroom, through a door, into a narrow corridor. Reeves stood in front of the now-closed door.

"Shall we find somewhere more private than this hallway where you can exercise your tongue, Helen?"

"Nae. I must go back to the ballroom." She waited for him to step aside. He did not.

"Do you have partners waiting for you there?"

"I have Lady Fitzhugh, my chaperone, and Lord Burchester."

"Ah, yes. Lord Burchester. I met him the other day. And this evening he has been making the rounds of the gentlemen, trying to find partners for you. Apparently, none of the men he has approached are his friends. It's almost as if he wants to pawn you off on people he doesn't know. Ashamed of you, no doubt."

"Let me pass, Lord Reeves. Ye dinnae want to be discovered in a hallway with a woman who cannae get another partner."

"You don't know what I want, Lady Kinmarloch."

"Ye dinnae want me, I assure ye."

"You're right. I don't want you. I want Kinmarloch. I want it as grazing land. And I want my son to be an earl. So we are going to stand here until someone finds us and you are compromised and have to marry me. I have arranged for a witness to your ruin. He should be here shortly."

"Ye think I would marry ye if I were compromised?"

"Yes, because no one else would ever have you."

She laughed. A laugh too high in pitch. She was close to breaking. "Yer a fool. Nae man wants me anyway. And I would never marry ye with yer plans for clearances when all I care for is Kinmarloch."

He raised his eyebrows. "I could put a child in you."

"Nae, Lord Reeves. How about I put something in ye instead?"

TWENTY-NINE

J ack pressed a rather large sum into the hand of the leader
of the musicians playing at the Titchfield Ball and made
it known who he was and what he wanted.

The man bowed and looked Jack over. "I suppose in
those clothes you'll blend in with the rest of us, Your Grace.
We'll put an extra chair in back of the bass viol. You'll have a
fairly good view of the ballroom from there. And no one looks
at the musicians."

"Good."

Jack carried in the bass viol himself, blocking his face, and
now sat behind the musicians tuning their instruments, his
hands on his knees, waiting to see Helen.

*Why am I here? I just want to see her, that's all, and not
have her see me. And then I'll go.*

The room began to fill with people. Helen was announced
and he spotted her figure sheathed in blue, but she was too far
away for him to see her face. Then she was meeting other
ladies, moving around the room with an older woman who
must be the chaperone Phineas had engaged for her.

Jack couldn't see Helen as well as he wanted, but he

was afraid to shift position. Phineas was speaking to various other men on the edges of the ballroom. Good, he was finding dance partners for Helen. Potential husbands.

The musicians started playing, and Phineas danced with Helen. Her jaw was jutting, and Jack knew she was trying to concentrate. He could see Phineas' mouth moving, talking incessantly. There. Helen had smiled politely. Once. Once was better than no times at all. And she was wearing his mother's jewelry he had sent her.

Why am I here? I'll stay for the next dance. Just to make sure she gets another partner. Just to see if she smiles again.

After the dance was over and Phineas had taken Helen back to her chaperone, Jack had a better view. Helen was close to where the musicians sat, and he could see her expression. She was under some strain, he could tell. It must be difficult for her to be here, to nod pleasantly and not to scowl. To hide herself and who she was.

And then her back straightened and her face reddened.

Jack followed her gaze to see what had caused the change in her. She was staring at the group of men Phineas had engaged in conversation.

She must know he's finding partners for her and she's embarrassed. He looked at the men. He knew a few casually and did not think much of them, including the blond Duke of Thornwick. But Jack had told Phineas to stay away from their mutual friends, hadn't he? So no one would happen to mention Jack Pike to Helen and let it slip he was the Duke of Dunmore. But surely there were better candidates than those fellows?

The men were looking at Helen and shaking their heads at Phineas.

She's a countess in her own goddamn right, you bleeding arseholes.

He looked back at Helen. Her face was carved from Aberdeen granite.

I did this. I made her do this. She didn't want this. I exposed her to these idiots who are making her feel badly about herself. Why am I here? You're the arsehole, Jack Pike.

He almost got up and left, not caring if someone saw him. But as he went to rise, his view of Helen was blocked by a man. A familiar man. Lord Feces. Jack kept his seat, his body tense.

Helen and Reeves spoke for perhaps half a minute, and he saw Helen take Reeves' arm and move to the center of the ballroom.

No.

If he had driven her to Reeves by writing that letter and by having her come to this ball, he would never forgive himself. He watched them dance. He was glad to see Helen's face continued to be stony. Then her mouth moved and she was finally speaking to Reeves. *I hope she's cutting him apart. Lopping off his head with a verbal claymore.*

The dance was over. Applause. The dancers began to mill about, chatting, laughing, returning to the periphery of the room, going for their glasses of lemonade or ratafia or stronger stuff.

He couldn't see Helen. He couldn't see Reeves. He stood up and searched the crowd. No flash of blue, that very particular blue he had made her wear.

Why am I here? I'm here to protect Helen.

He made his way to the front of the raised platform for the musicians. He didn't care who saw him. He needed to comb this ballroom until he found her and then he needed to get her out of here, away from these people, and then…he didn't know what then.

He jumped down from the platform to the ballroom floor

just as he had jumped off his ship to save the ship cat from drowning.

A jar. A much bigger jar than he had expected. Platform higher than he thought. Floor harder than water.

He took a step forward and immediately fell down, crashing into the couple who had been closest to the musicians when the dance ended.

"Pardon me, pardon me." He tried to get up and was surprised to find he could not support himself on his leg and he was on the floor again.

And then the pain. The unbelievably agonizing pain in his right ankle as he tried to stand. He crumpled to the floor again.

"Pardon me," he managed to get out again to the man he had tumbled down who was now up and helping his partner off the floor. Jack went to rise once more and again he could not. And the pain was worse.

"Helen!" he shouted. "Helen!"

He heard *Dunmore* and *His Grace*. He was recognized. It didn't matter. All that mattered was that he had to find his countess. He started crawling, dragging the excruciating ankle over the parquet floor. "Helen!"

Phineas was there, kneeling down, blocking his way. "Jack."

"Phin. You have to find Helen. Bring Helen here to me. She was with Lord Reeves. Go get her. Find her."

"Yes, Jack." Phineas disappeared.

Oh, my God. The pain.

He gave up crawling and collapsed flat to the floor. A phalanx of footmen surrounded him and stooped as if preparing to lift him.

"Don't fucking touch me," he snarled, lifting his head off the ground. "I'm waiting for the Countess of Kinmarloch."

The largest pair of shoes in London hove into view.

Edmund. And then the most perfectly polished pair of shoes. He looked up. George squatted down.

George's stern voice, taking charge as always. "Jack. We have to get you out of the ballroom. You are distressing the ladies with your screaming and your colorful language. And we need to have a doctor examine you. Edmund can pick you up or these footmen can. Your choice."

He allowed himself to be picked up by the footmen. Jack was all too sure Edmund was capable of slinging him over his shoulder and taking him out of the ballroom like he was a recalcitrant child with his arse pointing toward the ceiling.

"Don't touch my foot. Fuck!"

Edmund walked by Jack's side as he was being carried. Jack grabbed his arm. "Go find Phin. Take George. You have to help Phin find the Countess of Kinmarloch for me. Small woman. Blue dress. Brown hair."

It suddenly struck Jack as insane that those six words —*small woman blue dress brown hair*—comprised his description of Helen. But *brutally honest* and *eats me with her eyes* would sound like drivel.

Edmund nodded and turned away.

Find my thistle, Jack wanted to shout after him.

Jack was taken to a drawing room and put on a sofa. A doctor came in and removed Jack's hose and shoe while Jack howled and cursed. The doctor felt the deformed ankle. Much more firmly than was surely necessary, and Jack cursed some more.

"A fracture with an associated dislocation of the joint, Your Grace. I'll have to reduce the dislocation." He went into his bag. "I'll give you some morphia for the pain—"

"No morphia." Jack shook his head. "No morphia. I need my wits." He turned to one of the footmen standing nearby. "Do you know if anyone has found the Countess of Kinmarloch?"

"No, Your Grace."

"Well, goddamn it, go find out!"

The footman went to leave but the doctor held his hand out and stayed him. "I'm going to need you."

Another footman came in and spoke in the doctor's ear. The doctor turned to the man, astonished. "Another patient? Let me take care of His Grace quickly, and I'll come."

The doctor turned to Jack. "Are you certain you don't want morphia?" Jack shook his head, and the doctor turned to the footmen in the room. "Please keep His Grace from moving."

Five footmen held Jack's arms and his left leg and pressed his torso into the sofa as the doctor picked up Jack's right foot by its big toe. While Jack tried very hard not to scream, the doctor pulled on his heel and turned his foot. Jack felt the clunk of the joint. Then slowly, the pain went from excruciating to searing.

"There." The doctor put Jack's foot down on the sofa and went and picked up his bag. "Don't move, Your Grace, or we'll have to do it again. I won't mind, but you will. Your language reminds me of my time in the navy. I'll be back shortly, I hope."

The doctor left just as Edmund came in the door.

"Did you find her?" Then Jack noticed the gout of blood on Edmund's cravat. A cold wave of fear washed over him. "Whose blood is that?"

"Down, Jack. It's not from the countess. Phineas says the bleeding man's name is Reeves."

"Where's Lady Kinmarloch?"

"I don't know. Phineas and George are still looking for her. If they don't find her here, Phineas says he'll go to her rooms."

"Good." Then, "Why is Reeves bleeding?"

A small, grim smile from Edmund. The equivalent of a

broad grin from anybody else. "He won't say who did it to him but someone cut his face up very badly with a knife. Not deep cuts, but a lot of them. Very disfiguring. And he seems, uh, very frightened that the villain might come back and do it again. I had to shake him a bit, but he still wouldn't tell me who did it. And he was cupping his hands in front of his bollocks. Seems he was threatened with the removal of those."

His savage countess with her dirk.

I'm not here to protect Helen. I've gotten it all wrong from the beginning. That was never my job.

The doctor came back. "Messy. That'll take hours to sew up. But we'll get your ankle splinted and get you taken home, Your Grace. And I'll call tomorrow."

"I can't go home, I have to find someone."

"No, Your Grace. You have to go home. You can't walk, you can't travel. You are going to be in London, in your house, for the next four months. Otherwise, you might not heal properly."

"I don't give a damn about healing properly."

"Well, you should. Because I'm sure you'd like to be able to walk in the future."

Jack groaned, not from pain but from impotence. "Edmund."

"Do what the doctor says, Jack. I'll go help Phineas."

PHINEAS AND EDMUND came into Jack's bedchamber in his town house just as his own butler and coachman and three footmen were getting Jack settled in his bed. There had been a long delay in his transport back to his town house as he had been carried home in a litter, the doctor feeling that cobblestones under carriage wheels would endanger the ankle, despite the splint.

"Tell me, Phin."

"She wasn't at the ball, Jack. We looked everywhere. I found Reeves cut up as Edmund told you. So I went to her rooms. Empty, except for some jewels and some dresses. Including the one she was wearing tonight. With blood on it."

"Duncan, Mags. Were they there?"

Phineas shook his head. "No, the Highlander and the angel were gone, too."

"What are you doing here? You have to go look for them."

Phineas exchanged looks with Edmund. "I had my carriage take me to Hicks' Hall since it's the departure point for coaches going north. Two women, one with red hair, and a very tall man, also with red hair, got on the midnight mail coach."

Jack clutched at his waistcoat pocket and pulled out his watch. It was two o'clock in the morning. He fell back against the pillows.

Helen was well out of London. She would be in Bedfordshire by dawn.

She wasn't afraid of anything. What was she fleeing?

Reeves? Arrest?

No.

She's running away from me.

THIRTY

To Helen Boyd, the Countess of Kinmarloch.
My lady:

I was informed you have left London, but I hope this letter finds you safe at home in Kinmarloch.

I am writing to thank you for the return letter you sent via Captain Pike, and for the beginning of my education about the Highlands. I am following your advice and there will be no more clearances in Dunmore. In fact, I will see if it might be possible to have some of my farmers return unless they are happier where they are now.

I beg you will continue to endeavor to enlighten me as to the direction of the administration of Dunmore. I know it is a place for which you have a great affection and this, combined with your wisdom, can only lead to your having the best grasp as to what should be done there now and in the future.

Although I have no plans to marry (as I told you in my first letter), I hope you will consider yourself my proxy *duchess and tell me what I should do and the best way to do it. If you have the time and patience, of course.*

I have been much occupied of late with reading. I have taken up Mr. Walter Scott's "The Lady of the Lake." It concerns Scotland and the Highlands. Have you read it? I am only in the second canto of six and I am waiting for the action to get started since I was told it would have battles and bloodshed. But so far there has just been a hunt and a great deal of poetry. There is a Lady Ellen in the poem and I believe Helen, your name, is a form of Ellen, is it not? Lady Ellen is in love with a valiant young knight named Malcolm but a bloodthirsty Highland chief named Roderick wants her. Her father, good chap, says he will not commit her to a loveless marriage. I think Ellen and Malcolm will be betrothed by the end of the poem. What do you think?

There's a Scottish king in the poem, too—your King James V. He was the father of Mary, Queen of Scots, wasn't he? Right now in the poem, he is traveling in disguise, and I have heard there is a legend mooted about that he used to do just that. He would travel anonymously among his people to find out their burdens, the abuses they might suffer under their lords. Rather absurd, right? A king pretending to be someone else, a common man. But maybe his motives make up for his deceit? What do you think?

How is your weather? I understand it rains there frequently. Does your roof leak when it rains?

I hope, again, this letter finds you well. And I hope you will write to me again, if only to tell me how you are faring. I am interested in even the smallest detail of your life in Kinmarloch, and I hope you will indulge me.

> Yrs. sincerely,
> John MacNaughton,
> Duke of Dunmore.

PS I have heard our neighbor to the south, Lord Reeves, suffered some injuries recently. He has not named the perpetrator, but I suspect a farmer whom Reeves may have cleared from his lands in too forceful a manner. Lord Reeves has not been seen in public since his assault but has made it widely known he will not return to Scotland. From what I hear of Reeves from Captain Pike, I think our corner of the Highlands will be a better place for his absence. The man was lucky to escape with all his bits intact.

PPS Please send return correspondence to my club at the address below.

To the Duke of Dunmore, John MacNaughton.
My lord duke:

My life leaves me no time for reading. And in my keep where I lived until recently, any book would have been destroyed by damp. But even before that, I was not a great reader. My grandfather would read to me at times, and I liked that. As I told you before, I do not have much education.

I live in a new cottage now and it is very snug and no rain comes in which is a blessing. So, perhaps in the future, I will be able to have books and time for reading.

This is a long way of saying I have not read the poem "The Lady of the Lake."

I agree with you that in a poem the two lovers should be

*together at the end. Otherwise, it would be too much like
the world and not like a poem. And it's good the father in
the poem insists his daughter marry for love. Many noble-
men's daughters are not allowed that.*

*I have a young woman under my care named
Margaret who is very much in love. My dearest wish is she
will be able to marry her sweetheart, in time.*

*I hope your current devotion to reading does not mean
you are not well and cannot be active. Are you well?*

> *Yr. Friend,*
> *Helen Boyd.*

Dear Helen:

*You signed your last letter Helen Boyd so I am hoping I
may address you as Helen without giving offense.*

*And as to your question—I am well! I am well. Have
no worries on that point. I am merely circumscribed
temporarily. I am in London now and among my friends
here, which is good.*

*I hope you enjoy the book of the poem "The Lady of the
Lake" which I have sent with this letter.*

Are you well? Are you eating well?

> *Yr. Friend,*
> *John MacNaughton.*

What is the meaning of circumscribed?

*Thank you for the book which came with your letter.
I did try to read last night, but I fell asleep after only a*

few lines. I will try again tonight after writing this letter.

I am eating well, thank you. Are you eating well? I am glad you have your friends around you. Are they all gentlemen friends?

> *Yr. Friend,*
> *Helen Boyd.*

Circumscribed means limited or restrained. My friend George Danforth, the Baron Danforth, who makes a study of the origin of words says it comes from Latin. Circum means around (like a circle) and scribere means to write—so it is literally to draw a circle around something. I have a little circle drawn around me and cannot move from it. But I am well, I assure you.

Do not press yourself to read if you are tired. You should rest. The book will not run away even if it is not read.

But is it possible you are working too hard, Lady Kinmarloch? Is there anything I, or the people of Dunmore, can do to help?

I am eating well. Maybe too well, considering my sloth.

My friends are all men. They may be called gentlemen, but they are not. Our masculine talk is rough and unfit for ladies. And I find myself not interested in the ladies of London.

> *Yr. Friend,*
> *John MacNaughton.*

Do not restrain your language with me, Your Grace. We Scots are a rough, coarse bunch and I myself have been known to use foul language at times. In fact, sometimes I think I should have been a sailor, I have such a tendency to curse.

> Yr. Friend,
> Helen Boyd.

Have you found the waking hours to read "The Lady of the Lake"? I am anxious to hear what you think of the king in disguise. I will tell you Lady Ellen rejects the king when he makes a suit to her, wanting only to marry the man she loves. Of course, the king is in disguise at the time. Otherwise, perhaps she would have accepted him. But the king, I think, was wise to test her, to see if Lady Ellen wanted him without his crown.

Your mention of being a sailor made me realize you have not asked in your previous letters about our mutual acquaintance, Captain Pike. I know you met him on his trip to Dunmore and again in London. I hope you are still friends and you feel warmly toward him.

> Yr. Friend, John.

I am ashamed to admit I still have not read the poem you sent me. I find I am only interested in reading one thing—your letters. I do take the book out every evening with good intentions but do not progress beyond the first few verses. I just think I am not a good reader.

I am a good listener, however. I wish I were a Countess of Kinmarloch from five hundred years ago with a bard to recite stories to me.

And as to Captain Pike, he is a very worthy gentleman and was nothing but generosity itself to me during our acquaintance. I wish him well. Is he well?

Yr. Friend, Helen.

Do not be ashamed! I sent you the book so you would have some amusement. And, yes, so I might hear your thoughts on it. Pure selfishness on my part. I didn't mean to give you another task. Burn the blasted poem, if you wish!

Captain Pike is well and asks after you. He is worried about the sudden and heavy storms which come in Scotland. He wants to make sure your roof is snug.

Yr. Friend, John.

The roof is tight-fitting on my cottage. There is nary a leak. Please tell Captain Pike to have no concerns. All is well in Kinmarloch.

Yr. Friend, Helen.

In your last letter, you said all is well in Kinmarloch.

But you said nothing of your own health. Please tell me if
you are you well?

Yr. Friend, John.

You should have no concerns about me, Your Grace. I
am well, I am eating well, and the roof is snug.

Yr. Friend, Helen.

You mentioned a Miss Margaret at one time, in one of
your letters. Is she well?
And I have realized the cost of replying to my letters
must be very high. I do not want to cause expense by asking
you to answer me. Will you allow me to pay for the cost of
your post?

Yr. Friend, John.

I can afford the cost of the letters. Miss Margaret is
very well.

Yr. Friend, Helen.

When our correspondence first began, Captain Pike told

me you had hoped for a marriage for yourself soon. Have you had any suitors upon your return to Kinmarloch? Are there any men who have taken your fancy or captured your heart?

Yr. Friend, John.

I have not had a reply from you as quickly as your letters usually come. I hope you are well? And I hope I have not offended you in any way?

Yr. Friend, John.

I am concerned my letters are getting lost on their way to you. I have not heard back now in twice the time it usually takes for you to reply. Are you still receiving my letters? Is something wrong? Are you unwell in anyway? I am exceedingly anxious on your behalf and would appreciate a reply by the soonest return possible.

Yr. Friend, John.

THIRTY-ONE

P hineas sat with a small table in front of him, quill poised over foolscap.

"What next, Jack?"

"That's it. That's all." Jack moved a pile of books away from his still-splinted leg. The doctor said he was close to being able to put weight on it again, but not quite yet. Maybe next week.

The last fourteen weeks had been the most miserable of Jack's life. Worse than the lost months after his broken engagement to Elizabeth, when he had often found himself drunk or raging or copulating with whores. Sometimes all three, at once.

And yes, he had had some drunken stupors in the first week after the Titchfield ball and Helen's flight from London. But then the doctor had scolded him, warned Jack's household staff not to let him indulge, upbraided his friends for bringing him whisky.

"The care for your leg will mean nothing if you rise from this bed in four months as a habitual drunk, Your Grace. You will break the leg again or you'll break your skull or you'll become yellow and bloated. You'll die a young man in an old man's body."

Like my father did.

The doctor's admonition cut through the haze of Jack's pain and intoxication. Maybe because the man had been in the navy and was unfazed by Jack's surliness and curse words.

"What the hell am I to do then in this goddamn bed, Doctor? How am I going to survive this fucking prison sentence?"

"Your body cannot be active so you must make your mind active to compensate. You can see to the administration of your duchy from afar, can't you? And you should read. Read something that might involve you. Your duchy is in the Highlands? Read *The Lady of the Lake*, by Mr. Walter Scott, a Scottish poet. And you should write. Write letters to friends."

"My friends are here. In London. They don't need letters."

"Surely there is someone you know, far from London, who is doing something of interest to you. Someone who might take pity on you and write you back and tell you of his own life. So you can remember there is more to the world than this room and your pain."

Yes, there was such a person. Of course, there was.

Helen.

He drank no more whisky or wine or even small beer. He found himself sipping weak tea, all day, every day. Tea almost as weak as the tea he had drunk in the keep of the Countess of Kinmarloch.

He hired a new steward, a clever man who was frank and unapologetic. He instructed the steward to make sure the castle became a patron of the farmers and blacksmith of Kinmarloch. Money must flow to the earldom from Dunmore, but it must not appear to be charity.

He read extensively on the issue of clearances and then made offers to resettle farmers back in Dunmore. He had money enough to buy time for the duchy and the earldom. Time to find the livelihoods Helen had mentioned in her letter to the duke that she had written when she was still in London. Livelihoods that would support the people despite the barren soil and harsh conditions.

He had roped Phineas in. He had to. Phineas had penned the letter to Helen as the Duke of Dunmore, and that letter had not been found in the abandoned rooms. Helen could have taken the letter with her when she left London. She might compare the handwriting. The Duke of Dunmore must continue to write in Phineas' sloping script.

Because it must be the duke who wrote to Helen, not Captain Pike. Jack was sure Helen wouldn't answer any letters from the man who had fornicated with her and then put her up for sale on the marriage mart and exposed her to multiple indignities at the Titchfield ball.

He had difficulty exercising patience, waiting for her return letters. As soon as one arrived and he had read it a hundred times until he knew it by heart, he would thunder and bluster at his valet or his butler until someone went and fetched the Earl of Burchester so the Duke of Dunmore could reply to the Countess of Kinmarloch.

"You're trying me," Phineas had said a fortnight ago, dropping into a wing chair in Jack's bedchamber.

One of Jack's footmen, desperate not to return without the earl, had gone to the house of Phineas' new mistress, Lady Starling, and had him roused from her bed.

"Some of us are trying to conduct affairs with women in person, you know."

"Don't rub it in, Phin," Jack had growled. "Now, get ready to write."

"It's a good thing you saved my life years ago on the *Endeavor*, John MacNaughton. Otherwise, I would be breaking your other leg."

"John MacNaughton didn't save your life. Jack Pike did."

"You really must work toward seeing they are the same man. Because if you don't, how are you going to get Helen to see it?"

"What are you talking about?"

"I thought that was what you were trying to do with your letters. They're full of hints."

"No. They're not. They're friendly letters."

"The king in disguise in the poem? The love match? Not marrying for a title? She's not stupid."

"She has no idea, Phin. I would know if she knew. She can't lie, she can't deceive."

"You finally found an honest woman, eh, Jack? And you say she hates you? Pity."

"Pity? What pity?"

"I admit I didn't appreciate what you saw in her, at first. But now I do. From what you've told me about her, she worships your physical being even as she lays waste to your charming nonsense. A lethal combination for a man who craves love from behind the mask of a scoundrel."

"Phin, you have no conception. She knows I'm a scoundrel. There's no mask."

The earl laughed. "For a woman who labors as hard as you say she does, she's spending an awful lot of her time writing to the Duke of Dunmore. She must believe *he's* not a scoundrel."

"Exactly. That's why you're involved. Now, shut up and write what I tell you."

What he had dictated then had been the foolish letter to Helen where he had probed as to whether she had suitors, if she had found a man. He would never have asked such damn stupid questions if Phineas hadn't gotten him so riled. So needing. So wanting reassurance she was still free and some part of her belonged only to him.

She hadn't yet replied to that letter even though he had sent two more letters. Two rather begging letters.

Now, Phineas looked down at the foolscap and frowned. "That's all? You've had me write, *Helen,* full stop. *Don't get quiet,* full stop."

"Yes. Sign it, John. Just John."

"That's all you're going to write her?"

"She likes things unvarnished. She'll answer that."

Helen.

    Don't get quiet.

                John.

Ten days later, the very day the doctor told him he could start to walk on his right leg, he received her answer.

To John MacNaughton, the Duke of Dunmore.
My Lord Duke:

    I am happy to continue to advise you about your duchy, and I like reading your letters, but please do not mistake this correspondence for true intimacy.

    Although I wear breeches six days out of seven, although my language can be coarse (as I have told you), I am still a woman. And my womanly heart will only be open to one man—my husband. I must ask you not to expect me to reveal anything to you which should only be told to him.

                Yrs. Sincerely,
                Helen Boyd,
                Countess of Kinmarloch.

He paced his study that night, exercising the leg probably more than the doctor intended him to.

His epistolary friendship with Helen was over. She had cut him off, just as she had when she had held out her letter to the Duke of Dunmore, shoving it into his chest and telling him she couldn't be his lover anymore.

Helen knew her worth.

She wouldn't waste herself on a man who stayed hidden behind missives, lurking in London like the scoundrel he called himself. No matter that the man was doing everything he could to improve the lot of Dunmore and Kinmarloch.

She demanded a high price for the privilege of knowing her heart. And she was right to do so.

And the price—did he really think it was that high? He had lived years now behind the façade of a rakehell, concealing the man he was, the man he could be, the man he now wanted to be. Giving that up wouldn't be a price. It would be a reward.

And was there anything else in the world he wanted as much as he wanted her?

No.

But was he worthy of her?

No.

Did he have anything to offer her besides his money and his title?

He heard the case clock strike the hour. He took out his watch and looked at it. Midnight. The hour when he thought of her in Kinmarloch, in her bed, without him.

He came to three conclusions as the clock made its twelfth soft chime.

One. It didn't matter whether or not he was worthy. He must cast that into the wind and hope the *Anemoi* were kind to him.

Two. He had something to give her. Yes, his desire for her,

his cock, his tongue, his lips, his hands. But also something he didn't know he had to give before.

His love. He could name it now for what it was. Something more than admiration and respect. Something much greater than physical passion. Something that eclipsed possession, and even obsession. He didn't know the size of it but he suspected it was as limitless as a blue expanse of sky. And it belonged to her.

Three. His heart, his mind, his soul—every piece of him, apart from his body, was in Scotland.

The woman for him, the only woman for him, was in Scotland.

Therefore, he should be in Scotland.

THIRTY-TWO

Helen got into the boat, shoved off from the shore, and rowed into the middle of her loch. This was a luxury she allowed herself in these relatively warm days of summer. She went out in this little boat which was always by the empty hut at the edge of the loch. She rowed the way she had seen Jack Pike row on the River Thames when she had looked at him and thought of him as a young man in the navy and had imagined what a son of his might look like.

She could afford this now. This time and this strength to do something that brought no food to her table. The new steward of the duchy of Dunmore made a point of coming to Kinmarloch and buying from her farmers instead of at the market at Cumdairessie. And buying her own lambs as well. Duncan's father's forge was busy with work for the castle and the stable there.

There would be no want this winter in Kinmarloch. Everyone, barring illness or accident, should make it through. Including herself.

Duncan had come to her a month ago, frowning, worried. He had been offered a job at the castle as a farrier, but he had delayed accepting it, thinking Helen might feel abandoned. She had urged him to take the position.

"But can I still be yer honor guard, my lady, even if I work for the Duke of Dunmore?"

"Aye, Duncan. Ye will always be my honor guard. Take the post."

She had left the cottage quickly then, Mags sitting in a chair, her forgotten darning in her lap, Duncan hitching up the legs of his trousers in preparation for kneeling at her feet.

The wedding would be in two weeks.

Helen brought her oars up and got off her seat and lay down in the bottom of the boat. She looked up at the sky. She heard her name, but one often did hear odd things when one was out on the water. Ghost voices.

The sky was not the beautiful blue dome it sometimes was. Clouds scudded quickly across her view. Gray clouds, not white like the lace which edged the neck and the sleeves of the dress she was wearing today. It was the one dress she had taken with her from London since she had to have one to travel in.

She would have time to earn the money for a winter dress, herself. And so far, she had managed to keep this dress clean. She touched the lace around the neckline of the dress.

She heard her name again and felt an odd sensation all over her body. She held her forearm up in front of her face and could see each individual hair was erect. The air was full of menace. There must be a fast-approaching squall, blown off the sea, with no warning.

The boat rocked with a sudden wave.

She sat up from the bottom of the boat and thought she saw a figure along the edge of the loch, waving both arms at her. But she knew she must be quick so she turned and took her seat and got her oars in the water and began rowing.

Within seconds, there was torrential rain. Heavier and more violent than the rainstorm she and Jack Pike had driven her cart through from Cumdairessie to Kinmarloch when the roof of the keep had collapsed.

Flashes of lightning and cracks of thunder. Wind and white tops on waves which had not been there just moments ago.

She fought the oars, panting, unsure if she was still directed toward the nearest shore. The rain pelted her eyes and splashed into her open mouth. The bottom of her boat began to fill with water from the rain and from waves coming over the sides.

She pulled on her oars. She bent her strong back and she pulled. She pulled. She pulled. She twisted her body, trying to see where she was going, trying to find the shoreline. She could see nothing but rain and a wild, tossing loch.

The water in the boat covered her feet, her ankles, and was creeping up her calves. Her mind was empty of everything but the need to pull, to get to land, to pull.

A big wave came up and the boat did not ride it but dipped under it and the boat was completely full of water and going away from her into the down deep and she was surrounded by water and her tired arms were thrashing and water was going into her mouth.

She sank down under the surface.

A jerk. Something strong around her waist. Her head up above the waves. Gasping. A body next to hers, holding her against him.

The most beautiful man she had ever seen.

He turned her away from him and yoked an arm around her chest and she had no sense of movement, only water on her face from waves and the rain. The crack of thunder. Her own thudding heart.

But he must have been moving because she was being dragged over something solid and she was lying on land. She clutched the earth next to her. She was safe.

His face over hers. "Helen."

She put muddy hands to his cheeks. "*Mo luran.*"

She was being lifted off the ground and carried. She grabbed his shoulders, turned her face into his chest, wanting to bury herself in him.

Then there was no more rain falling on her face or body. He had taken her into the little hut on the shore. He laid her on the earthen floor and now their bodies were not touching. He knelt next to her, his chest heaving. The rain thrummed heavy on the thatched roof.

She struggled to sit up. "Jack Pike."

"Rest, Helen. Rest."

She found his hand and clutched it, lifted it, brought it to her chest and lay back.

They stayed that way for some time, her lying, him kneeling, looking in each other's eyes, unable to draw breath fully. She held his hand over her heart as the thunder rolled and boomed.

Jack's cheeks were smeared with mud where she had touched him. He was still the sunrise and the stars, but there was something different about him besides the mud. He had pain in his eyes and all she wanted to do was wipe it away, like it was the mud on his face.

But she didn't know how she could do that.

And she didn't know how to be in the same place as the man she loved.

Finally, she spoke. "I dinnae know how to swim."

"No."

"Ye saved me."

He shook his head. "No more rowing until you learn how to swim."

"Aye. Thank ye."

A deep breath and she sat up and let go of his hand. "Yer here, Jack Pike."

"Yes."

"Ye said ye would never come to Scotland again. I thought ye meant it. I thought I could count on it."

THOSE FIERCE BLUE HALF-MOON EYES. Her wet hair, plastered to her head. A drop of water at the tip of her nose.

Jack got off his knees and sat cross-legged. He winced a little, feeling some strain in his right calf. The bone was strong now, but he had not used the muscles of the leg in a long time and he had just done the most vigorous kicking of his life.

"I didn't know my own mind. About a lot of things."

"Aye."

"I was dishonest. To myself."

"Aye."

"And to you."

She was suddenly very still. Jack felt like the air between them was solid, crystalline.

Minutes ago, his entire life's happiness had hinged on getting to her before she became lifeless and sank to the bottom of the loch. And now his whole future depended on how she took what he said next.

"From the moment you met me, Helen, you knew I was less than sincere."

"Nae, I—" He raised his eyebrows and she grimaced. "Aye."

"You knew I was a flatterer and a flirt and a philanderer, but you didn't know how much of a liar I was."

He looked away. He had steeled himself for this and now he couldn't even look her in the eyes when he told her.

"I have to tell you something."

"Nae, ye dinnae have to—"

"I am the Duke of Dunmore. I am John MacNaughton." A crack of thunder. "You have every right to be angry."

He forced himself to look at her. Her chin was trembling and he did not know if it was from cold or rage or some other emotion.

"I lied. I deceived you. Innocently at first, but I kept the deception going. I was unfair to you."

He couldn't read her eyes. He wanted Helen to say something, give him some clue about how she was receiving his confession, but she stayed silent.

"I wanted you, Helen, so I kept lying to you. And I fell in love with you. But I didn't know it. Or I did know, but I didn't want to know it because I didn't think I could love anybody and I thought you couldn't love me—"

She must have lunged at him from her seated position because suddenly he was lying on the ground and she was on top of him.

"Ye. Fell. In. Love. With me?"

"Yes."

She kissed his mouth, his nose, his cheeks, his eyes. She kissed him like she had gasped for air when he had found her and brought her up to the surface of the loch. Frantically.

"Jack." She said between kisses. "Jack."

He stroked her wet hair, trying to calm her. Finally, she stopped kissing him and just sat atop him, looking down at him, her own face now smeared with mud from his.

"Do ye still love me?" she asked.

"Yes."

She shook her head as if she still didn't believe him. He grabbed both of her hands.

"I love you more than ever, Helen Boyd. Your last letter. I want your heart. I'll do anything I can to get it."

"Do ye know I love you?"

His breath seized in his chest. "No."

"Well, then ye are a very stupid man. Because I do love ye. I have loved ye ever since ye named me. Ye called me a thistle and then I knew ye knew me, Jack Pike."

The thing he had said to her in her bed, his impulsive truth she had accused him of rehearsing. Now, he knew what that look in her eyes had meant. And she was giving him that same look now.

"I don't deserve your love, little thistle." He reached up and put his hand over her heart again. It was racing, beating a tattoo against her chest.

"It dinnae matter if ye deserve it. Ye have it and ye cannae give it away."

Here it was. He hadn't planned for it to be this way. On his long trip north, he had developed some harebrained notion of coming to her cottage at four in the morning and bundling her up and putting her on a horse in front of him and taking her up one of the Benrancree mountains to see the summer stars and then the sunrise.

But maybe this was more fitting. The rain. Both of them soaking wet. The mud on their faces. Her sitting on top of him.

"Will you marry me, Helen Boyd, Countess of Kinmarloch?"

She squinted at him, suddenly prickly. "Who is asking me? Jack Pike, the most beautiful man in the world, or John Mac-Naughton, the Duke of Dunmore, the man who promises to save the people of Kinmarloch?"

"Whichever one is going to get yes for an answer."

"And I will agree to marry whichever one promises to be a good husband."

He sat up and took her face in his hands.

"I thought you would hate me."

"I never hated ye. Never. Ye know that. I hated that I wanted ye and I thought I couldnae have ye."

"You're not angry about my deception?"

"Aye. I was angry at first."

"At first? For how long? Three seconds?"

Her brow furrowed into a scowl. "Do ye think ye are marrying a fool? I have known Jack Pike was John MacNaughton ever since that letter came to me. In London. From the duke. Where ye said ye widnae marry. Ye used that word *purported*. A purported scoundrel. Said ye widnae be a good husband. It was in a different hand than yers, but I knew Jack Pike had written that letter."

She had known in London. It was why she had told him she couldn't be Jack Pike's lover any longer. Because she knew he was talking about himself in the letter.

"Why didn't you say something then? Punish me? Rip me to shreds for lying to you?"

"I knew I loved ye. But ye dinnae want to marry me, and I thought I would have to marry some other man. But if I let ye continue as ye were, being Jack Pike, I could keep ye out of Scotland as long as ye thought ye were fooling me. 'Twas selfish because the duchy needs its duke here. But. I. Couldnae…" Her eyes filled with tears and she trembled. "I couldnae bear the thought ye would be so near me, in the future, here. It was painful to hide my thoughts from ye. 'Tis nae my way. And 'twas hard nae to lie with ye again, to touch ye and kiss ye. But I knew it would be far more painful and hard to have ye near me for the rest of my life when I would be married to some other man I dinnae love. Ye must forgive me for lying to ye." Her tears ran down her face, streaking the mud on her cheeks.

"Helen, only you would ask for forgiveness for going along with my lie. I'm the one who should be begging for your forgiveness. For the lies, for not knowing my own heart sooner, for sending you to that ball—"

Her fingers came up and pressed against his lips.

"Hush. I forgive ye. If ye'll kiss me."

He leaned forward. Her fingers fell away. He kissed that cider-flavored mouth he thought he would never get to kiss again. He kissed her softly and slowly, making sure he took her lips from every possible angle, their tongues sliding over each other in a dance far more intimate than a waltz.

He kissed her as if kissing was all they would ever share. He kissed her as if she had not yet accepted him and he might convince her with his kiss. He kissed her as if time had stopped and they were the only two people in the world. Because it had. And they were.

He made her be the one to break away, to pull her mouth from his to breathe. He would never again be the one to end a kiss between them. Ever. He put his forehead against hers.

"And you're really not angry at me now, Helen?"

Her panting turned into a little laugh and she leaned away from him. "How can I be angry, *mo luran*? When I am getting everything I ever wanted. The man I love and the man who will help me fulfill my duty. And, oh, yes, the sunrise and the stars in my bed every night for the rest of my life."

"Every night?"

"Every night."

"God, I love you, Helen."

He crushed her to him as tightly as he could and buried his face in her neck. Her arms were around him, her strong hands gripping his back. He was home. She was his home. His prickly home.

"I will never deceive you again, Helen."

"Good. I believe ye."

He raised his head and looked in her eyes. "You believe I won't lie to you again?"

"Aye."

"Then you have to believe this, Helen Boyd. You're beautiful." He cupped her muddy face in his hands. "You're beautiful. You're beautiful. You've always been beautiful."

She gazed at him. "I believe ye, Jack Pike."

"Good."

Her eyes widened. "But do I have to call ye John now?"

"You better call me Jack Pike. Always Jack Pike when we're in our bed." He seized her around her waist and lifted her off his lap and got to his feet, drawing her up with him.

"But we're nae in a bed now, are we?"

"Close enough. From now on, any place in Dunmore or Kinmarloch will qualify as our bed." He ran his hands over her back, her bottom, her hips, her abdomen, and ended at her breasts, the nipples pointed and hard under his palms. He wanted those nipples in his mouth now.

"I think I should get you out of these wet clothes."

"And I think I should do the same for ye."

Her hands went to his fall even as he was reaching around her back for the buttons of her dress.

"I want to consummate our marriage right now, Helen."

"Ye know I want the same, *mo luran.*"

Oh, yes. There was that. One last thing. Now that he had her promise, he would ask. He clasped her wrists together with one of his hands and brought them to his chest.

"You must tell me."

"Tell ye what?"

"What does *mo luran* mean?"

She bit her lip. She looked away. "My pretty boy."

"Not man? Not pretty man? Or handsome man?"

She shook her head.

"So you named your dog Pretty Boy?"

"Aye."

"And you named me the same."

She stared at him, eating him with her eyes. "The dog is just Pretty Boy. Yer *my* pretty boy."

He let go of her wrists and grabbed her head and kissed her. A deep, long kiss, his hands not letting her move from him, owning his savage countess. Yes, he was hers, but he wanted her to be his, as well.

Her hands pushed against his abdomen so he reluctantly let go of her head and she got her mouth free to gasp, "Yer… yer nae angry?"

He chuckled softly. "How can I be angry, Helen? When I am getting everything I ever wanted." He groped her bottom briefly before unbuttoning the last button on the back of her muddy dress. "And something I didn't know I wanted."

"What didn't ye know ye wanted, Jack?"

He growled. "I didn't know." He took her dress off over her head. "That I would want." The chemise followed. "To share a name with a dog."

And then there was very little talking between the two wet and muddy people in the hut by the shore of the loch in Kinmarloch.

Only kissing.

Unlimited kissing.

And *dàireadh*.

FIRST EPILOGUE

E veryone agreed the bride was the loveliest bride in the history of Kinmarloch, if not the entirety of Scotland. And the groom was very tall.

It was a wedding most would remember well since the Duke of Dunmore himself walked the bride to her groom inside the small kirk. And many people saw the duke wink at one of the witnesses when he turned away from the bride at the altar. But only one person saw the Countess of Kinmarloch's grin in return. That one person was the duke, of course.

Then the duke and the countess seemed to be looking at each other a great deal during the wedding breakfast which was out-of-doors a little way down the hill from the cottage which sat next to the keep. All the food and drink had been put on trestle tables. And when the fiddle began to play and there was dancing, the duke claimed the countess for his partner for every dance except his dance with the bride and the countess' dance with the groom. And then, just before the redheaded newlyweds left in the duke's carriage, to go to Dunmore Castle where the duke had offered to host them until

their own cottage could be completed, neither the duke nor
the countess could be found anywhere.

"Jack, are ye mad?" Helen sputtered. "'Tis the middle of
the day. 'Tis the middle of the wedding breakfast."

Jack had pulled her into the keep and closed the door and
pushed her against one of the stone walls and was pinning her
there with his body.

"I thought you looked a little sad." He stroked her neck
with his fingers.

"I'm selfish. I'll miss Mags in the cottage."

"You won't be living in the cottage for that much longer."

"Aye."

"Cheer up, Helen. You'll still have me."

Yes, she would. The most beautiful man in the world.
Who made her feel beautiful.

"Aye, *mo luran.*"

"And I'm jealous of the bride and groom. They're going to
have fun in the middle of the day. Why can't we?"

The sounds of laughter and fiddle music filtered in. Bright
shafts of sunlight came through the not-yet-repaired roof of
the keep, and the gold flecks in Jack's hair glinted. He grinned
and Helen could feel his length against her and immediately an
ache started in her nether regions.

Jack ran his fingers over the skin of her chest, around the
lace on the neckline of the dress which she had worked very
hard to get clean enough to wear to this morning's wedding.

"I don't remember you being averse to my touching you in
the middle of the day before, Helen." He leaned down and
licked the shell of her ear. Her stomach flipped over.

She put her hands on his shoulders. "I cannae get my dress
dirty. And that was in London."

"I won't get your dress dirty, I promise. Not today anyway.

And only in London, you say? How about the middle of a stormy day, a fortnight ago?" His hands were on her breasts now, pinching her nipples through her dress.

"Ah-aye." She felt her own breathing become ragged as sharp sensations from the tips of her breasts raced to her groin. "By the loch. But I had just escaped mortal danger. Is it any wonder I would fall into the arms of the man who saved me?"

"And the day after that." His lips just barely touching hers. "And all the days between then and yesterday."

"I dinnae need reminding that ye make me a wanton woman, Jack Pike."

"Mmmmm." His hands slid down from her breasts along her sides and cupped her hips. His brown eyes had a wicked gleam in them as he looked down at her. "I want you to be *my* wanton woman, Helen."

"I am." She felt herself dissolving.

"Only mine." He lifted her leg to his waist and curled it around him.

"I am."

"Now and forever." Still holding her leg, he lifted her skirts with his other hand and touched her maidenhair and then his fingers were in her folds, caressing her.

"Ah, aye…" A finger grazed her small hardness and she inhaled sharply as all rational thought fled her mind. All resolve. "Oh, Jack, I must have ye, please."

He grinned. "No."

A finger at her entrance. Now inside her, stroking in and out of her, curled to hit the place that made her wild and boneless and wanting to scream.

"What are…ye doing?"

"I'm touching you." The finger was joined by another and the pace of the stroking increased.

"Ye are torturing me."

"Yes."

"I need ye, Jack."

"No."

She groaned. "What are ye doing?"

"I told you. I'm touching you. And I'm torturing you."

"Why?"

His mouth on her ear. "I want to announce our engagement now that Mags and Duncan are married. And I want a date for our wedding, Helen. You give me a day for the kirk, and I'll give you my cock."

She knew she wanted time for a dress. Time to lay in food for a feast for all of Dunmore and Kinmarloch, too. She knew she should be thinking of these things but somehow all she could think of were his fingers inside her, their movement, and how much better it would be if his member replaced his fingers.

His voice went on, low and purring. "It's simple, my thistle. A date. Then cock."

"Aye. Michaelmas then," she gasped.

The fingers became rougher, thrusting in and out of her more vigorously, his thumb coming up to stroke her little hardness. Her head lolled.

"It's August right now, thistle. Why are you saying Michaelmas?"

"I cannae…think."

"Let me suggest next week. Three days from now. We're in Scotland, after all. No need for banns or a license."

"I cannae think…but I think…fine. Next week." She pulled down his face so she could kiss his grinning mouth and his fingers were out of her and he must have unbuttoned his fall because his shaft thrust into her and she gasped against his mouth.

Both of her legs encircled his waist and both his hands were under her haunches, pulling her onto him as he pushed into her. She wrapped her arms around his neck.

"I'm glad…I've found a way…to win an argument, Helen."

"Aye, *mo luran*, 'tis unfair."

"You have your dirk, my lady, and I have my cock."

He pushed her against the wall again and was moving in and out of her more rapidly, filling her, thrilling her, tearing at her mouth with his. She could feel a release building deep inside her and she abandoned herself to it and to him completely as waves of pleasure ripped through her body. She clutched and quivered and writhed against him as her muscles contracted around his cock. When she stilled, he stilled in his thrusting, too, and she was limp, her legs still around his waist but only just barely holding on to him.

"Let me kiss you, Helen." She brought her face to his, her eyes closed in the wake of her ecstasy, and he kissed her lips, her cheeks, her nose, her forehead.

"I thought," she said.

"You thought what?"

"I thought the Duke of Dunmore dinnae like the mention of sharp objects and genitals in the same sentence."

Jack now began to move again, pushing into her. "There are always…exceptions to be made for wives."

She opened her eyes and tugged on his hair. "Wife."

He growled. "Yes. Wife. I'm going to release now."

She growled back. "Aye, Jack. We must make an heir. 'Tis our duty." She rocked her hips against him.

"Yes. Our duty. We must make…many heirs. Over…and over…and over again."

"Aye. I love ye. I want yer sons and daughters. Do yer duty, Jack Pike."

He panted. A drop of sweat ran down his temple and onto his cheek and she licked it off him, savoring the salty taste of her man.

"I love you, Helen Boyd. I only need one more thing from you."

"What's that?"

He took her mouth in a kiss that fanned the embers of her desire back into licking flames. And the kiss went on so long she found herself reaching a peak once again just as his own muscles went rigid and he filled her and shuddered against her mouth.

Then he staggered and she unwrapped her legs and slid off of him and down, thinking he might buckle.

He put his hands on the wall above her head, leaning, gasping for air.

She reached up and caressed his cheekbones and his lips with her callused fingers.

"Yer getting old, Jack Pike. What are ye now? Almost five and thirty? Maybe we should do this lying down next time in a bed. Save yer knees and back."

"Fuck my knees and back."

"Aye. We must keep up with the *dàireadh* everywhere and the foul language. For now. Get our fill before we must stop." She pulled down her skirts.

"Stop?" He had begun to button his fall but now he halted and looked at her.

"Yer nae thinking I'll have my bairns exposed to our wicked ways? We'll raise them properly with nae cursing and nae *dàireadh* outside the bedchamber."

"I understand the cursing, but the other?" He put his hands on her waist. "*Mo leannan*, my wife-to-be. You are the Countess of Kinmarloch. You will be the Duchess of Dunmore. You will rule my heart forever, and I'll be true to you forever. You will make the important decisions about the earldom and the duchy, my lady. But there will be one thing you should leave to me."

She raised her eyebrows. "Ye want to be lord of the rutting, is that it, Jack Pike?" She pretended her reluctance. "Aye, I will agree to that."

"Yes, you will." He grinned his wicked grin and kissed her again.

Helen had learned long ago, after all, that men didn't like to be told to do things or feel they must. And although her betrothed was the most beautiful man she had ever seen, he was still a man.

And as a countess in her own right, she was very happy to afford her husband a privilege or two. Because she knew, and she knew he knew, too, that only Jack Pike was foolhardy enough to pluck a thistle bare-handed and brave enough to make it his.

More

REGARDING FELICITY NIVEN'S NEWSLETTER
AND THE BED ME BOOKS

Sign up for author Felicity Niven's newsletter at www.felicityniven.com/bedmeduke to get news about upcoming romance releases and free novels, novellas, and stories including a **free second epilogue** to *Bed Me, Duke*, a short story about Jack and Helen that takes place a dozen years after they say "I do." This second epilogue is available exclusively to newsletter subscribers. (Even if you are already subscribed, you still have to sign up at the website above to get the free second epilogue).

The Bed Me Books are Regency romance novels with steam and happily-ever-after endings. Each book in the series functions as a stand-alone, although there are some interconnected characters and overlapping timelines. And each book in the series begins with a woman making a seemingly simple request to a man: "Bed me." Of course, nothing is simple before, during, or after the bedding, and soon these gentlemen are in deep trouble, their hearts well and truly lost to the women in question.

There is a sneak peek look at George and Phoebe's love

story **Bed Me, Baron**, the second book of the series, in the pages ahead.

AUTHOR'S NOTES

Helen and Jack are third cousins (meaning they had the same great-great-grandparents). Marriage between *first* cousins was not only legal but also rather common in this time period in England, so no one would have batted an eye at a marriage between *third* cousins. And modern readers shouldn't bat an eye either. On average, third cousins share 0.78% of their DNA, and third cousins are not considered to have a consanguineous relationship.

The Highland Clearances took place between 1750 and 1860. The forced removal of tenants from land in Scotland occurred largely so that more profitable sheep-grazing could replace farms. Houses were sometimes burned so evicted tenants could not return. In 1814, a steward for the duchy of Sutherland was charged with arson and culpable homicide when a woman died after her son-in-law's house was burned; the steward was ultimately acquitted.

BED ME, BARON: PREVIEW

After twenty-two years, someone has to make a move.

Lady Phoebe Finch, the youngest of the Duke of Abingdon's daughters, is done waiting. She's a grown woman and ready to be a wife and a mother. If it means giving up on the man she's loved all her life, so be it!

Baron Danforth taught Lady Phoebe Finch to walk when she was one. He taught her chess when she was eight. He's like a big brother to her, surely. But when his dear Phoebe comes to him for bedding lessons, George Danforth must confront the truth—his best and oldest friend is not only the most alluring woman in the world, she's also the love of his life.

And she's engaged. To a man that's not him.

When you've blundered everything, stalemate isn't an option.

Bed Me, Baron is book two in the *The Bed Me Books* series.

Prologue: 1805. Duchy of Abingdon.

George found Phoebe in the blackness of the priest hole. She wasn't afraid of the dark. Of course, she wasn't. Her name meant light. He had taught her that.

He had to stoop as he came in, holding a candle. He stifled a shudder as he sat beside her. The candlelight made the priest hole tolerable for him. Just barely.

"I've been looking for you," he said.

A sob from her.

"Why are you crying, Phee?"

"I'm not pretty!" she howled.

He let her cry for a few minutes until she got tired and began hiccoughing instead.

"I don't like it when you cry. I really wish you wouldn't." Then an idea struck him. "See here. From now on, when you feel like crying, come to me, and I'll tell you if you really have a reason to cry or not."

She snuffled and looked at him in the flickering light. "I'm never going to get married."

"Why do you say that?"

"Abigail said I looked like a little frog and Judith and Deborah said I am ever-so much shorter and fatter than they were when they were my age."

Phoebe's leap from her older sisters' comments to the conclusions that she was both ugly and condemned to spinsterhood made no sense to George. But she was only eight. And a girl. His own six-year-old sister mystified him, too.

He folded himself into a cross-legged position. "All right, Phee. I'll tell you the truth. I didn't want to, because it might go to your head. You must promise not to let it."

She wiped her face with her hands, leaving dirty smudges on her round cheeks. "I promise."

"You are uncommonly pretty."

"Really?"

"Yes. And you'll have no problem getting married. You'll have a husband if you want one."

"Will you marry me, George?"

"No, of course not."

The corners of her mouth turned down and new tears began to fill her eyes and brim over.

"Stop that. You're much too young for me. You're only eight, and I'm twelve. And the lady never asks the gentleman. It must be the other way around."

She snuffled again. "That doesn't seem fair."

He shrugged. "It's the way things are."

"When I am closer to you in age, will you ask me?"

"You will never be closer to me in age, Phee. We will always be four years apart. When you are twelve, I will be sixteen and will have already met my wife."

"Yes." A tremble to her chin.

"And you can't ask me to ask you. That's the same thing as asking me."

"Yes." This was followed by a sob. And then another one. She looked down at her own lap. "I'm s-s-sorry."

"But." He paused. Did he really want to promise this? Anything to get her to stop crying. "When we are very old, if we haven't married anyone else, I will ask you."

She lifted her head. "Wh-what is very old?"

"Twenty."

"When I am twenty or you are twenty?"

"You. Twenty isn't old for a man. But you must promise not to cry anymore."

She stared at him. No new tears came. But George could see that her nose was still running and her face looked wet and sticky and dirty all at the same time. He went into his pocket and pulled out a handkerchief.

"Here."

She took it and wiped her face and her nose. She held it out to give it back, but he shook his head.

"You keep it, Bumblephee."

"Th-thank you." She played with the corners of the handkerchief.

"Now, I have an idea. What do you say to my teaching you how to play chess this afternoon?"

"Isn't chess for men? And very hard?" Her lower lip stuck out and her tone was petulant.

"There's a queen in chess. If there's already a woman in the game, it can't be just for men."

"A queen?" Suddenly, Phoebe seemed very interested.

"Two queens. A black one and a white one. And they're very powerful. As for it being difficult? The rules are simple. You'll be able to learn them this afternoon. Shall we go see if your father will let us use his chessboard in the library?"

"Yes, please, George." She leaned over and put her lips against his cheek. A kiss.

He got up very quickly then, holding the candle he had brought with him, careful to stay leaning over and not to bump his head on the low ceiling. He held out his other hand to her and she took it and stood up, too, and they made their way out of the priest hole into the bright sunlight of the upstairs hallway.

Chapter 1: June, 1819. London.

George Danforth had been out of sorts all week. The damnable thing was he had no idea why, and he had never been a man to suffer ignorance with good grace.

He paced the study of his London town house, reviewing the possible causes of his unease.

Of course, there were always the looming philosophical questions that haunted him at night when shadows gathered in the corners of both his bedchamber and his mind. Questions about his place and purpose in the world. But that wasn't what was bothering him right now. In fact, those worries seemed rather silly and irrelevant at the moment.

There was something else unnerving him. Something new. Something pressing.

He had no financial worries. Yes, he had unexpectedly had to spend a good part of last month away from London due to some flooding in his barony. But no lives had been lost and everything had been managed as well as it could be under the circumstances.

His sister Alice, the person most likely to plague him, was being remarkably well-behaved despite having been left alone in London for some weeks. He had heard no reports of a new scandal.

He felt physically well. True, in the last few days, he hadn't slept more than a few hours a night and his appetite had been poor. But that was *because* he was out of sorts. His lack of sleep and his picking at his food were results, not causes. He was in a fine fettle. Despite being in town, he was well able to exercise, riding early every morning on Hampstead Heath and indulging in some long bouts of fencing three afternoons a week. But this week, the pounding of his heart and the use of his muscles had brought him no respite from the mysterious, gnawing thing that kept him from sleeping and eating.

He had enjoyed *the chair*, the best chair, the perfect chair, at his club the last four days. Frequently, he and Phineas Edge, the Earl of Burchester, competed for *the chair*. This spoke well of *the chair* since the earl was a self-proclaimed hedonist. But Phineas was currently out of town which meant George had been able to claim *the chair* easily, without any teasing from his absent friend who was also very much a rogue.

And on Monday, George had won his weekly chess match against Lady Phoebe Finch, his oldest and best friend in all the world. Handily.

Therefore, he should be in a good mood. Everything was in order, and he sought order even as he craved control. An iron grip on himself and on those matters that concerned him.

But he wasn't in a good mood, and he hadn't been for the last several days.

Something was wrong.

Maybe the nagging disquiet he felt derived from the fact that his win at the chessboard on Monday hadn't been due to his own skill. Instead, it was almost certainly owing to Lady Phoebe's rather slapdash play that evening. She had been more scattered than usual, putting her fingers to her mouth several times before remembering and jerking them down.

In retrospect, it was understandable that she had been preoccupied. Her surprising engagement to the Duke of Thornwick had been announced the next day. She had likely been anxious on Monday evening about the impending announcement of her nuptials.

Come to think of it, his own disagreeable mood had started the same day her betrothal was made public. Tuesday. Peculiar.

His thoughts about the timing of his perturbation were interrupted by a knock on the door in his study that led to the special entrance.

He wasn't expecting a knock. He had never had a knock at that door. The women who came through that door didn't knock.

A familiar voice said, "It's me, George."

He opened the door, and now he was even more out of sorts.

Lady Phoebe Finch was unannounced, tripping lightly into his study on a Friday afternoon. Not the right day. Not the right time.

And she had come through the special entrance that had its own staircase. The special entrance from the back garden off the alley that obviated the need for a servant to let her in. The special private entrance that only his mistresses used.

Phoebe had previously always come in through the front door of the Danforth town house, laughing with his butler Wynn, accidentally dropping her wrap or her reticule or her gloves on the floor of the hall, popping down to the kitchen to chat with Mrs. Hay and to snatch a few biscuits before coming to his study where she would leave crumbs on the carpet which he would have a chambermaid come and sweep up after she left.

Wrong day. Wrong time. Wrong entrance. Wrong, wrong, wrong.

"I want a rematch, George. Let's play." She put down her reticule and took off her gloves.

"We play chess on Mondays, Phee." He picked up her dropped glove and handed it to her.

"I know. But I thought, just once, you might indulge in a change of routine." She untied the ribbons of her bonnet.

Once more, he picked up a glove and handed it to her. "Why? Are you busy on Monday?"

She took off her bonnet. "No, I will also come on Monday to play."

"You want to play an extra game?"

"Yes." She unbuttoned her silk spencer and shrugged her way out of it. "But I'd like to change the rules."

He ignored the dropped glove this third time. He was provoked by what she had just said.

"Change the rules?" Yet another unprecedented thing. "Use some of those bizarre Italian castling rules?"

"No, I misspoke. I didn't mean the rules of the game. I meant I'd like to lay a wager."

"Blast, Phee, use your words precisely. A wager is entirely different from an alteration in the play of the game."

"Calm yourself, George."

He resumed his pacing. "I am calm. I'm just not myself this week. And I don't know why. Maybe because it's been so hot. It's a puzzle."

"Has anything happened?"

"No."

"Nothing's wrong with Alice, is there?"

"No. Alice is the same as usual. Alice is Alice."

"May I sit, George?"

He noticed then that she was still standing.

"Phee, you know you don't have to wait for an invitation from me. I'm such a rude fool, I'd likely leave you standing forever."

She smiled and said teasingly, "Yes, Lord Danforth," as she made an elaborate curtsy.

He liked to see her smile. It did lift him, take him out of himself a bit. "My only desire is that you should take your ease in my presence, Lady Phoebe."

He bowed deeply with a flourish and his wig came off his head. He clutched at his bald pate, a split-second too late.

Well, it didn't matter. If he had known Phoebe was coming, he would have already taken off the wig. But he usually wore his dark wig on a Friday at home, since that was his afternoon for his mistress and even though Lady Starling wasn't coming today, he had kept it on since, after all, it was still Friday whether his mistress came or not.

But Phoebe saw him without the wig more often than she saw him with it. He had known her since she was born, after all. He still remembered meeting her as a baby for the first time, leaning over her basket.

She had been the bald one then, and he had sported a full head of dark-brown curls. How he missed those curls. Because by the time he was eighteen and had become the Baron Danforth in the wake of his father's death, his curls had already started to thin. And now, eight years later, he was completely bald. She on the other hand had the same thick, long, dark-blonde tresses—albeit now pinned up—that she had started growing after shedding her wisps of baby hair.

He had taken to wearing a wig when he was twenty-two. But he never wore one when he played chess in his study. Or when he wrote his speeches for the House of Lords or worked on one of his etymological monographs. He thought better without a wig, some notion of air getting to his brain.

He picked the wig up off the floor and put it on his desk. He'd take it to his valet Morton after Lady Phoebe left.

She had taken her seat in her usual chair.

"Shall I ring for some tea or sherry, Bumblephee? Surely some biscuits?"

She rocked back and forth a little. "I'd rather you didn't. In fact, I'd rather no one else know that I'm here."

He raised an eyebrow. "Oh?"

"Yes. Mother thinks I went to Lady Huxley's whist party early with your sister. I didn't lie, exactly. I just misled her."

Odder and odder. Phoebe was exceptionally transparent. It was one of his few advantages when playing chess against her. He always knew when she was three or fewer moves away from a planned check. He could sense her excitement no matter how hard she tried to hide it.

How strange she should mislead her mother. Why couldn't Phoebe just have said she was coming for a game? Even though her mother frowned on their chess matches, her father would have allowed it.

Well, no matter. The opportunity to get an extra game with his most dangerous opponent? It more than made up for the fact that his mistress was out of town. If George Danforth had been a demonstrative man, he would have rubbed his hands together in glee.

But he wasn't. Instead, he put the chess table in place and began to arrange the pieces on the board.

"What's this wager then?"

"If you win, you can have my copy of the first edition of Cawdrey's *Table Alphabeticall* that Uncle Seth left me."

"I can?" He had coveted that book for years. "What if you win?"

She studied the pattern of the carpet. "You will bed me."

There was a silence. George could hear a far distant clanging in the alley behind the town house. Some coal for the kitchen being delivered, perhaps. Or ice.

"I will what?"

"Bed me." She raised her head and met his eyes. "You will take me to your bed. Now. This afternoon. Immediately after the game."

He collapsed into his own wing chair.

"I know this afternoon is the time your mistress usually comes to you. But I also know that Lady Starling is not in town at present. Perhaps bedding me might be a substitute so your routine will be less disrupted than usual."

His breath was gone. His mind was blank.

"I'll give you draw odds, George."

When they played chess, White always went first. Draw odds meant she would play White but, as Black, a draw would count as a win in his favor.

He said nothing, still not really able to comprehend her proposal. Her lewd bet. The odds she was offering him.

She shifted in her chair. "Fine. Pawn and move, then."

This meant that he would play White and she would give up a Black pawn before the start of play.

"Phee." He coughed. "I don't understand."

"You know I announced my engagement this week."

"Yes."

She clasped her hands together tightly, something he knew she did when ungloved to keep her fingernails out of her own mouth. "I suddenly realized that I know nothing about pleasing my future husband in the marital bed."

Oh. Foolish girl.

He leaned forward. "Phee. That is usual. In fact, it is assumed and considered desirable."

She raised her head and stared at him levelly. "It's not desirable for me, George. You know I hate not knowing how to do something."

That was true. Phoebe didn't like to fail. It was what made her such a worthy rival.

She stood. "I need bedding lessons. You are the logical person to give them to me. What do you say to the wager?"

"You must give me a moment, Phee."

She smiled even as her voice betrayed her with a slight quaver. "Yes, I suppose it's a bit like Sir Josiah asking you to bed him."

Sir Josiah Bastable was George's standing Wednesday night chess game. He was, if it were possible, an even slower and more methodical player than George himself. Sir Josiah was also well over fifty, portly, and had breath that regularly reeked of onions.

She went on. "Although I do like to think that I probably rank higher than Sir Josiah in your choice of bed partners."

Of course she did. But was that truly the standard by which she measured herself? *Oh, Phee.*

She lifted one foot and brought it down with a small thud on the carpet. Was that an impatient stamp from his little Phoebe?

"Fine," she said. "Pawn and two moves."

Phoebe would lose a pawn and he would play White and make the first two moves in a row.

He was silent.

"Knight odds," she offered, her expression stony. This

meant she would lose a knight before play even started. She stood in front of him, fidgeting with her fingers, waiting.

"Give me queen odds." As soon as the words were out of his mouth, he wanted to claw them back. Had he lost all sense of himself? All sense of *her*?

Wait. There was no need for panic. He took a deep breath. Queen odds was an extremely safe bet for him. They were a well-matched pair at chess, despite her impulsive daring and his considered caution. If Lady Phoebe had no queen, he should beat her easily. The rare first edition dictionary would be his. There would be no bedding of his best and oldest friend.

"Fine," she said and resumed her seat.

She was queenless but as the odds giver, she was White and went first.

Very quickly, George lost his surety that he would win. Even with no queen, Phoebe's play was nimble. He, on the other hand, seemed to be playing in a heavy fog, one that confused him and twisted his thoughts. *He* was the one that was distracted today.

Because now when Phoebe moved a piece on the board, he saw her hand and thought of those fingers—with their nails that she had worked so hard to grow—clutching at his back as he lay atop her, thrusting into her.

He was vile. Vile.

He looked only once at her face during the game. He saw two strands of her dark blonde hair that had escaped her hairpins, her serious mouth, her pink cheeks, and he was adrift in a sea of fantasy that involved her hair tumbling down completely, her mouth moaning in ecstasy, her cheeks flushing a deep red.

It was madness.

And then she looked up at him, fierce and angry about something, her brown eyes on him, boring into him, and he had to close his own eyes and when he opened them again, he made sure to look at the chessboard and only at the chessboard.

Utter madness.

She was the most aggressive she'd ever been in the game, attacking him relentlessly, fearlessly, her pawns brutally battering his king into submission.

She won.

Of course, she did. The real question was—did he let her? He didn't think so.

He looked at her again as she checkmated him. Her face was still creased with anger, an emotion he wasn't used to seeing there.

She leaned back in her chair and steepled her fingers.

"I didn't know I was so unattractive."

"What? You're not—"

"You offered me a handicap that guaranteed that you were almost certain to win, George. You must be very averse to bedding me."

He wondered if he should reveal that he thought he might have, without meaning to, let her win. But he couldn't do that without insulting her chess play which had been brilliant and ruthless this afternoon, in a way that his own had never been and never could be.

And he knew it wasn't true. He hadn't let her win. He just had not been capable of winning today.

He leaned back in his chair and steepled his own fingers, mirroring her. Surely, she had learned that unfeminine pose from him since he had assumed it so often during her chess lessons when they were children.

"There are two alternate theories. First, you are such a good player that you needed a crippling handicap. My mistake was not making your handicap more severe, say queenside odds." Phoebe would have lost all her pieces on the side of the queen, save her pawns.

She let out a little snort.

"My other theory as to why I might have lost is that you are…uh…actually *too* enticing and the gentleman in question —that is, me—was preoccupied by the possibility of what might happen after the game."

Phoebe tilted her head and scrutinized him. "Your play *was* poor today. Did you lose on purpose?"

"I don't think so."

"But you're not sure?"

"I must wonder. But I remind you that I lost even after you gave me queen odds. And I assure you that whatever the cause—your skill, my preoccupation with the outcome, my possible secret wish to lose—all only reflect on you in the most complimentary manner."

He thought now she would laugh and tell him this had all been a good joke on him. She'd say his sister Alice had put her up to this prank. Phoebe was unpredictable at times; one more reason why she was such a good chess player. Given her frank and honest nature, a drawn-out joke like this would be a stretch for her, but not an impossibility. Yes, now she would giggle and gloat over her win and get up and go out the door, leaving behind one of her gloves and he would have to put it in his desk drawer until she returned on Monday for their regular game. When she would leave a different glove behind.

But no.

She stood suddenly. "Let's go into your bedchamber."

This was no joke.

George's mind floated free, detached. It watched his body stand and walk and open the door that connected his study to the room where he slept. And where he bedded his mistresses.

ACKNOWLEDGMENTS

My deepest and most fervent thanks to those who read this novel in early stages: Alexandra Gall, Shannon Lawson, Alexandra Vasti, Lisa Jones, and Sharon Gunn. You are the most generous of friends and readers.

However, all errors are mine, and mine alone.

About the Author

Felicity Niven is a hopeful romantic. Writing Regency romance is her third career after two degrees from Harvard. And you know what they say about third things? Yep, it's a charm. She splits her time between the temperate South in the winter and the cool Great Lakes in the summer and thinks there can be no greater comforts than a pot of soup on the stove, a set of clean sheets on the bed, and a Jimmy Stewart film on a screen in the living room. She is the author of ***The Lovelocks of London*** series: ***When Ardor Blooms*** (prequel novella), ***Convergence of Desire***, ***Clandestine Passion***, and ***A Perilous Flirtation*** as well as ***The Bed Me Books*** series.

Made in United States
Orlando, FL
01 July 2023

34677335R00190